**A New Breed
of Undersea Warriors
Duel for the World's Most
Dangerous Prize . . .**

Captain Peter MacKenzie: After years of extraordinary leadership, the most victorious submarine commander in the fleet has a new job: training America's warriors for the next century. On the *Jacksonville*, it's time for him to step back and loose the reins—until the action gets hotter than any he's ever seen . . .

Captain Pari Avilov: Commander of the *Northern Star*, he's a legendary Soviet hero, the unpredictable genius they call the Hawk. Now he's been blackmailed into committing the most daring and treacherous act ever attempted on board a submarine . . .

FULL FATHOM FIVE

"A whirlwind pace . . . The novel is also aided by the author's impressive knowledge of his subject matter, particularly submarine workings and detail."

—*West Coast Review of Books*

A CONSPIRACY OF EAGLES

"A fast-paced and engaging thriller . . ."

—*Publishers Weekly*

Admiral Rushkov: The commander of Russia's Black Sea fleet has watched a powerful empire crumble around him. Now he engineers a desperate ploy he hopes will not only save his career but make him rich in the process . . .

Captain Zilah: He looks more like a fierce desert chieftain than a naval officer, but the commander of the Russian sub *Adri* has a single mission: make sure Captain Avilov pilots the *Northern Star* safely to his Cuban destination. Failure would mean ruin . . .

BLIND PROPHET

"A gripper from beginning to end."

—*Newsday*

"One of the best international thrillers to appear in recent years."

—*Library Journal*

"Bart Davis seamlessly blends high technology with the age-old problems of men in combat."
—Gerry Carroll, author of *North SAR*

The "Top Gun" Officers: For Mark Bell, Jamie Flynn, Reggie Carter and Jess Moran, Andros Island in the Bahamas is where their destinies will be written. There, the undersea combat exercises will make or break their dreams of command. Then the game on the *Jacksonville* turns real—and they'll be lucky to surface alive . . .

Fasah al-Zawi: The Libyan representative harbors his own dreams of power, from New York to Riyadh to Tel Aviv. Only acquisition of the *Northern Star* can make them come true. Only Peter MacKenzie and his elite group of young officers on board the *Jacksonville* can shatter them . . .

BLACK WIDOW

"Chilling authenticity . . . a ruthless, dynamic novel."
—*Yorkshire Post*

TAKEOVER

"A first-class thriller which encourages frantic reading."
—*Liverpool Daily Post*

Books by Bart Davis

Atlantic Run*
Blind Prophet
A Conspiracy of Eagles
Destroy the Kentucky*
The Doomsday Exercise
Full Fathom Five
Raise the Red Dawn*
Takeover

*Published by POCKET BOOKS

ATLANTIC RUN

BART DAVIS

POCKET **STAR** BOOKS

New York   London   Toronto   Sydney   Tokyo   Singapore

An *Original* Publication of POCKET BOOKS

A Pocket Star Book published by
POCKET BOOKS, a division of Simon & Schuster Inc.
1230 Avenue of the Americas, New York, NY 10020

Copyright © 1993 by Bart Davis

ISBN: 0-671-76904-9

First Pocket Books printing May 1993

10 9 8 7 6 5 4 3 2 1

POCKET STAR BOOKS and colophon are registered trademarks of Simon & Schuster Inc.

Cover art by Jeff Mangiat

Printed in the U.S.A.

For Paul D. McCarthy,
the dean of editors

ACKNOWLEDGMENTS

For several days in May I sailed on board the fast attack submarine U.S.S. *Jacksonville* (SSN-699) off Andros Island in the Bahamas. I'll never forget handling the stern planes during a dive, or standing on the sail while we raced through the ocean, or waking to the noise of a fire (drill) coming over the PA. I experienced the character of dedicated officers, and of men who rise to their inspiration by giving their best. They made a deep impression on me.

For their help in researching this novel I am indebted to Captain Tim Traverso, *Jacksonville's* supremely calm and confident commander; his XO, LCDR Pete Flynn, whose endless patience in answering my questions was never a strain regardless of his workload; Chief Engineer LCDR J. L. Lovering, Nav/Ops Lt. P. W. Siegrist, DCA Lt. K. L. Harrington, COB MMCS (SS) Bob Tacha, and the rest of the crew.

PAO LCDR Dave Morris was my constant guide and companion. He saw to my best interests and aided us all in our understandings. Also, his vocal renditions were the stuff of which legends are made, to say the least.

My sincere appreciation to VADM Roger Bacon, OP-02; RADM Brent Baker, Chief of Information; VADM John H.

ACKNOWLEDGMENTS

Fetterman, Jr., Chief of Naval Education and Training, who believed in my task and first granted permission for the underway embark.

At AUTEC itself I was the guest of Mr. Jay Ostaffe, Program Manager; and CMDR Brian Covington, OIC of the AUTEC Range. They enlarged my understading of the important job AUTEC does.

Mr. George S. Murphy told some of the best submarine stories I've ever heard at lunch one day. And my thanks to Capt. Stan Sirmans (ret) and CMDR John Alexander (ret), who first pointed me in the right direction.

The essential contribution to this novel was made by my friend, RADM J. Weldon Koenig (ret), now president and CEO of P.T.S. Technical Services in Austin, Texas. Weldon has been gracious enough to spend endless hours with me plotting the submarine tactics in *Full Fathom Five, Raise the Red Dawn, Destroy the Kentucky,* and *Atlantic Run.* The tricks of the trade are his, as is the steadiness and moral fiber of Peter MacKenzie. He is a father, husband, and business-man, and I often reach him as he's winging through yet another airport, skipping the how-are-yous to jump to something like, "Okay, Weldon, I've got these three subs, see, and one of them has to . . ."

I went to Weldon early in the writing of *Atlantic Run* to understand how submarine commanding officers are made. He is uniquely qualified to explain it. Over a thirty-year career he rose from ensign to admiral, and he is one of the most highly decorated submariners of our day. He has commanded both fast-attack and ballistic missile subma-rines, served as Commander, Submarine Squadron 8; Com-mander, Submarine Squadron 6, Director of Submarine Distribution, Washington, D.C.; and Director of Logistics and Security Assistance for the Commander-in-Chief of the Pacific Fleet, Admiral William J. Crowe. He has received two Meritorious Service awards, two Legion of Merits, and the Superior Service Medal. His final posting was Com-

ACKNOWLEDGMENTS

mander of the Naval Training Center, Orlando, Florida. He continues to contribute to my appreciation of the sacrifices submariners make, and to increase the support for their vital mission. He is one of the finest men I have ever known.

I want to thank Gerry Carroll, the brilliant author of *North SAR,* for his help with the helo portions of the novel. He made the incomprehensible comprehensible because he is the genuine article.

Curtiss P. MacDonald, of Varied Directions International, which produced *Steel Boats, Iron Men,* was kind enough to provide additional submarine videotape.

Commander Paul J. Ryan's fine article, *"Preparing for Submarine Command," The Submarine Review* (June 1991), helped me, too.

And especially, my love and thanks to:

Mr. Bob Binns, who always has the answers.

Brandon T. Davis, Esq., who returned Mac to me.

Mr. Robert Gottlieb, of the William Morris Agency, who continues to be right and to guide me in spite of my stubbornness. I value him immensely.

Mr. Paul McCarthy, to whom this book is dedicated for too many reasons to name here.

And Sharon and Jordan and Ally, always my most beloved.

ATLANTIC RUN

Prologue

Sabaña Key, Cuba

HIS NAME WASN'T HAMED ABU SHARIF, IT WAS DAVID EPSTEIN, but the Arab name was as familiar to him as Libya, the country in which he had spent most of his adult life as a deep cover Mossad agent.

Epstein pried a leech off his leg and flicked it back into the dank water. He hated this damn swamp on Sabaña Key off the coast of Cuba. Epstein had dark Semitic features—penetrating eyes, olive skin, full lips, and tight black hair like steel wool. His mother was a Sephardic Jew who had immigrated to Israel from North Africa. In college he was often taken for an Arab exchange student. He stopped to pry off another leech. It was a long way from there to this fetid swamp.

The soldiers were closer. He had to get to the transmitter the Mossad agent brought before Sayid's men did. Sayid was the security chief, a tough, well-trained man. The direction finder was supposed to take Epstein right to the transmitter, but, like a lot of things in life, it didn't live up to its billing. He cursed their bad luck. The truth was there had been too little time to set this up correctly. He was on another matter completely, and it was only by accident he had stumbled onto what Fasah al-Zawi, his boss in the Libyan Intelligence Service, was up to.

When al-Zawi told Epstein—Colonel Hamed abu Sharif, to his countrymen—he was going to Sabaña Key, Epstein assumed he was just delivering money to another terrorist base. Acquiring and transporting hard currency was his specialty. But seventy-five million dollars was a big enough figure to make Epstein take a second look.

Another agent had been dropped here hastily after Epstein alerted his Israeli handlers. His job was to get communications gear to Epstein. Maybe, being in a hurry, they had sent someone inexperienced. He had tried to reach Epstein in spite of Epstein's doggedly showing the "don't approach" sign. The man was spotted and was now the object of pursuit. This endangered Epstein. It also angered him. Twenty years had taught him the most important survival trait of all was patience. Wait. Don't rush. Never act precipitately. Now he had to.

The Mossad agent found him before he had gone much further. He was crouched on a mossy spit of land between two trees, gun in hand, obviously afraid. He was young, brown-haired, maybe twenty-one, nice-looking. A stranger. Epstein privately thought they had no business sending one so young, conveniently forgetting he had been a year younger when they sent him to Tripoli. He wanted to yell at the boy and demand an explanation, but that was pointless. What difference did it make now?

"Give me the transmitter," Epstein said sharply.

"Look, I'm really sorry, sir. I—"

"The transmitter. Now."

The boy handed him a tiny satellite-relay phone, a little black square no bigger than a pack of cigarettes. Epstein keyed in a number, got the connection, and spoke quietly for a few moments. Behind him in the swamp he could hear Sayid and the others coming. He only had seconds. *The Northern Star. Akula-class submarine. Two weeks. July first.*

He told them as much as he knew, as much as he had time for, and signed off.

The boy put the phone back in his breast pocket.

"Fire your gun twice," Epstein commanded.

"But"—the boy shook his head—"they'll hear—"

"Can't you follow even the simplest orders?" Epstein said furiously. "I said shoot!"

Stung, the boy fired two rounds, then looked back to Epstein for approval. It was sad, really, Epstein thought. As if that was going to make it all right.

Epstein drew his own gun and shot the boy through the heart, smashing the phone in his breast pocket.

"Over here," Epstein shouted. "I got him."

They came running. Sayid checked the boy's pulse, then searched him, muttering about how he would have liked this one alive. But they had all heard the shots fired, so no one could blame him. Sayid examined the smashed transmitter unhappily. The man must have made a report. They searched his camp, found nothing else, and left the body where it was for the swamp creatures to digest.

Epstein hid his profound sadness. The sight of the dead boy lying on the mossy ground without even so much as a kind word to send him to God would haunt him for a long time. His complicity was like a knife in his soul. He was deeply sorry, but sadly the boy's death had been ordained from the moment he betrayed his presence here. Sayid would have caught him soon enough and, lacking sophisticated equipment, would simply have hung him up and begun hacking off pieces till he talked. He would have, too. Everyone did. Unless they took the poison. So either way the boy was dead.

Sayid put an arm around him and jokingly told him to aim for the kneecaps next time. Hamed abu Sharif made a funny/hurt face and told him that's where he *had* been aiming. Sayid roared.

Epstein fought the temptation to go back and bury the

3

boy. His soul was torn in half. What gave him the right to do what he did? He regained his balance. Never forget the reason, the greater good. Mossad would analyze the information and call in the Americans. They were the only ones who could stop the *Northern Star* from reaching Sabaña Key and falling into Libyan hands.

Hamed abu Sharif slogged along toward camp with the others. Outwardly he joined in their lighthearted banter, complaining about the heat, the bugs, and the lack of women.

Inside, all the way back, David Epstein recited kaddish, the Jewish prayer for the dead.

Chapter One

Ukraine

THE WIND SWEPT IN FROM THE BLACK SEA OVER THE ONCE-GREAT piers at Sevastopol and took twenty degrees off the temperature of what should have been a glorious June day. Senior Captain First Rank Pari Avilov sealed his black slicker tighter and selected his incoming channel markers from the sail of the *Northern Star,* his *Akula*-class attack submarine.

"Right ten degrees rudder," Avilov said into the headset mike connecting him to the control room. "Make minimum turns."

Avilov's touch was soft. *Northern Star* moved through the harbor chop like a languid otter.

Something darted across the horizon, and Avilov's eye jerked to track it. Not a bird, just the same damn gray spot that had been appearing in his peripheral vision with ever greater regularity, followed by a brief pain in his head. Avilov probed his scalp trying to find the spot where it originated but it seemed always just out of reach. Maddening.

"Are you all right, Pari?"

Senior Lieutenant Yuri Pachenko, Avilov's first officer,

was a game, dark-eyed, black-haired little man with quick movements and a wrestler's shoulders. He had been scanning the water ahead through binoculars for submerged debris. Now he looked concerned.

"The fresh air gives me a headache the first few hours, Yuri," Avilov said, waving it off. Pachenko had served under him almost two years now, and despite their age difference they had become close friends.

Pachenko accepted the explanation and went back to scanning the harbor. He had come to know his captain well. Pari Ivanovich Avilov was the finest submarine commander in the fleet. His legendary exploits and tactical brilliance had earned him the nickname *Orgule,* the Hawk. It was appropriate physically, too. Avilov's prominent nose curved down like a beak. He had a crown of silver hair. And his sharp azure eyes fixed a man like prey. Even at fifty-three Avilov retained the fluid strength of that powerful hunting bird. He had been known to pluck a crewman who wasn't doing his job right out of his chair.

"Who do we report to?" asked Pachenko. "Do you know yet?"

"I have no orders other than the ones you know about," said Avilov. "Return to base immediately. Come home." He frowned. "Home. What does that even mean now?"

"It means you pick a side," said Pachenko soberly. "That's democracy."

A radio technician scampered up the sail ladder and thrust a transmission out. "Captain."

Avilov read it. "We've been summoned."

Pachenko took the paper and frowned. "What the hell is the Unified High Commission for Naval Affairs?"

"I don't know. It changes every week. But it's cosigned by Admiral Rushkov. If he's involved, Russia hasn't given up the Black Sea Fleet yet."

"There won't be much left to lose if this keeps up," Pachenko said sadly. "Look at it."

6

Ships of every size and class lay mothballed in the harbor losing more of their fighting edge every day. It wasn't a port, it was a graveyard. The *Northern Star* sailed silently past idle sub tenders and patrol boats standing by like lost relatives at a funeral. Pier cranes drooped in the sky untended, ungainly things whose time had come and gone. A crisscrossed web of transfer lines and guy wires creaked back and forth in the wind giving voice to the harbor's sad rusting song.

My song, too, thought Avilov bleakly. He was at the end of his career. Normally he and his wife, Katcha, would have retired to the lovely cottage in the provinces the fleet had promised him. But what good were those promises now? The economy was bankrupt. Money was worthless. On some bases they'd had to turn barracks into communal apartments for fifteen or twenty families, all of them huddled behind makeshift plywood walls with one kitchen and bathroom. Was that his future?

"Engines back one third, rudder amidships," ordered Avilov. *Northern Star* touched the pier gently, and crewmen secured lines from her deck cleats to the dock. "All engines stop. Secure the underway watch."

"Pari?" Pachenko motioned to the gray military sedan stopped on the road above the pier.

Avilov spoke to his navigator through the headset mike. "Pytor, you have the duty. Station the in-port watch, and let the rest of the crew go ashore. Yuri and I will be back in a few hours. Wait for us."

"Yes, Captain."

The watch guard saluted them as they crossed over the gangplank and onto dry land for the first time in weeks. Avilov hated taking his first steps on land. They separated him from his ship and consigned him to his earthbound life, a transition he never made easily or without some small regret.

The car's driver was a stocky civilian. Ordinarily a military driver would have come.

"Captain Avilov?" he asked.

"And Senior Lieutenant Pachenko. Just where exactly is the Unified High Commission for Naval Affairs?"

"Outside the city, com . . . sir."

"Let's go, then," said Avilov, pulling the door shut himself.

They sped onto Primorsky Boulevard and headed east along the coast. They passed the fleet's water sports center. Pachenko drummed his fingers impatiently.

"What's bothering you?" Avilov asked idly.

"There was no message from Irina and Katcha. You think they got to the spa all right?"

"Can I tell you something?" Avilov asked mildly.

"What?"

"You are getting to be an old lady with your worries." Avilov held his forehead and feigned a headache. "Your wife is more competent than you are at details. More than mine even, and Katcha sorts socks by their age. One thing I know. If I had your Irina as my exec, we would have eaten more fruit this trip, hmm?"

"I did not forget the canned peaches," Pachenko fumed. "But even if I did—not that I'm taking responsibility, mind you—but even if I did, how can a perfect record be spoiled by something as mundane as peaches?"

Avilov had to laugh. "It marks what I am sure is a decline in my professional standards, but I've omitted it from your fitness report."

"Future generations will sing of you," muttered Pachenko.

Only the occasional spa or villa dotted the road now. They pulled into a private drive. Carefully trimmed shrubs lined it, leading to a modern white structure whose glass walls overlooked the sea. A sparkling blue pool sat alongside. A Mercedes and a Rolls were in the garage. There was the immediate impression of wealth and power. Avilov caught Pachenko's look. Where the hell were they?

"This way, please," said the driver.

In the house, curved poured-concrete walls led them into the living room which looked out to sea. Multicolored woods. Ceramic vases and sculptures. A cantilevered deck around the room. Vast windows and a system of terraces leading right down to the water. It was a house a man could work a lifetime for and still not be able to afford. Avilov commanded a billion-ruble ship capable of destroying a small country should he desire to, but he felt instantly and completely out of his depth in this house.

"It makes a man think, eh, Captain Avilov?"

Avilov had been so mesmerized by the house he hadn't realized there was anybody else there. Admiral Vladimir Rushkov was up on the deck facing the sea. Avilov came to attention and saluted.

"It is quite something, this house," Rushkov continued. "Built with different values from the ones we devoted our lives to. Stand at ease, Pari Ivanovich. You, too, Senior Lieutenant."

Avilov relaxed his stance. Rushkov was commander of the Black Sea Fleet, a squat, powerful man with a great head, thick neck, and wide shoulders. He was the veteran of a score of successful naval campaigns, and his intellect was legendary. But he was of the old guard, and many in the new government wanted to unseat him. Rumor had it his days were numbered.

"Something to drink?" suggested Rushkov. "You, too, Senior Lieutenant Pachenko."

"No, thank you, Admiral," said Avilov. Pachenko declined and sat cautiously. It never paid to relax in the lion's den.

Rushkov came down and made himself a drink. He seemed in a good mood. "Remember that operation you commanded on the African coast, Pari Ivanovich?"

Avilov permitted himself to smile. "Yes, Admiral."

Rushkov's black eyes sparkled. He turned to Pachenko.

"A thing of beauty, Senior Lieutenant. We had to get a Spetsnaz commando team in to dispatch an enemy commander, but the Americans had the country locked up tight. The Hawk sneaked past an entire battle group and dropped off the team, then sailed back out under a pair of fishing trawlers tethered to his main cleats. When the Americans finally realized what was going on he put a torpedo into their support tanker and escaped in the fire and confusion." He winked at Avilov. "Those were the days, eh?"

"They had their moments," Avilov agreed. There was danger here. He felt it but didn't know why.

"All gone now," Rushkov continued sadly. "We and the Americans. Like two subs caught in a race to dive deeper and deeper. But they were able to pull out, while we crashed into the bottom. Our time is over. You saw the ships at Sevastopol. There are similar junk piles at Cam Ranh Bay and Najin, even at Kola Bay. How long before those units are just worthless hulks? And consider this, Pari Ivanovich. We are very much like those ships. Military officers lived privileged lives, cared for and pampered. How long before we are worthless hulks, too?"

"We'll always be needed, Admiral," said Avilov.

"You're shortsighted," mocked Rushkov. "We've already been abandoned. But I am not going to let the politicians consign me to the same graveyard as my ships."

Avilov shrugged. "I am only a submarine commander, Admiral. These matters don't concern me."

"Ah, but they do, Pari Ivanovich," said Rushkov. "They concern you directly. Tell me what you feel in this house. Don't lie, I watched your face."

Avilov hesitated. Rushkov's dark eyes never left him. Avilov felt Pachenko watching him, too. "I feel . . . small."

There was a sigh of pleasure from Rushkov, almost gratitude, as if Avilov had said I suffer the same weakness. I am an addict, too.

Rushkov gestured around them. "There are men for

whom this house is but a bauble on a string of baubles to be dropped in the ocean if they wish," Rushkov said. "Would you like to be one of them, Pari Ivanovich?"

Avilov was startled. Only an hour before he'd been worrying he would end up one of the old men who sat on the benches in the parks talking about past glories and begging their children for bread and the occasional vodka. Now Rushkov was offering him riches?

Rushkov switched to English. It took Avilov a moment to make the change in his head. "Come. I want you to meet some people."

Avilov followed him into the library. Pachenko came behind, silent and unreadable.

Two men were waiting. "Permit me to introduce Mr. Fasah al-Zawi," Rushkov said, and Avilov shook his hand. "And Mr. Franklin Lerner. They have come a long way to meet you."

"Good of you to come," said al-Zawi, a portly Arab with intense dark eyes, black hair, and a small, neat mustache. His gray business suit and shoes alone would have cost Avilov several months' pay. He extended a perfectly manicured hand with a gold and diamond Rolex, and Avilov shook it.

Rushkov said, "Pari Ivanovich, Mr. Lerner is an arms dealer. Ordinarily his agreements are with the Ministry of Defense. The breakup has induced him to work with those of us who have more direct control over things. Mr. al-Zawi is his client."

Lerner was well over six feet, with brown eyes and hair. His skin was so tan it looked like polished wood. He looked fresh from lunch at the country club. "It's a pleasure to meet the man they call the Hawk. You've got quite a record, Captain."

Avilov nodded. Flattery from this man was meaningless. He would speak the same way to an ax murderer just to sell him a sharper blade.

Lerner went on. "My father used to be in the cattle business in Dallas. Do you know where that is?"

"Texas."

"Right on the money. One time we bought a herd and left them in one of our corrals while we hired a crew. Unfortunately, the fencing hadn't been tended to properly, and the cattle got out. They ran off a lot of weight and most of our profit before we got them back. It taught me a lesson. It's one thing to have, another to keep. Are you interested in being rich, Captain Avilov?"

"To be honest, I have never thought a great deal about it."

"I'm a pretty fair judge of character, sir," said Lerner, "and I say you thought about it the minute you walked in here. The old Soviet Union sold arms all over the world. America still does. The difference is *you* stand to profit from it for the first time."

"What do you want exactly?" asked Avilov.

Al-Zawi's cultured voice spoke of attending universities in other lands. "The Libyan government has bought a Pantera modified *Akula* nuclear attack submarine, Captain Avilov. Your submarine, the *Northern Star.*"

"Impossible," said Avilov flatly.

"Seventy-five million dollars," said Lerner, throwing out the number as easily as if he had just quoted a price for shoes. "You and your lieutenant will be paid three million dollars and one million dollars respectively for delivering it to our base on Sabaña Key in Cuba." Lerner smiled expansively. "It's that old free market economy you keep hearing so much about."

"Why not the Middle East?" asked Avilov.

"The *Northern Star* will never operate from Libya," said al-Zawi. "She is meant for . . . special missions."

"Missions Libya might not wish to be connected to?"

"You are a smart man, Captain," said al-Zawi. "Be smart a while longer and you'll profit greatly."

"It is a day-to-day thing whether I control this fleet or the president of Ukraine does," said Rushkov. "The *Star* must be out of here within the week. When you are two hundred miles off Sabaña Key you will cause a fire to break out forcing you to abandon ship. The crew will do quite well in those warm waters until they're picked up. Bravely, you'll go down with your ship. The *Northern Star* will be presumed lost at sea. In reality, you'll finish the run to Sabaña Key."

"You could order a hundred other officers to sail the *Star* to Cuba. Why offer millions for what you could get for free?"

Lerner twisted the links of his watch, the first nervous gesture Avilov had seen in the man. "The Americans have learned the *Star* is coming. A Mossad agent made it to Sabaña Key, and suddenly there is unprecedented naval activity in the Atlantic. The connection is obvious. The man who takes the *Northern Star* across the Atlantic must be able to beat the Americans. The man we had was good, but not the best. *You're* the best. You've beaten them before. That's why you're here."

Avilov had to admit he was tempted. One last fight against his old adversaries. A great battle against desperate odds. And the money. He imagined giving his wife and children fine schools. Cars. Beautiful clothing. What did Americans call it? Yes . . . the good life. For one final Atlantic run.

"I'd say three million's pretty good pay even for this trip, wouldn't you?" said Lerner.

"I can't say it isn't." Avilov caught Pachenko's nod and went on. "But a naval officer carries out the policies of his government. That's what we owe the people for all our training and privileges. You want the *Star* for one purpose, Mr. al-Zawi, and we both know it. Terrorism." He heard their sharp intake of breath. "You can't have her."

Lerner was fast, but Avilov was faster. He had pegged the bulge under the cashmere jacket for a handgun. When Lerner came up from his chair with his hand inside his jacket Avilov sprang out of his seat and went low, hitting

13

him hard in the abdomen. Lerner doubled over, and Avilov grabbed the gun and held it on them.

"Yuri, put in a call to the Minister of Defense in Moscow and tell him what you have just heard."

"Yes, sir!" said Pachenko gladly, dialing. "I guess you aren't so old and slow after all. For a moment I thought—"

"For a moment I thought so, too."

Lerner got off the floor, glaring. Rushkov just shook his head as if a bright pupil had suddenly turned stupid. "Put down the phone. Pari Ivanovich, there is something you should see. Then he may call if you wish. Please, for your own sake."

Lerner used two fingers to extract a plain white envelope, which he tossed over. He waited silently, smoothing out his clothes. Avilov handed the gun to Pachenko so he could open the envelope. The first item stopped him cold.

Lerner's voice was smug. "You are the last piece in a puzzle it has taken me a year of my life and considerable money to arrange. When Admiral Rushkov showed me your file I knew this was going to be a hard sell, as we say. So I figured I'd make sure the fences were strong enough this time. What do you think, Captain? Are they?"

"What is it, Pari?" demanded Pachenko.

Avilov passed him the envelope. Simple 35mm color prints showed his wife and youngest son, Misha, cavorting on a beach in Cuba, along with Pachenko's wife, Irina, and their daughter Kara. Other shots showed them shopping in Havana, eating, riding. The pictures weren't fakes. Avilov had made port there enough times over the years to know the city. There was a handwritten note.

Dearest Pari,
   How wonderful to surprise us with such a vacation! Too bad our daughter couldn't come, but marriage and work have her too busy. As you can see from the

photos, Misha and Irina and Kara and I are having a wonderful time. The weather is gorgeous! They told us you and Yuri will be coming soon to the military base on Sabaña Key, and we will meet you there. Thank you again for the wonderful *surprise!*

All my love,
Katcha

"This is why they didn't call," Avilov said. He returned the gun to Lerner.

"You understand now?" asked the American.

Avilov nodded. "The story about fences. You were telling me this."

"Yes. And something else, too."

The barrel of his gun crashed into Avilov's head, and pain seared through his skull. His vision shattered into a million fragments and then went black. When he came to he was being supported by Pachenko.

"I never leave a score unsettled," said Lerner. He turned to Pachenko. "You'll do as your captain says? Remember, your family's out there, too."

"I am Captain Avilov's man," said Pachenko proudly, and then just as clearly, "you filthy bastard."

Lerner smarted, then shrugged. You couldn't hit everyone for every little thing. "Captain Avilov, I want you to have as much to gain, and to lose, as the rest of us. Sail the *Northern Star* into Sabaña Key by July first and you're a rich man. I give you my word your family will be waiting on the pier to see you surface. I also give you my word that if you cross me, you'll never see them again."

Rushkov handed Avilov a packet of authorizations. "Take on supplies and weapons. Anything else you think you'll need. My intelligence reports say you won't run into major opposition until the western Med."

Gray dots were still dancing in Avilov's field of vision.

Behind them the ocean grew darker as the sun set. The house with all its treasures had turned violet as the sun's final colors reflected off the sea. Pachenko took his elbow, leading him.

"We will not meet again, Pari Ivanovich," Rushkov said. "Good luck on your Atlantic run. Remember how much depends on it."

Chapter Two

The Bahamas

THE NAVY TRANSPORT PLANE DROPPED TOWARD THE SPARSE, sandy island nestled in the mottled green waters of Grand Bahama Bank.

"There it is, Lieutenant. Andros Island," the navy pilot needled him. "Destiny."

Lt. Mark Bell sighed. What the hell response could you make to that wiseass crack? It was too damn true.

Andros island was the site of the navy's Atlantic Undersea Test and Evaluation Center (AUTEC). It represented the last leg of a journey that had started six months earlier for Bell and the other submarine Prospective Commanding Officers—PCOs—on the plane. This was final exam week. They would be tested here in actual undersea combat in the deep blue waters off Andros Island. It was war, and only the winners went on to become commanding officers.

"It's not my *destiny* I'm worried about," Bell said gamely. "I just stepped on the Cracker Jack box your wings came in."

Bell hoped his nervous tension didn't show. His stomach had been sour ever since they'd left Norfolk Naval Base that morning, having completed Advanced Weapons Training. It had been a dream-filled sleepless night. His own private nightmare still followed him like a homing torpedo. Even now the thought of boarding a sub again brought back painful memories. Would he ever shake them? And could he command if he didn't?

Destiny. The pilot didn't know how close he'd come.

"You Bubbleheads are all alike," the pilot said, chuckling. "Up here you're just fish out of water." He pointed to the gold dolphins on Bell's chest and elbowed his copilot, enjoying his own humor. "Fish out of water, get it?"

Bell went aft.

He expected to find his classmates working. In fact, Carter was engrossed in an engineering manual. Flynn was plugged into a Walkman, eyes closed, humming a rock tune, totally self-assured. Nothing fazed Flynn. He had been his usual "Lemme at 'em" self all morning. If the transport plane had been any later, Flynn would have swum to Andros.

"Heading in, girls," came the pilot's jocular voice over the loudspeaker.

The plane hit the airstrip and slammed to a stop. "Let's get a move on, Brother Bell," Flynn said cheerily. "Our new master awaits."

"Anxious to meet him, Jamie?" asked Bell, trying to smooth out the wrinkles in his khaki uniform.

"Are you kidding? MacKenzie's the best, the only captain ever to fight in two navies," Flynn reminded him as they passed through the wooden building housing customs. "The goddamned Russians gave him a medal."

"Three enemy kills to his credit. One American, too, if you count the *Kentucky*," Carter said, sliding on his shades. He had no wrinkles in his uniform. "We might be the luckiest PCOs in history to be here when he drew this billet."

"Or the most intimidated," said Bell. "How the hell do you impress this guy?"

"You start by getting into his car so he can get out of this god-awful sun and back into his air-conditioned office," said an amused voice behind them. "I'm Captain MacKenzie, your senior PCO instructor. Welcome to Andros Island."

Bell smothered a curse and snapped to attention. Carter whipped off his shades and jerked erect. Flynn hopped over his bag and cut a sharp salute. All three stood stiffly in the hot sun.

MacKenzie smiled. He couldn't help it. The little pups were so full of hope, so innocent of what it really meant to be in command of a submarine. Yet they wanted it badly enough to have devoted years to the demanding journey from ensign to commanding officer, gaining hard-won practical experience and dozens of scientific and tactical certificates along the way. Each was a combination of youthful arrogance, bright promise, and veteran pride.

And from where he stood they didn't know jack shit about anything.

"At ease, gentlemen." He stuck out his hand. "Not very sporting of me to sneak up on you like that."

"Lieutenant Commander James Grady Flynn. Pleased to meet you, Captain."

"Mr. Flynn." Flynn had the face of a film star. Firm jaw, straight nose, green eyes, jet-black hair. A little bit of slouch from having it come too easy. The other two called him Jamie. Not James. That was good. Friends meant loyalty.

"Pleasure, sir," said Carter, stepping over. "I was on the *Baton Rouge* when you gave us the slip in the eastern Med. We sure didn't know it was you in command of that Russian sub."

"It was a remarkable experience, Mr. Carter. Taught me a great deal." MacKenzie sized up LCDR Reginald Carter, the bright Afro-American Annapolis grad from Georgia. He had top marks for efficiency and performance. Top ten percent of his class. Near-genius IQ.

Bell stepped up, putting his hand out almost as an afterthought. "Lieutenant Bell, sir. Pleased to meet you."

"Thank you, Lieutenant. You've healed, I take it?"

"Yes, sir. Clean bill of health. You don't have to worry about me, sir."

He said it defensively. MacKenzie knew several senior captains who claimed Bell was the best officer they'd ever served with, a rare blend of natural ability and hard worker. His being here at twenty-nine was testimony to their regard. But self-doubt clouded the lean boy's dark eyes. MacKenzie didn't know what he'd been through because the files had been sealed; there was only the rumor that it would have disqualified most men. Maybe that gave Bell an edge. It took more than ability to succeed here. It took character.

"Gentlemen, dinner tonight is at seventeen hundred down at the beach. Attire is casual. Short-sleeve shirts are fine. You'll meet everybody there. Nothing's scheduled this afternoon so I'll drop you at the BOQ to relax and look around."

The public road terminated at AUTEC's main gate where they went through a security check. The base was one square mile with the western side on the water. Trailers and apartments were painted light pastels. The Bachelor Officers Quarters was sided with yellow corrugated steel. Children rode bicycles, and men and women strolled to work along the main street of this small "town" of two thousand, mostly engineers and communications experts who ran the AUTEC range. The vegetation was lush, the horizon reached up to a vaulted cloudless sky, and shades of green water melded into azure blue.

"Sir?"

"Yes, Mr. Carter?"

"PCO classes usually have four candidates. We're still at three."

"I'm hoping a fourth officer will be here by the start of the underway tomorrow."

"Which sub will be ours, Captain?" asked Flynn.

"The *Jacksonville*. She's already here. You'll get your operational orders and be notified of your targets when we board."

MacKenzie felt their energy. They were anxious to prove themselves. The academics—learning the administrative tasks of a commanding officer, intelligence training, order writing, legal work—all these were over. Now it was for the money. Only Bell restrained himself. He had MacKenzie's sympathy. In a way, someone like Bell made it easier for him to be here.

He'd been hurt when his old friend Ben Garver, Chief of Naval Operations, "suggested" it was time he passed on his hard-won knowledge to the next generation of submarine captains. Men like Flynn, Bell, and Carter were supposed to be the best of a smart new breed, trained differently, America's warriors for the next century. MacKenzie had to accept change. If he didn't, despite his unequaled talent and reputation, he would be swept away like so many others whose stubborn clinging to past glories had turned them from heroes into relics.

MacKenzie caught his reflection in the mirror. He didn't *feel* old. Sure, his dark hair was showing some gray. And the lines around his pale gray eyes had grown deeper. But the planes of his face were still lean and strong, a blend of his Scottish immigrant ancestors and the Midwestern women they had married. Imbued in his line was a respect for freedom, honesty, thrift, and hard work, a drive for competence in all things, and a love of life stemming from boundless optimism, which, given America, seemed self-evident.

To the PCOs he was the bold Captain MacKenzie, the most victorious commander in the fleet. His inner reality was vastly different. He wasn't sure he knew how to change.

What happens to a man when he finds the perfect job, loves it with all his might, becomes the best at it, and then has it taken away? He had come to Andros Island less than a week before. Everything was still brand new. It was his job not only to train them, but to *educate* them in the subtle ways of command. He decided to do that he first had to know them as people.

"Tell me, Mr. Bell. Is it true what I've heard?"

"Depends, sir. Can you tell me what you've heard? Been a long time since I threw a football, if that's what you mean."

"Actually, I meant your literary bent. The T is for Twain, isn't it?" MacKenzie drove around a line of kids returning home from school. "Rumor has it you have all of Mark Twain's books in your head."

Bell shook his head. "Not the way you mean it, sir. You can't give me the page number and have me read it straight out of the book or anything. My dad just liked us to memorize a lot of what Twain wrote. We'd do it when he was away on cruise. It was our way of being closer, picturing him in his cabin reading the same passages. We'd have contests when he got home."

"Go ahead, sir. Test him," said Flynn from the back. "He's got one for every occasion."

"All right," agreed MacKenzie. "Mr. Bell, do the honors. A salute to Andros Island and what lies ahead."

Bell concentrated for a moment. Then something sparkled in his eyes, and the tiniest smile broke the corners of his mouth. For the first time MacKenzie saw an inner quality of the man, and it seemed to include not only wry humor beneath that hard New England hide, but a tough, rebellious intelligence as well.

"Very well, sir," said Bell. "A tribute to PCO final training. From Huck Finn. *'I was a-trembling because I'd got to decide forever betwixt two things, and I knowed it. I studied for a minute, sort of holding my breath, and then says to myself, 'All right, then, I'll go to hell.'* "

Chapter Three

300 miles east of the North Carolina coast

THE OCEAN DEPTHS WERE TOO MURKY TO GET ANY KIND OF CLEAR TV picture, so LCDR Moran cut the front floods and backed off to let the silt settle on the sub. The downed U.S.S. *Grayling* was in a tough position, covered by tons of ocean silt thrown up by her too-rapid impact with the bottom. If too much silt covered the escape hatch, they couldn't dock *Avalon,* a Deep Submergence Rescue Vehicle. Their hydraulic robot arm could move a ton of rock, but it was useless with the fine stuff.

"I'm going to try a back blow, Phil," said Moran.

Lt. Phil Levin, the copilot, was monitoring the gauges closely. The DSRV was low on battery power. "Maybe we should go back to Mother for a recharge."

"We got ten minutes?" asked Moran.

Levin frowned. "That's pushing it."

Moran looked out the viewport trying to discern the position of the downed sub. If the horizontal angle wasn't too sharp they could settle over the *Grayling*'s escape trunk and dewater their skirt to make a tight enough seal to transfer twenty-four men at a time into *Avalon.* Too great an angle, the seal would rupture.

23

Whatever they were going to do, it had to be done quickly. They were over nineteen hundred feet down, close to the sub's crush depth. A hundred and twenty-eight men were breathing smoke from the fire in the engine room that had sent her to the bottom. The whole area was laced with trenches that had bottom depths well below the sub's crush depth. Luckily, the captain had been able to bottom his ship on a plateau. Another fifty feet and *Grayling* would have been over the edge. Moran had to be damn careful. A shock might send the sub sliding into the trench. Adding to their problems, the captain had been injured in the incident and now the XO, Commander Kelly, was in charge. Moran could hear fear in his voice. He was close to cracking, failing to use proper procedures for an accident of this kind. You never knew who could stand the heat until the kitchen was on fire.

"Avalon, we've got fumes spreading," came Kelly's worried voice over the speaker. "The fan room is unable to clear."

"Grayling, Avalon," radioed Moran. "Can you get your portable fans and filters to clear the air?"

"Negative, *Avalon,* they are inoperable. You've got to make your mate now."

"Sure enough, Mr. Kelly," Moran tried to soothe the XO, "but first things first. Got to clear the hatch. Try ventilating with air from the air banks."

"Don't tell me how to run my ship, *Avalon.* I said *now.* That is a direct order. Do you hear me? I repeat. Now. Confirm."

Moran cut the radio and turned to Levin. "Sing this bastard some kind of song while I set this up, will you?"

Levin chuckled and muttered something under his breath that sounded like "schmuck." Most everything Levin said that came from his Jewish origins sounded like he was clearing his throat. Moran wasn't even sure Levin really *was* Jewish, coming from Nebraska.

"I'm gonna back around and blow the trunk clear. Keep us in trim and watch you don't catch the arm on anything."

Levin keyed in the mike, "Mr. Kelly, this is Lt. Levin. We are complying. Out."

Moran said wryly, "Succinct."

"It's about damn time," came Kelly's voice angrily.

Levin shook his head. "He's losing it."

Deftly Moran swung the DSRV around on its own axis to line up the props with the escape trunk.

"*Avalon,* where are you?" radioed Kelly frantically. "Sonar reports you're moving away. *Avalon.* Come back!"

"Ignore that asshole," said Moran tightly. "Tell me, Phil. How many Jews are there in Nebraska?"

"Eleven at last count. There were more, but the salmon died. Can't have Jews without smoked salmon. It was an ecological as well as a religious tragedy."

They bantered without really listening, concentrating on their delicate tasks while Moran set up the only maneuver possible to get those men off the sub. *Everybody came home.* That was their motto, though Levin was on record as preferring *We pick up and deliver.* Moran watched the screens closely. The mating decal over the escape trunk had to be there. Yeah. Right there.

"Got it, Phil. Hold her there. Full thrust."

The engines screamed up to full power and the prop wash sluiced over the *Grayling's* hull. Bit by bit the silt cleared. Levin moved the larger debris with the hydraulic arm. With some of the weight shifting, *Grayling* came up straighter, giving them a better shot at her trunk.

"Some days you eat the bear," Levin said admiringly.

"Is that kosher?" Moran wondered.

"What are you doing, *Avalon?*" radioed Kelly, yelling. "The ship's rocking. We're close to the edge, damn it. Do you want to send us over? Cease this action immediately."

"Clear to dock," said Levin.

"Acknowledged. Here we go."

"Avalon, do you hear me!?"

Moran picked up the mike. "It's a little tough to hear you, Mr. Kelly, what with all this jockeying about going on," Moran said politely. "Now would you mind hanging on? We're coming in."

Six trips did it, with the last being roomy enough to let Levin joke with the final group that they were in first class. The XO, Kelly, was in that group, stewing angrily, complaining about everything from the damp blankets to the wait while Moran and Levin had recharged *Avalon*'s batteries at their mother craft, Submarine Rescue Ship ASR-22 *Ortolan,* out of Charleston. Moran took it stoically. The after-action report would be enough to condemn Kelly. The radio traffic was part of *Ortolan*'s record. Little else would be needed. A pity. No PCO school for this XO. He had been tested and found wanting. This was as far as Mr. Kelly would go.

Moran experienced a pang of wistfulness. *Avalon* was a very special craft, able to go where no ordinary sub could, but the thought of commanding a nuclear attack sub—being out there under the ice with the big boys—that was an undeniable lure, something Moran had wanted since joining the navy, and the elusiveness of that goal still made for an inner sense of restless unhappiness. Sub command was effectively closed off and unobtainable, for no good reason, as far as Moran could see. There would be no attack runs or underwater combat, no way for Moran, now thirty, to attain command. The wistfulness changed to a stab of anger. Kelly wasn't the only one who had gone as far as he could go.

Kelly's unpleasantness grew as they rose to the surface. He muttered about incompetence, displaying a special anger toward Moran. The rest of the men ignored him and tried to let Moran know how grateful they felt. Moran was okay about the job. Maybe being truly happy was too much to ask for. Best be content and go about it.

"Home sweet home," Levin said happily as they surfaced and the submariners exited the topside hatch.

"Nice work, Phil," affirmed Moran. "Is CINCLANT sending a team down right away, do you know?"

"I heard they're coming. Figure we'll have to take 'em down later. Watch it. Here we go." Levin keyed the mike. "Affirmative lift, Mother."

The big grappling crane on the mother ship pulled *Avalon* out of the water. Levin levered himself out of the hatch into the fresh air. Moran climbed after, gratefully stretching limbs that were cramped and aching after so many hours behind the wheel.

Levin, ham that he was, took a bow as the submarine and ASR crews applauded. Moran waved. The ASR skipper gave a long blast on the horn. The navy might lose a ton of money today, but every precious life had been saved. No one ever argued that balance.

What happened next came quickly, and Moran should have figured it. There was ample evidence Kelly wasn't going to put it down. One minute the clean sea air was blowing the mustiness out of Moran's lungs, and the next a hulking shape dropped from the superstructure to *Avalon*'s deck with a wrench in his hand. Levin only had time for a hasty, "Jess, duck!" before Kelly rammed him aside. Levin hit the deck hard, and Kelly charged with the wrench held high like a club, fury in his eyes.

Everything's tough on the south side of Chicago, even sports. Twenty years ago Moran was a kid wanting to play on the neighborhood baseball team and some jerky kid decided maybe it wasn't such a good idea. He tried to back up his opinion with a baseball bat, wielding it just like Kelly, chopping down like an ax to crush Moran's skull. But then as now Moran had always figured the opposition. A lot of work with the local gangs resulted in a special combination of boxing, karate, and just plain dirty street fighting. The boy with the baseball bat ended up eating it. He was only the first to underestimate the strength in Moran's five-foot-six-inch body.

Moran spun *into* Kelly, driving an elbow deep into his midsection. Kelly's breath exploded out of him. Moran grabbed his wrist and twisted it so he either bent over or it broke. The wrench clattered to the deck. Moran hammered him in the neck with all the force one hundred and twenty pounds could muster, which in Moran's case was considerable. Kelly dropped. There was cheering from above. Levin had risen, apparently unhurt. Moran was content to let it go.

"Very nicely done," said a woman's voice close by. "Very nice indeed, Commander."

A woman's voice? Here? Moran turned, curious. An absolutely breathtaking woman stood there with an appreciative smile on her face. She was in her late thirties or early forties, it was hard to tell exactly. Tall and striking. Her jet-black hair was pulled back as tight as piano wire showing off her dark eyes, straight nose, and full red mouth. Aristocratic was the word that described her. She was wearing an expensive Italian black wool suit with stockings and heels and a patterned leather belt. A gold necklace adorned her open-collared red silk blouse. She fit in on the ASR like a diamond in a mud puddle, but she seemed totally relaxed and comfortable. Moran felt dirty and cheap next to her.

The woman extended her hand. "I'm Justine MacKenzie. It's a pleasure to meet you, Commander Moran."

"Er . . . thank you, ma'am." Moran wiped at the oil-stained navy coveralls. "I'm sorry I'm not . . . Excuse me, sir!" Moran jerked to attention, totally nonplussed. It was a credit to this woman's incredible presence that she had made Moran ignore the admiral standing behind her. He had enough ribbons on his chest to support a medal shop, and Moran suddenly realized that he was the Chief of Naval Operations, four-star Admiral Ben Garver. Christ! The CNO? Here? What the hell was going on?

Justine motioned to Kelly lying on the deck. "What do

you figure, Ben? He has maybe seventy pounds on her? I haven't seen natural timing like that since—well, since *I* was that young, if you'll excuse the immodesty."

"You've got a long way to go before you've got a foot in the grave," admonished Garver affectionately. "At ease, Moran. My compliments to you and your copilot."

"Thank you, sir," responded Commander Jessica Moran. She pulled off her cap and shook out her blond hair. She desperately needed a shower and a change of clothes. Her face was sweat-streaked, and she wore no makeup—a sharp contrast, she couldn't help noticing, to the perfect grooming of the MacKenzie woman. What remained of her femininity rebelled at standing anywhere near enough to induce comparisons. God, could you imagine looking like that? And wearing those clothes? Ahh, but, Moran consoled herself, could she have driven *Avalon* to hell and back, or taken Kelly? No way. No damn way at all.

Comparing herself to Justine and wondering why the woman had slipped off her shoes, Moran forgot all about Kelly. It wasn't until someone shouted that she realized he was coming at her again, but before she could do anything Justine had moved past her and intercepted Kelly in mid-charge. Her foot lashed out faster than a cobra strike, toes back, smashing the ball of her foot up under his chin with enough force to jerk his head straight up and glaze his eyes.

Kelly stood there wavering. Justine was poised and balanced like a deadly ballerina. She took no notice of her skirt bunched up to mid-thigh or the ship's crew hanging off the superstructure whistling and ogling. She spoke to Jessica alone, as if lecturing in a classroom. "Your strike was good, but that nerve-bundle paralysis only lasts for five minutes or so. *This* is the spot to fully disable." Her stiff fingers speared out *shuto* style and struck somewhere along Kelly's back. He sank to his knees in pain, unable to lift his arms. Justine raised her hands and said simply, "This will kill."

"Justine." It was Garver.

"Hmm? Oh, sorry, Ben. I wasn't actually—"

"I know. But there'll be plenty of time for this later."

"Right. Sorry."

"Actually," Garver said good-naturedly, "I'm always delighted to see you in action. I so rarely have the opportunity."

So much for feeling superior, Jessica thought. *Sure* she couldn't take Kelly. Garver put the XO in custody. Show over, the crew got back to work.

Exhaustion was setting in, and she was starting to feel kind of detached, as if it weren't really happening to her. She decided she wouldn't run her usual fifteen miles. Maybe she'd just wake up in bed and find that *Grayling,* Kelly, this beautiful, deadly woman, and the CNO were all just part of a weird dream. She followed them to the captain's cabin. The sharp click of Justine's heels on the steel deck plates wasn't a sound you often heard out in the Atlantic Ocean. They knocked her out more than anything. They were so delicate. So womanly. She stared morosely at her own thick boots. More dreaminess. Best just flow along with things. Besides, what could happen that was any stranger?

There was the usual nautical decor, reference books, and framed photos of ships and kids in the captain's cabin. Garver took a chair and gestured for Jessica to take one, too. Justine perched up on the desk, playing idly with a dagger-type letter opener. Moran could have sworn she was testing it for balance.

"Commander Moran," began Garver, "these are changing times. As Chief of Naval Operations I am responsible for helping the navy respond to those changes. Your qualifications make possible something we've been discussing for a long time."

"Too long, if you ask me," said Justine pointedly.

Garver sighed. "Be that as it may. Commander Moran, do you know what takes place on Andros Island?"

Moran's head snapped up. If it was a dream . . . scratch

that, it had to be a dream. Where else but in her head could what Garver was suggesting be possible? She'd had the same training as any submariner in Nuclear Power School to drive the NR-1, the nuclear-powered version of *Avalon*. In fact, she was fully qualified for subs but had been held back because she was a woman. Yet why else would Garver be here? Justine was looking at her steadily. Despite the short time they'd been together, Jessica felt like she had an ally.

"Yes, sir. I do know what takes place there. PCO final training. Is that what this is all about?"

Garver was still talking an hour later, and Jessica Moran was still listening.

MacKenzie got the wire from Garver and Justine after he dropped the PCOs at the Q.

Final candidate tested and confirmed. On our way.

MacKenzie checked his watch. Commander Jessica Moran would be on the island in less than an hour, along with his wife, Justine.

Now they were four.

Chapter Four

Andros Island

AUTEC Control Center

COMMANDER FRANK "RED" CADO WAS WAITING FOR BEN Garver when he strode in, just back from the *Ortolan*. Garver had dropped off Justine and delivered Jessica Moran to her PCOI, Peter MacKenzie.

Cado was wearing a look Garver could only interpret as relief and concern mixed in equal parts. "The *Dallas* had a fix on the *Northern Star* in the Med, sir."

"Christ, that ends a lot of worrying," Garver said to his senior aide.

"But they lost her," amended Cado. "She probably got through Gibraltar into the Atlantic."

That was bad news. Avilov had a big ocean to hide in. "Send the rest of the subs. I want a screen so tight it could sift flour," Garver said firmly. "What do you think about adding the battle group?"

"We've got five destroyers already in the search area, two other fast attack submarines besides the *Augusta*, and all the helo squadrons and Orions we own. The *Northern Star* isn't going to get through."

"I don't want to have to eat those words. What does Legal say about us stopping her?"

Cado shrugged. "They'd be a damn sight happier if Admiral Rushkov gave us the go-ahead. So far he hasn't. We're looking for precedents."

"Which means do it and we'll justify it later."

"Right. You think Rushkov is in on it?"

Garver was thoughtful. "Could be. All this time we've been worrying about them selling the little stuff. SAMs, battlefield nukes, warheads." He shook his head sadly, "No one ever figured someone might try to sell a whole damned sub. What do we know about this Avilov?"

"Here's the profile. It's gone out to all the COs."

Garver took the folder. "Summarize it."

Cado spoke thoughtfully. "They call him the Hawk. He's their best. Speculation is he was responsible for that oiler sunk off the African coast a few years back. A slick, tough, veteran commander with a complete bag of tricks. His ship is one of their newest and quietest. He will be very difficult to stop. If it's any comfort, CIA thinks he might not be a willing accomplice."

"Why?"

"CIA Station Moscow found something out updating his dossier. Katcha Avilov told her neighbors she and her son Misha were going on vacation in Havana with his senior lieutenant's family. She'd been told they would meet Avilov and Pachenko when they got to Sabaña Key."

"Guests or hostages?"

"There are a lot cheaper hotel rooms. Insurance, at the least."

"It only makes it worse," said Garver. "His family's at stake."

The problem was that there were too many approaches to Cuba to set up an effective screen. It was like trying to answer the question, Which way to Chicago? "Make sure every CO in the operation gets a complete report on current thinking. Tell them in no uncertain terms that if we lose the *Northern Star* I'll have somebody's ass for an ottoman."

"Yes, sir."

The phone on his desk buzzed. "Sir? It's Arthur Winestock at CIA," his secretary called in.

"Put him through." Garver hit the speaker phone and motioned for Cado to stay. "Arthur? Nice to hear from you. Red's here with me."

"Seems like we only meet in the middle of crises," said Winestock's cultured voice over the speaker. "This line is secure?"

"It is," said Garver.

"What's the status of the *Northern Star?*"

"One of my subs made contact. We're trying to nail it down."

"We have to do better than try, Ben. We've got additional product. We're not going to get any help from the Russians on this. It looks like Rushkov was part of the sale."

Garver grimaced. "A little freelance capitalism?"

"To the tune of seventy-five million dollars. We can't let this one go. If it pays off, there'll be plenty of others wanting to do it, too."

"Weapons R Us," said Garver without humor.

"We've confirmed that the *Northern Star* is carrying SS-NX-21 nuclear-tipped cruise missiles," said Winestock. "Ben, the president is getting signals from the Secretary of State that maybe we could have peace in the region in ten years or so if no one does anything major-league stupid like setting off a nuclear bomb. He feels strongly the sub cannot be allowed to reach Cuba. The president would like you to take personal charge of this one. Upgrade the stop-and-hold to a kill order."

"And here I thought the Cold War was over," said Garver dryly.

Winestock didn't flinch. "Sure."

Garver scissored two fingers at Cado. Cut the order. Cado left the office in a hurry.

"Er . . . Ben," Winestock said hesitantly, "I don't want to

step on your turf, but do you think we might get MacKenzie in on this one?"

Garver thought it over. It was exactly the kind of operation Mac liked best. A cunning adversary. Tough odds. A difficult mission. But where did it stop? It would remain a dangerous world for the foreseeable future. There would always be another mission, and more after that. You couldn't build a force on one man. The navy needed others to take his place. The time had come to take Mac out of operations, and Garver wasn't going to put him back in if he could help it.

"It would only prolong the agony, Arthur. He's got to stay with the PCOs."

"Up to you," said Winestock simply. "But it'd be a hell of an education for them, wouldn't it?"

A slow smile crept over Garver's face. It was an interesting thought. Maybe . . . "Might be, Arthur. Might be at that. Let me ponder it."

"Sure." The line went dead.

Garver thought about MacKenzie for a long time after.

BOQ

How silent and good. Sink down. Forget. No more faces. How easy. Forget the bodies in the water . . . the bodies in the water . . . the thing coming at him . . . waving . . . waving!

Bell woke with a start. His body was bathed in sweat, trembling after the same haunting nightmare. He swung his feet off the bed and held his face in his hands till the shakes stopped. He looked in the mirror. A frightened man stared back. He didn't want to spend any more time alone, so he took a shower and got dressed. He needed to walk. To *breathe.*

There was a frame house down on the beach with a bar and an outside deck. He got a cold beer and walked down to the water. It rippled onto pure white sand. The fear had subsided. The dream was past. But could he command? That was the question. Could he ever command again?

He stared out at the blue water and thought about finally being here. As a kid the sportswriters had called him the original fish out of water, a northerner becoming quarterback in the South. He showed them all when he took his team all the way to a bowl championship. But the real notoriety came when he turned down big pro money to join the navy. He had worked to become a sub commander ever since. And make no mistake about it, command was what this was all about. He hadn't joined the navy to be anything less. None of them had. He wanted to be the one who made the decisions, who stood on the bridge directing the power of that huge black whale of a ship, to be the man other men turned to in times of need.

Like his father.

He tossed some sand into the water, an old ritual for him. Farewell to the dead and dying.

"I usually find the bar first," said Flynn, coming up behind him. "Penny for your thoughts, XO. You worried?"

Flynn was decked out in a gaudy Hawaiian-print shirt, a bottle of beer in his big fist. The older man's green eyes were kind. They'd all been together too long for there to be any derision in the question.

"Just trying to get my head right, Jamie. My coach'd always yell, 'Get your head right, Bell. Doubts'll kill ya faster than women or booze.'"

Flynn looked horrified. "Life without either is too horrible to contemplate."

Bell laughed. "I can't imagine *you're* worried."

"Nah, I feel ready. I was a good goddamned XO. But who the hell knows? My last CO used to shake his head and say 'Flynn, there's as much difference between a CO and an XO as there is between an XO and a civilian.' What the hell did he mean?"

"He meant there's no one else to turn to," Carter said, joining them.

"Busy beach," observed Bell. "How you doing, Reg?"

"Well, part of me is calm. Part of me can't wait to get into action. And I suppose there's a part in there that feels some trepidation."

"He didn't ask you for everything you ever felt since childhood, Reg," said Flynn dryly. "A simple 'not bad' would have done it." Abruptly Flynn's attitude changed. "Well, well, well. If you gentlemen will excuse me . . ."

A female jogger in black spandex running shorts and a red tank top was running down the beach. Her blond hair was tied into a ponytail. Her breasts bobbed as she ran. The total effect was intriguing.

Flynn moved out on an intercept track. The woman had bright blue eyes and skin like milk. She was drenched from running. About twenty feet away he tripped and went down in the sand, clutching his ankle. She stopped to help him as he tried to stand, and he gravely consented to let her put her shoulder under his arm and walk him to the deck. Conversation ensued, bodies touching.

"Masterful," acknowledged Bell.

"Greatness is a pleasure to watch in any field," Carter agreed.

Bell saw something on the sand and picked it up. "Reg?"

Carter took a quick look at it and grinned. "You weren't thinking . . ."

"I'm ashamed to say I was."

Carter grinned and saluted. "Battle stations."

For a man who could toss a football fifty feet through a swinging tire ten times out of ten, even figuring the harmless little sand lizard wasn't evenly balanced, the ten-foot toss was a gimme. It landed squarely on the back of Flynn's neck and dropped into his shirt at the same moment Carter called out, "Scorpion!"

In one unusual movement Flynn twisted around frantically and shoved a hand up under his shirt, trying not to put any weight on his "sore" right ankle, which was extremely difficult because his left foot had come off the ground when he tried to grab the "scorpion" down his back. The end result was a kind of hopping, waving, stumbling dance down the beach culminating in a back-first dive onto the sand to extricate the harmless lizard.

Seeing Bell and Carter grinning broadly, Flynn realized what they had done. He was choked with rage. He searched for words dark enough to convey his fury and advanced with murder in his eyes, finally getting out, "You miserable sons of—"

Bell pointed.

Flynn had forgotten his limp. A disgusted look came over the woman's face. He tried to recover with a rueful smile. "I just wanted to meet you. I guess there were better ways. I'm sorry."

"You got that right," she said contemptuously. "Tell me your name so I can steer clear in the future, huh?"

"I'm Jamie Flynn. This is Reggie Carter, and my candidate for lizard thrower is Mark Bell."

Her face changed to disbelief. "You're the other PCOs."

"How did you know?"

"I'm Commander Jessica Moran. Off the DSRV *Avalon*. I joined the class today."

"You're the fourth man . . . person?" gasped Carter. They all stood there in shock.

Flynn said, "Nobody told us you were a—"

Her stance grew defensive. "A what?" she demanded.

"A DSRV pilot," supplied Bell diplomatically. He offered her his hand. "Welcome aboard, ma'am."

"Jessica." They all shook on it.

"Tell us about yourself," Flynn said.

"What's to tell? I hit the big three-oh this year," she said without a grimace. "Born Chicago, Illinois. Academy '86."

"You went to Annapolis?" asked Carter.

"Twenty-second Company. I held my own. Wasn't any tougher than my old neighborhood, and a lot cleaner. You, Reg?"

"Academy '79. I'm thirty-six, former XO of the *Baton Rouge*. A wife, two kids, and a mortgage that's a killer. Did you know a guy named Paulson at Annapolis?"

"Big dude? Refused to cut his Afro?"

"I forgot about that," said Carter. "My radical cousin."

"And you, Jamie?"

"Not a great deal to tell, lass," Flynn began modestly.

Bell couldn't believe his ears. Flynn humble? He was more earnest than Bell had ever seen. And he talked to Jessica without using his patented lines, possibly the greatest gesture of respect Bell had ever seen him make. Ironically, he realized Jessica must have thought it was another ploy.

"You do have a wide variety of tactics, don't you?" she said, laughing. "Jamie, your rep precedes you. Remember a little redhead named Joyce when you were posted in San Diego? She and I roomed together at the Academy. Those were some hot letters she wrote me till you walked off with somebody else. Mark?"

"Born Bedford Falls, Maine. Ole Miss, '80. Former XO of the *Simon Bolivar.*"

"What was a Yankee doing in Mississippi?"

"Playing football."

A light went on in her eyes. "You're that Mark Bell. I remember the big deal they made about you. Like football was heaven, and you'd given up a free pass."

He laughed. "That's just about the way they put it."

"Was it the right thing?"

"I've never been more certain. Want to know what Twain said?"

"Mark Twain, the writer? Sure."

"*'Always do right. This will gratify some people and astonish the rest.'*"

She giggled. "Do more."

"'*A round man cannot be expected to fit into a square hole. He must be given time to modify his shape.*'"

Jessica found herself fitting in and relaxed. "I'll say this, you guys do make an impression. Look, I'm gonna finish my run. See you all at dinner. And Jamie? Maybe you could do that dance again. Just once?" She took off down the beach.

Flynn stared after her. A self-deprecating smile curled the corners of his mouth. "God, that's one interesting woman. And a PCO yet. By the way, I'm gonna check if killing your classmates is an accepted tactic."

Bell clapped him on the back. "I think—"

Flynn pushed him into the sand.

The fish fry was held in a clearing filled with picnic tables and benches by the beach. Fallen pine needles made a soft blanket on the sand for families to spread out picnic style. Colored lights strung in the trees gave the clearing a festive air, typically tropical, informal and relaxed.

Bell, Flynn, and Carter stepped up to the bar, driftwood planks nailed between two trees and faced with shingles.

"Scotch," said Bell, looking to Carter.

"Jack and soda, thanks."

Flynn said "Irish whiskey," and Bell said, "Of course. '*Give an Irishman lager for a month, and he's a dead man. An Irishman is lined with copper, and beer corrodes it. But whiskey polishes the copper and is the saving of him.*'"

"Wisdom," Flynn agreed magnanimously.

Bell was about to put money on the bar when a navy pilot with a chewed-up stogie clenched between his teeth stepped up next to him and slapped down a twenty.

"I'm buying, Lieutenant," he said. "Commander Bill Colby, CO of the *Forestal*'s HS 15." Colby wore a shirt even gaudier than Flynn's, and a cowboy hat with a feather in the crown. He peered through the smoke gathered under the brim. "These are my pilots. It's kind of a tradition around

40

here us buying drinks tonight, 'cause tomorrow during combat we're going to be out for your asses." Colby's men looked at the PCOs like lobsters in a tank before dinner.

"You know this guy, Mark?" asked Flynn.

Bell shook his head.

Helicopter Anti-submarine Squadron 15's Sea King SH-3 helos were carrier-based anti-submarine warfare (ASW) units. They had a marvelous track record at locating submarines. One of the pilots, a guy with a black stubble and an even blacker cigar—obviously *de rigeur* in Colby's squadron—blew smoke Bell's way. "We eat Bubbleheads and spit out the pits. You got something to say about that?"

"What's your name?" Bell asked.

"Rico. Lt. Frankie Rico, hotshot."

"Well, Frank, I'm sure intimidated all to hell," said Bell. He turned back to the bar and put his money down. "Take it out of this."

Colby shoved his money forward. "I said I'm paying."

Flynn looked at him coldly. "Take a hike, Tex."

"I'm from New Mexico, pretty boy. We think Texas sucks."

"That's a little technical for me," said Flynn pleasantly. "Sort of like the difference between a call girl and a whore."

There was the instantaneous crowding in that might have led to a fight had not Jessica Moran stepped up to the bar and said, "Well, classmates, making more friends, I see."

"Now might not be the time, Commander," Flynn said quietly.

"I dunno. We the PCOs?" she asked.

"Well, sure," Flynn said.

"They the ASW units?"

Flynn grinned. "I see your point." This girl was something, he thought.

Bell said, "Gentleman, meet Commander Moran. Our team's secret weapon."

41

Colby was staring. "I see it, but I don't believe it. What the hell is this navy coming to? If you think—"

Carter held up a hand. "Now, now, sexist remarks aren't allowed, haven't you heard? Not that I expect a giant bag of wind like you to make any."

They surged in again, but Jessica was an unknown quantity and she parted them like the Red Sea by moving to the bar and ordering a shot of whiskey, which she downed in one gulp.

"I am in love," Flynn said dreamily.

Carter said, "Why exactly do you want to buy us drinks anyway, Commander?"

"Like I said, tradition. First night the pilots buy. After that, whoever takes the prize buys." He added slyly, "Plus a hundred a man, a *man,* at the end. Got it?"

"HS 15 hasn't bought in a long time," said Rico happily. The others nodded.

"I wouldn't buy these guys a—" Flynn began, but Bell stopped him. "MacKenzie know about this?" he asked.

"Nobody has to know, unless you girls tell him," said Colby.

Bell took a quick poll. Carter shrugged. He would play it either way. Flynn was ready to fight, sending signals that he'd be happy to take the first punch. Jessica's stance said she was with the team. Bell studied the amber liquid in his glass for a moment, then stuck out his hand to Colby. "You got yourself a bet."

"Mark?" Carter said questioningly.

Colby grinned and stuck out his hand. "Good man."

Bell held his hand. "On one condition."

Colby's eyes narrowed. "What?"

"A slight change in stakes." Bell explained what he had in mind. "Call it a side bet."

Flynn's mouth dropped open. Carter smiled. Colby's men looked dubious, but Colby took out his cigar and observed mildly, "Could be a historical event. It's a deal, Lieutenant. Let's go, boys."

MacKenzie watched the helo pilots give his PCOs a hard time. They had given *him* one, a long time ago during his PCO days.

He had spent an hour with Jessica Moran getting to know her and was impressed by her strength of purpose and mental toughness. She was a welcome addition, and if being female posed problems, he hadn't seen any yet. What interested him now was confirmation of a relationship the prior instructors at Norfolk had written about. In spite of his past and his youth, when Colby pressed the PCOs, they looked to Bell. Further confirmation the younger man was a natural leader.

MacKenzie sidled over to the bar. "Dewar's, John."

"Right, Captain."

"Evening, sir," said Carter.

"Sir," said the rest simultaneously.

"I see you've all met. Again I want to welcome you to PCO training, Commander."

"Thank you, sir."

"What do you think of the carrier boys?" MacKenzie asked innocently.

"One or two I wouldn't mind drowning," said Flynn darkly.

MacKenzie laughed.

"Captain, sir?" A seaman came up. "Can you tell me where I can find Commander Carter?"

"Right there." MacKenzie pointed. He handed Carter a note.

"What is it, Mr. Carter?"

"The base commander wants to see me in his office, sir."

"At this hour?"

"Something about dependent insurance forms. I don't

know." Carter shrugged. "God forbid we don't have the right forms."

"We have a briefing at twenty-one hundred tonight. Don't be late."

"Yes, sir. See you there."

The lights were out in the administration building and Carter checked the message to make sure he had the right time. Odd being called this way.

"Come in, Commander. Over here."

A shadowy uniformed figure down the hall went into an office. Carter followed. The nameplate on the door read OIC 2/Simmons, but Carter knew this office didn't belong to the man who stood in front of him any more than anything on this base did, except that in a way he owned it all. Carter had a bad feeling. Something wasn't right. He brought his arm up in a fast salute.

"Sir!"

"At ease, Commander Carter. Thank you for coming."

Carter knew Admiral Walton Ransom. He was the closest thing to a warlord the navy had. In his world, political power meant funding, and funding meant control, so he had cultivated Senate and House members and anyone else who could affect the outcome of a budget vote. He gave junkets and parties and set up terrific photo ops for politicians to greet returning Marines for the newspapers back home. In return they handed him the power of the purse.

Some officers idolized Ransom, others saw in him the worst kind of cult figure. He was the kind of man who rises to the top in any field, part visionary, part ruthless schemer, and the tally was evenly split on which part dominated. One thing everybody agreed on: Ransom never forgot a friend and always, always, *always* got even with his enemies.

Carter was instantly on his guard.

"You know who I am?"

"Yes, sir."

Ransom folded his ascetically thin frame into the desk chair, crossed his legs, and put his hands in his lap. He looked Carter over slowly. "Curious as to why you're here?"

What the fuck was going on? "Sir, I'm sure you have a good reason."

Ransom laughed at that. "One of the best, near as I can tell. You'll come to realize that if you live as long as I have. I want you to punish a man for me, Commander Carter. No, don't ask who. I'll tell you who in good time. I want you to fix it so he has no chance of surviving in this man's navy. That's a dandy reason, isn't it?"

"I don't understand, sir."

Ransom waved that off. "Did you know I had a son, Mr. Carter?"

"No, sir."

"Well, I did. He died. On a submarine. The *Thornton,* to be precise. Criminal negligence caused his death and the death of a hundred and twenty-nine other men. Oh, they didn't call it that at the hearing. But with the CO running her at that speed in those waters? Just a matter of time before she tore her guts out on those reefs and went down with all hands."

Carter steeled himself. "Navigational failure."

"What?"

"Sir, we studied the *Thornton* at the Academy. SEALs dived on the wreck and found that the inertial guidance system had . . ." Carter stopped.

Ransom had grown completely still. His arms and legs looked frozen. Carter wondered if there was any circulation left in those scrawny old limbs. "Sir, are you all right?"

It took a moment for Ransom to answer, as if he was winding up the strength. His eyes were as dry as dust. "There are two kinds of thinkers in my organization, mister. You got any idea where that kind of thinking puts you?"

"Sir, I can guess."

Ransom's eyes were cold. "You want a command of your

own, you get your thinking straight, or as God is my judge the best post you'll ever have will make commanding a rowboat seem glamorous. I'm as good as my word, son. If you know me at all, you know that."

Cold sweat slid down Carter's sides. He rallied his courage. "You're asking me to commit an illegal act. I'm going to report you to the appropriate authorities."

"Very good, son. Right response. But think it over. You've got a wife and kids. Be nice for them if Daddy got that special posting in Paris, or Washington. Flag rank is within reach for a smart, good-looking man like you. With me and my people behind you pulling strings it's only a few years to full captain. Another couple to rear admiral. Later on a vice presidency at one of our contractors. Ahh . . . I guessed right, didn't I? A career in big business appeals to you."

Carter tried to make light of it. The truth was that Ransom had just laid out his life's dream. That he could deliver it so easily made a mockery of hard work, of the effort needed to get there. But the truth was that everybody knew there wasn't a defense contractor in the nation that wouldn't do anything the gaunt, wizened seventy-year-old admiral asked, any time he asked it, no questions, *sir*.

"Listen to me, Reginald. I can call you that. Old man's prerogative. You know my power. I can deliver good or evil. Have you ever asked yourself what a report of you having sex with another man would do to your ambitions?"

"What? Jesus, Admiral, not even you could—"

"Oh, but I could. In fact, it's easy," Ransom said. "I know a hundred men who would swear you were their lover. Loyalty's an easy thing to buy, son. Only thing cheaper is sex. You think it'd be tough to frame you? Christ, how do you think we get certain votes? The only difference between a politician and a snake is that the snake bites for a reason. Wake up, son. These are your options. Great success or eternal damnation. You can't have it both ways."

"Why me?" Carter asked plaintively.

Ransom shrugged. "You're vulnerable. Straight as an arrow. Wife and kids." His aged face grew hard as stone. "I loved my son more than anything on this earth, and I've waited ten years to pay back the man who killed him. You're going to help me."

"Sir, everyone on board the *Thornton* died."

Ransom's flinty eyes were suddenly alight with fury. "'I the Lord your God am a jealous God, visiting the sins of the fathers upon the children.' Exodus 20:5. Captain Robert Bell had a son who grew up, and mine didn't."

"Bell? Mark Bell? That's who you're after?"

"Imagine my concern when I discovered he wants to be a captain, just like his daddy. This is probably a public service."

"You're mad."

"I've considered that." Ransom's eyes were clear and dry again. "But who's to say?"

Father?

"Eh?" Ransom looked around.

"Sir?" said Carter, confused.

Father, so many times have we talked about this. I've asked you not to. And in my name you agreed. Will you love me less now, at the end?

"Not less. More!" Ransom cried. "That's why I have to do it now. While there's time."

I am the best part of you. Forgive him.

"I tried to. I even held back like you asked, but if Congress doesn't extend my term again, I might not be able to . . ." He stopped suddenly, staring vacantly.

Carter couldn't figure out who Ransom was talking to. There was no one else in the room. It was eerie. The man was insane, still wanting revenge even after all these years. An eye for an eye regardless of justice. The psychopath's song.

Ransom shuddered and seemed to come back into focus. The vacant look left his eyes. He turned back to Carter as if nothing at all had happened and handed him a thick folder from the desk. It was a restricted file filled with medical and psychological records in connection with a judicial hearing, the kind of material only someone as powerful as Ransom could gain access to. Carter saw the first few words, OFFICIAL INQUIRY INTO THE EVENTS OF . . . , and the name, LT. MARK T. BELL.

"Listen to me, Reginald," said Ransom. "Here's what you're going to do."

Chapter Five

AUTEC Control Center

IT IS AXIOMATIC OF THE SEA THAT WHEN THINGS CHANGE THEY
become deadlier. MacKenzie, Flynn, Carter, Bell, and
Moran were called into the conference room by Red Cado.
Garver was already at the long table. There was tension in
the air.

"Sit, everybody," Garver said. "Go ahead, Red."

Cado turned on a slide projector and a picture of Captain
Avilov came on the screen.

"Mac, you got the *Northern Star* briefing?"

"Yes, sir."

Garver turned to the PCOs. "This is Captain Pari
Ivanovich Avilov. The very best sub commander in the
Russian navy. A week ago the CIA received word that his
Akula submarine, the *Northern Star,* was sold to Libya and
he was sailing it across the Atlantic to Cuba. I needn't
remind you what a sub like that could do to the balance of
power in the Middle East. Or of the other terrorist purposes
to which she could be put. We won't permit it. A kill order
has been issued. Mac, what can you add about Avilov?"

"He's a superb veteran. I heard about him when I was in
Russia. They call him the Hawk. Totally unconventional

49

and unpredictable. A genius at doing what you'd expect least. There isn't a submariner over there who doesn't claim he's their very best."

Garver nodded. "Evidently the claims are true. We had him and lost him. Twice. I'm telling you all this because I think you deserve an explanation. I'm sorry, ladies and gentlemen. Due to this situation, PCO exercises are terminated. Combat exercises will be rescheduled when this is over. Mac, you are relieved as PCO instructor. I want you on my staff."

"Yes, sir," said MacKenzie, hating the idea.

"Sir, with your permission. What happens to us?" Flynn asked.

"You'll return to Norfolk for reassignment. We'll put together another class in a few months. We need every available ship. The *Augusta,* the *Key West,* and the *Cincinnati* are already on station. The *Jacksonville* and *Phoenix* will be going out, too."

MacKenzie admired their discipline. He himself wanted to rail at the unfairness of Garver's pronouncement because ships were going to sea against an enemy and he wasn't going with them. The PCOs' frustration was evident. It was a bitter thing to have the final phase of your training canceled on the eve of your coming of age. Terribly unfair. But they were professionals, and not a word was said.

A thought hit him. It was one borne of desperation. Maybe it was selfish, too, but it could work. And it could take him *back.* The idea grew into a certainty.

"Admiral," he said. "No man learns faster than when the stakes are for real. You know it as well as I do, sir."

"What are you driving at, Mac?"

"Avilov is as creative a captain as there is. Sir, the PCOs have been groomed to be something new. Flexible. Not bound by traditional thinking."

He's finally seeing it, thought Garver happily. "So?"

"So let me conduct their final training on board the

Jacksonville as part of the search. Let us go after Avilov. Their kind of training might make the difference against him. A wild card. Why not play it?"

"The unblooded top guns." Garver thought it over. "You're willing to use them as your approach team and not be in command yourself? You believe in them that much?"

"Yes, sir. I've read their training reports. I think they can do it. I'm willing to bet on them."

"What do they say?"

MacKenzie turned to the PCOs. Carter was silent. Bell had turned pale as a ghost. Jessica looked uncertain, and even Flynn's ebullience had waned.

"This is the difference between an exercise and the real thing," he said. "What you're feeling right now. There's a real enemy out there. It makes your hands sweat and your chest get tight. No more brave talk, just responsibility. Practice is over. Put your money where your mouth is, let's see what you're made of—there are a hundred different ways to say it. It all means pressure. No more points on a score sheet. We put our faith in you, and if you're wrong, we don't come home. Mr. Bell, you want the conn under those conditions? You of all people know what it can cost."

"Yes, sir. I do. I'll stay."

"Very well. Mr. Carter?"

"I appreciate your confidence in us. Yes, sir."

"Mr. Flynn."

"I'm already packed, Captain."

"Miss Moran?"

"I didn't come here to go home empty-handed. Yes, sir."

He turned back to Garver. "Admiral, I think I've got a team."

"Very well, Mac. Under those conditions."

Cado cut the operations orders and handed them to MacKenzie.

FM:CINCLANTFLT
TO:MACKENZIE, CO, U.S.S. *JACKSONVILLE*
<u>SUBJ:SEEK AND DESTROY MISSION</u>

Effective immediately:

1. JACKSONVILLE REASSIGNED TO SEEK *AKULA*-CLASS
   PANTERA-MODIFIED SUBMARINE *NORTHERN STAR* EN
   ROUTE GIBRALTAR TO SABAÑA KEY.
2. PROCEED AT BEST SONAR SPEED TO INTERCEPT AND
   DESTROY *NORTHERN STAR.*
3. ALL AVAILABLE CONVENTIONAL WEAPONS AUTHORIZED
   AND RELEASED.

MacKenzie felt his first pangs of doubt. The PCOs and his
own need for command pulled at him. He wondered if they
could survive his being pulled in opposite directions.

"Go get the *Northern Star,*" Garver said.

Chapter Six

Northern Star

AVILOV HAD MANAGED TO SLIP THE *STAR* THROUGH THE STRAITS of Gilbraltar and into the North Atlantic, but now he faced a gauntlet of ships that would surely have intimidated a lesser man. He was tending to the endless paperwork that is the bane of all commanding officers when Pachenko knocked on his door.

"Come in, Yuri."

Pachenko sat on the bunk. "How is your head?"

Avilov hadn't told Pachenko about the crippling headaches that had begun within hours of Lerner hitting him. "My head is not our problem. So many ships. It's going to be tougher now."

Pachenko said, "You'll get us there, I have no doubt. But what will we do then? We are finished the moment we deliver the *Star,* and we both knew it."

"Sadly, true. Lerner isn't going to pay for something he'll already own. That implies honor. We have from now till we reach Sabaña Key to figure out how to beat him."

"It was interesting about the money," Pachenko mused aloud. "He really thought you would take it. Odd how some people think it's easy to do bad things. Criminal things. Just pick up a fallen wallet in the street and put it in your pocket. But the wallet burns a hole in your pocket, and the money makes you afraid. Good things do not come of it," Pachenko finished simply. The big muscles of his shoulders moved under his black uniform. "He made a mistake taking our families."

Avilov nodded. "Twelve days to get to Sabaña Key. Some small margin of safety. Now come to the control room. I want to take a look around."

It happened when he stood up. The gray spots danced into his field of vision again, but this time they spread until they covered it all. He lost his balance and would have fallen had not Pachenko shot off the bunk and steadied him.

"What is it, Pari?"

Avilov reached out blindly. Everything was fragmented, as if someone had torn pieces from his field of vision. "Help me sit," he managed.

Pachenko got him to the bunk and started for the door. "I'll get the doctor."

"No!" Avilov clenched his eyes tightly. The pain was a dagger under his skull. He pressed his head between his hands to make it go away.

"This has been going on for a long time now, hasn't it?" Pachenko said. "Like the other day on the sail."

"Yes . . . but never this bad."

"We have to get you to a hospital."

"And what happens to our families?"

"I can take the ship into Sabaña Key," insisted Pachenko.

Avilov's voice was a pained rasp. "I can't turn over this responsibility."

"You could die."

"If I fall, you will take command. Not a moment sooner." Avilov held his head. The pain was blinding. He couldn't think.

Pachenko had one last argument. "Radio Rushkov to send a MedEvac. He'll see you're not faking. He'll have to cancel the mission."

The pain made it so hard to concentrate. "No. No one must know."

"Why not?"

The pain was making him short-tempered. "Think it through, Yuri. If the mission is canceled, our families have no hostage value."

Pachenko shook his head sadly. "What do we do?"

Avilov's peripheral vision was completely gone. Most of the center was gray and blurred. "I don't know yet. If it gets no worse . . ." The pain was diminishing. He could start to concentrate. He stood up, and his head did not spin, but the open doorway was only a dark blur inside a lighter one.

"What can you see now?" asked Pachenko.

"Not very much, I'm afraid."

"This is crazy," said Pachenko. "How can you possibly command?"

Avilov caressed the painted bulkhead like an old lover. "If you think about it, Yuri, the *Star* and I are kind of alike now. She has no eyes. Only sound to guide her. If she can do it, why can't I?"

Pachenko said flatly, "This is no metaphor to play with like some drunken poet. It's our lives and the lives of our families, and all the men on this ship. Can you command?"

"I don't know yet," said Avilov honestly. "I'm going to try."

The intercom crackled. "Captain, control room. Could you come up here?"

"This is the captain. I'm on my way."

Avilov took Pachenko's arm. "You've always been my friend, Yuri. Now be my guide as well. Help me to the control room."

* * *

"The captain has command," announced Avilov. "Pytor, give me a report." He steadied himself against the main scope.

"There were no more fires in the galley's deep fryer, sir. I consider this a good sign of the crew's progress," responded Lt. Pytor Stepov. "Airbanks fully charged. Speed ten knots, depth four zero zero meters, course two seven zero."

People liked Stepov because he was funny. He had a natural timing that made even the most ordinary pronouncements and observations humorous. A simple "sounds like a tuna" from the portly, bald navigator with the thick Tartar mustache and myopic eyes could reduce the sonar operator to tears. It would never be a rated category in a fitness report, but it had been warmly cited by all of Stepov's superiors.

"Sonar says we were acquired by an American submarine, Captain," Stepov continued. "We had it on our screens for about ten minutes. As per your standing orders I gave the command to reduce speed and made our depth four hundred meters. I cannot say with any certainty we lost her." He pulled off his spectacles and cleaned them on the handkerchief which always hung out of his back pocket, blinking a few times. "I have never seen such surface activity, Captain."

"As I told you, the vaccine we are carrying will save many Cuban lives. The anti–Castro forces in the American government are opposed to this mission. You see the result."

"If anyone can get us through, it's you, Captain."

"Thank you, Pytor. Did we get enough of a signature to identify the contact?"

"Sonar says she is the Los Angeles–class submarine U.S.S. *Augusta.*"

"Pytor, let me see the area charts."

Stepov spread them out on his table. Avilov used the periscope for balance and to guide him around. "We need someplace to hide."

"I've been working on it. Look at this formation. What do you think?"

The chart was a blur. Try as he might, Avilov could not focus on the tiny lines and notations. He bluffed. "I think the thoughts of a captain. If you wish ever to become one, you will tell me what *you* think."

Stepov was happy for the opportunity to demonstrate his skill. "There's a flat shelf three hundred meters deep, at least a hundred meters wide. Perfect cover. Even if he hits us with active sonar all he'll get is the cliff formation. We sit till he goes away."

Pachenko stepped in and provided confirmation. "Our navigator thinks like a captain. It's a good choice."

"Very well. Set a course, Pytor," ordered Avilov.

"Come right to three five zero."

"Helm, slow turn to new course three five zero. Pavel, make your depth two hundred sixty meters."

"Two hundred sixty meters," confirmed Lt. Pavel Mishkin, the diving officer. A small man with a stony face, Mishkin was Stepov's perfect foil. He went about his job with almost grim concentration and considered jokes in the control room mortal sins.

"Coming to three five zero, Captain," reported the helm.

"We are over the ledge, Captain," said Stepov.

"Very well. Prepare to bottom. All stop," ordered Avilov. "Take us down slowly. Engine room, rig equipment for maximum quiet rotation. Shut down the reactor and secure all pumps."

With a deep crunching sound the *Star* settled onto the ledge at three hundred meters.

"Now we wait," said Avilov.

U.S.S. *Augusta*

Captain Vince Scotti ordered his "tail" out.

The towed array of passive hydrophones spun off the reel

and streamed out a tube leading aft from the port horizontal stabilizer. The inch-thick cable unreeled back over twenty-five hundred feet deploying almost a hundred more hydrophones into the sea. Scotti wanted the extra sonar sensitivity. Even though they had lost contact, deep in his bones he felt that the *Northern Star* was still somewhere in these waters, closer then they wanted him to believe.

"Still nothing, skipper," reported sonar. "Think he's gone?"

"Keep your ears on, Mr. Connors," said Scotti. "He's out there somewhere."

"Aye, sir."

Every sub in the North Atlantic had been looking for the *Northern Star* since the OP-Immediate operation order had come down from CINCLANT. Almost overnight they had put more destroyers and ASW platforms in the Atlantic than anyone had seen in years. Scotti didn't know what made this sub so special, but he figured someone must attach a helluva lot of importance to it.

"You think he bottomed?" asked Paul Lane, his XO. He rubbed a hand through his blond crew cut and answered his own query. "Guy's supposed to be a tricky bastard. Could well be."

"This area's got enough ridges and caverns to hide a fleet of subs in," Scotti said flatly. "Nobody runs that quick and stays that silent, modifications or no. He's still here somewhere."

"From the *Cincinnati,* skipper," said the radio officer. "They're on station. Ready to patrol on your order."

"Where's the *Key West?*"

"They'll be on station in ten minutes," said Lane.

Scotti set his trap carefully, a movement here, a drift, slowly setting up an inner patrol zone with the *Cincinnati* and *Key West.* The destroyers were well back in the outer zone. This took their noise out of the area, which aided the sub's sonar. It also created an important secondary screen should the *Northern Star* try to make a break for it. He had to prevent that. The waters here were too deep and the bottom features too tricky. If they lost Avilov, they would probably not pick him up again.

"*Key West* reports they're on station, sir."

Scotti had put the *Cincinnati* at three hundred feet, the *Augusta* at six hundred, the *Key West* at one thousand, each at the trisect points of a big circle hopefully surrounding the enemy sub. Each would proceed at very slow speed, tails out, alert for the *Star*'s slightest sound. If she moved at all, they'd nail her.

"Fire control, status of all tubes."

"Tubes one through four loaded with Mk-48 torpedoes and flooded, Captain."

"Very well," said Scotti. "Radio, send to *Key West* and *Cincinnati*: Commence search."

Chapter Seven

THE PCOs BOARDED THE RETRIEVER BOAT FOR THE *JACKSON-ville* at dawn. They talked little, shivering with anticipation like hunting dogs anxious to get the scent and run.

The *Jacksonville* was a black shape on the pale gray sea at sunrise. Its sail planes extended out like arms over the water. She was making four knots. The breeze was light. It was a wondrous feeling to have your purpose coincide with that of such a great sleek ship. Harnessed crewmen on the sub put a rope ladder over the side. A deckhand on the retriever boat tossed them a line. It fell short.

Carter grabbed it out of his hands, surprising MacKenzie. "I'll do it," Carter snapped.

"Yes, sir," said the man, glowering.

There is a feeling of compression when you first descend into a submarine, a sense that quiet, throbbing power has encased you in its grasp. Every inch is meant for business. The corridors are less than a yard wide, the ceiling a snaky mass of electrical cables and conduits painted white to create the impression of height. Laminate paneled walls are bare but for the occasional commendation, safety poster, or piece of fire fighting equipment.

MacKenzie reexperienced the exhilaration of coming on board, a sense that the mighty vessel awaited only his orders to dive deep into the sea where its true power and advantage lay.

The *Jacksonville's* engineering officer, Lt. Cmdr. Kyle Fayette, met them in the corridor. "Good morning, Captain MacKenzie. Welcome to the *Jacksonville,* the finest ship in the fleet."

"Thank you, Mr. Fayette, I have no doubt she is," MacKenzie said. "You three go ahead," he added, and he strode off to inspect his ship.

The wardroom was the officers' dining compartment. It held a table big enough for ten officers to sit, which also made it the conference room, the site of disciplinary hearings, and the operating room if the need ever arose. Brass hooks secured the chairs in case of extensive rolling. Under each was an EAB—emergency air breather mask.

"You okay, Reg?" asked Bell. He seemed jumpy.

"Stomach," said Carter irritably. "Something I ate."

"Get set for crow," Flynn smirked.

"You and what navy?" Carter rejoined.

"Down, boys," said Moran.

MacKenzie came in happily. "I've just been looking around. She's a fine ship. Tom Travers did a great job getting her back into shape after the refit."

"I'm glad to hear you say that, sir," remarked a voice from the hatch. "We worked hard when we knew you were coming."

"Mr. Randall," MacKenzie said delightedly. "I haven't seen you since our *Seawolf* days. How are you?"

"Fine, sir. It's a real pleasure to serve with you again."

"Mr. Randall, meet my approach team, PCOs Reggie Carter, Jamie Flynn, Jessica Moran, and Mark Bell. They're going to show us how it's done."

"Be surprised if they had anything to show *you,* sir," said Randall, smoothing down the shock of red hair that sprouted on his head. He had a young face, blue eyes, and an engaging smile. His respect and affection for MacKenzie was obvious.

"Lt. Randall is the best diving officer in the fleet," said MacKenzie.

"Thank you, sir. We're cleared to sail," said Randall.

MacKenzie had thought long and hard about how he would compose the team. "Mr. Bell, you're approach officer. Mr. Carter, you're plot coordinator. Miss Moran, fire control. Mr. Flynn, XO. We'll rotate assignments as our mission permits. Mr. Randall, report to your station."

"Aye, sir." Randall left the wardroom.

"Captain?"

"Yes, Mr. Bell?"

"We all wanted to say—well, we talked, and we wanted you to know that we appreciate your faith in us."

"We won't let you down, sir," said Jessica Moran.

MacKenzie looked at them. So young and fresh. So untested. And he was taking them into war. He wondered if they would all come back from the search for the *Northern Star*. "Just remember there isn't a CO in the fleet who hasn't felt what you're feeling. But you all know you're good, or you wouldn't be here. Some advice: nothing fancy at first. Take it slow. Get your balance."

"Yes, sir."

"All right, my pirates. Take us out."

Bell stepped up on the periscope platform in the conn.

"Mr. Bell," said Randall, taking his place behind the helmsman and planesman. "Chief Crowley is the chief of the watch. Mr. Springfield is your navigator."

"Hello, sir."

"Mr. Springfield. Chief," Bell acknowledged.

MacKenzie said, "Mr. Bell, you have the conn."

Bell took a deep breath and acknowledged the transfer of command with the required response, "I have the conn, sir." He wondered if the air conditioning was on the blink, it felt so damn hot. Steady down, he told himself.

The approach team was in charge of the attack. The approach officer was the boss of the team. He gave the orders. He received constant information from the fire control coordinator and updates on the ever-changing tactical picture from the plot coordinator.

Randall stood directly in front of Bell, eyes on the wall of gauges in front of him. Like most of the men he wore comfortable sneakers, and a sweater over the blue jumpsuit to ward off the chills.

Navigator Springfield was at the chart table behind the scopes. His main concerns were the ship's position and keeping them aware of the bottom and other physical dangers.

Jessica Moran took her seat at the fire control station on the right side of the compartment. She set the course, speed, and enabling range of the torpedoes in the four torpedo tubes amidships and tracked their targets.

Carter's plotting station was next to the navigator's. He was sometimes called the keeper of the facts and was responsible for drawing the written chart of any engagement. If Moran's fire control computers were ever destroyed, a shot would have to be made from his hand-drawn plot.

Sonar was the final element crucial to an attack. The sonar officer was also on the approach officer's phone circuit, glued to his screens in the sonar room just off the conn.

When they went to battle stations there would be almost thirty-five people in the conn, a space no bigger than a small living room.

"The area is clear," said Bell firmly, making a complete rotation with the periscope, "Mr. Flynn, status of the ship."

"The ship is ready to get underway and prepared for dive except for the deck."

Bell hit the intercom. "Engine room, this is the captain. Stand by to answer maneuvering orders."

"Ready to answer all bells, Captain. We're here to serve."

"Straight board, Captain," reported the chief. "All hatches secure." Critical. It was considered very bad form to leave any hatches open during a dive.

"Conn, Sonar. No contacts, skipper. All clear."

"Sounding," said Bell.

"Seven six three fathoms."

"Helm, steady on course zero nine zero."

"Zero nine zero, aye."

"Topside clear and rigged for dive," Flynn reported.

Bell felt exuberant despite all the tension. All his life he would remember taking *Jacksonville* out under his command for the very first time.

"Submerge the ship," Bell ordered. "Mr. Randall, make your depth two zero zero feet. Five degree down bubble."

"Two zero zero feet, five degree down bubble, aye."

The navy-blue Bahama waters closed over the *Jacksonville*.

"All ahead two thirds. Helm, steady on course zero nine zero. Reg, to the plot table. Jamie, you and Jessica, too."

"Aye, sir."

MacKenzie moved with them, watching from the sidelines.

"Give us the positions, Reg," Bell said.

"Here's the battle group," said Carter, showing them on the charts the position of every ship.

Even as he spoke, Ransom's ghostly fingers reached out and touched him. He had wanted to pick up the phone and call MacKenzie twenty times during the night, but he didn't. He was in torment. Ransom was like a tapeworm. He felt like two people, fragmented for the first time in his life. The outward man did all the normal things, the hidden man schemed and plotted. He felt dirtied having been forced to peer into Mark Bell's private life through his medical files. It was a small service, and Carter had heard rumors of Bell's trouble in Australia, but they paled before the reality. It said a lot about Mark's character that he'd managed to survive what he'd been through, much less make it back to command. Ransom wanted Carter to use those wounds to break him, knowing they were Bell's greatest vulnerability. Physical pain wasn't his goal; he wanted the destruction of Bell's very soul. In the end Carter had caved in. *There are a hundred men who would swear . . .* But could he actually do it? The thought sickened him. He had to find a way out before it came to that.

"The carrier *Forestal* is here at the point of a triangle," Carter said. "Two Farragut-class destroyers aft, the *MacDonough* and the *Mahan,* two Ticonderoga-class cruisers abeam, the *Monterey* and the *Leyte Gulf.* There's an oiler and some other replenishment ships close in. The helos are in the air." He pointed to a distant quadrant of ocean. "The *Star* was sighted here, where *Augusta* is."

Bell looked over the tactical picture and came to a decision. "Helm, steer two three five. We'll parallel the battle group."

"Two three five, aye."

Bell picked up the intercom and dialed the MC channel, all ship. "This is the captain speaking. Good morning, *Jacksonville.* I can already see I have a fine ship to serve on. Be prepared for All Back Emergency commencing shortly. Make sure everything is secure. Captain out."

Suddenly reversing spin on the main engine at high speed cavitated the water like an explosion. The noise of the collapsing bubbles would be picked up by any sonars in the area. Flynn said in his best brogue, "Begorrah, they'll hear that all the way to Norfolk."

"Let's hope the *Northern Star* hears it, too," said Bell mildly. "All ahead flank, maintain course two three five. All Back Emergency. Run the reactor at one hundred and ten percent. Cooling pumps on max."

"Engine room, aye."

Bell was deliberately abandoning stealth, the submarine's main advantage, to lay a false trail. He ran the maneuver five more times, every twenty minutes, until the string of noisy "pops" made it appear his true course was 235.

"Now we change. Mr. Flynn, rig for ultra quiet."

"Ultra quiet, aye."

"Engineering, switch to emergency propulsion motor. Mr. Randall, make your depth one two zero zero feet. Five degree down bubble. Nice and easy. No cavitation."

"One two zero zero feet, aye."

"Explain your plan, Mark," MacKenzie requested.

"Sir, the battle group is moving southwest, and I hope we've convinced everybody we're moving along with it. Now I'm going to change direction and come in on their other side."

"Why?"

"Sir, if Avilov manages to get past *Augusta*, he'll be facing all those ships. You said he was a genius at doing what you expect least. I'm thinking if he runs true to form, where's the least likely place for him to go if he gets through?"

"You tell me."

"Right in the middle of them. Hide in all that noise and slide along with the carrier, drop off when he can. I'd like to get there first. The *Mahan*'s the slower of the two destroyers. See how she falls back. Here. And here. Let's sneak in and hide under her and wait. See if he shows."

"So you figure if the *Mahan*'s leaving a hole in the screen and we see it, Avilov might see it, too. Sonar, can you verify?"

"Sir, we've picked that up. He has to kick in his boilers every hour or so. Big increase in noise."

MacKenzie had to admire the perceptiveness. He looked back to Bell. "Why alone?"

"He might not be suspecting a solitary unit. But more

than that, sir. Would it make any sense if I told you it just feels right?"

Christ, MacKenzie wondered to himself, could Bell be one of the intuitive ones? So early in his career? Did he have that much gut sense?

"Let's find out if what feels right *is* right, Mr. Bell," MacKenzie said. "Proceed."

"Aye, sir. Helm, bring her around slowly. Engine room, secure EPM. All ahead two thirds. Rely on natural flow for cooling. No pumps. No cavitation."

"One third, aye, natural flow."

Bell sat back for a moment. He couldn't see anything he had failed to do. The ship was running to a good tactical position from which it stood a chance of moving in on the carrier undetected. They were running near silently. So what was bothering him?

"Captain Bell, might you want some weapons if we run into any hostiles?" MacKenzie asked, gently chiding.

Shit. "Miss Moran," he said hurriedly. "Status of torpedo tubes."

"Sir, tubes one through four are empty as a poor man's pocket."

"Torpedo room, load tubes one through four with Mk-48 torpedoes." Fine thing, thought Bell, forgetting to ask for a weapons check. That'd be great—run into trouble and first have to load your tubes.

They set up their approach. It was a good team. Flynn ran the ship like a consummate conductor. Moran's analytical mind was just what he needed as fire control boss, and Carter's calm cover-all-the-bases style made him a great plot coordinator.

For Bell, it happened when they were six hours out. Suddenly the conn seemed to shrink. A terrible lassitude came over him, and he feared he would pass out. Out there in the water, just beyond the hull. *Bodies in the water . . .*

bodies in the water and the thing coming at him . . . waving . . . waving! He saw them! So close! He felt the claustrophobia come on. He fought for control, to stop feeling he had to claw through the steel hull plates to get to the surface.

"Mr. Bell, are you all right?" MacKenzie asked.

"Yes, sir," Bell managed. He had to pull out of it. Banish the demons. He clamped down on his turmoil.

"When's the last time you ate?"

"Last night, sir."

"Get some food. Miss Moran, take over."

"Aye, sir."

Bell had to control himself and walk calmly, difficult when all the demons of hell were pursuing.

Chapter Eight

Northern Star

PACHENKO TURNED AVILOV TOWARDS THE CONTROL ROOM. "How many steps to the first hatch?" he asked quietly.

"Twenty," Avilov responded impatiently. "It was twenty yesterday and the day before that as well. It can't change, can it?"

Pachenko ignored his truculence. "Reach up, catch the lip, and remember to lift your foot or you'll trip."

"Then another twelve to the control room," finished Avilov in an equally low tone. "I'm going blind, Yuri, not stupid. After two days and endless trips I remember. Haven't I done it perfectly the last ten times?"

"On a ship that's not moving where no one is racing down the corridors to man their stations. Don't get cocky, Pari Ivanovich. Eleven o'clock. Seaman Karansky."

"Hello, Captain," greeted the man as he passed.

"Fine day, Seaman Karansky," acknowledged Avilov to the blur. "Not too much longer in this vacation spot, eh?"

"No one can keep the Hawk in a cage if he doesn't want to be," said Karansky confidently, but then he looked quizzical. "Can I ask why you are doing so much counting everywhere?"

"Measuring for the new computer systems."

"Oh."

Avilov sniffed the air. "Yuri, have you found any liquor on board?"

"None, why?"

"Because he had some on his breath. Check his bunk later, would you?"

"Of course. But I didn't smell anything." He stared at Avilov. "Is what I've always heard true, that your other senses improve to compensate for your loss of vision?"

"In a way," said Avilov, thoughtful. "I can't hear a pin drop a mile away. It's more like when you work unused muscles they get stronger. I'm paying more attention to things now. Sounds under sounds. Aftersmells."

"Let's go through this again."

Avilov straightened. "No more. It is twelve steps to the control room, ninety from here to engineering. I know I can walk the stairways with my eyes closed because I have done it." Avilov took four steps forward and his hand slapped out. "Intercom." He missed the box by six inches.

"Wonderful," said Pachenko dryly.

It didn't throw Avilov. He felt along the bulkhead and stabbed the button. "Engine room, this is the captain."

"Yes, Captain?"

"What is the status of our batteries?"

"Fully charged."

"Thank you. Captain out." He turned to Pachenko. "See?"

"I see one of us is convinced. The hardheaded one."

"It's been days, Yuri. We have to get out of here."

"You aren't ready."

"The longer we wait, the more ships they bring. They could even blockade Cuba. Don't tell me no. They already did it once. The first of the month is only ten days away now. We have to go, and we have to go *soon.*"

There was a time for arguments, then you were either in or out. Pachenko decided. "On your order, Captain."

Avilov's face softened. Through a small spot in his vision he could see Pachenko's face. It was a comforting sight. "Twelve," said Avilov walking off. "Eleven . . . ten . . ."

They went to the sonar room and listened through headphones to the noises in the water.

"We've identified five destroyers and three Los Angeles–class subs," said Lt. Ivan Pushkin, the chief sonar officer. Pushkin had served with Avilov almost as long as Pachenko had. He understood sound as well as any concert musician, and he worked hard at his craft. No matter what the rotation or duty roster, he had never let Avilov go into battle without his own steady presence in the sonar room.

Avilov smelled the cologne Pushkin was using, and the substance he used to smooth down his thick black hair, so much like porcupine quills. He heard a tiny click in Pushkin's knee every time Pushkin stood and wondered if he was hearing the first signs of arthritis. He felt for the chair in front of the number-two console and sank into it.

"I've never seen anything like this before, Captain," said Pushkin. "So many ships. It must be a very important vaccine."

"It is. Is there talk among the crew? Be honest with me, Ivan."

"Some talk," said Pushkin hesitantly. "Not a lot. It's—well, just that there are so many enemy ships out there, and the Hawk walks the corridors . . . counting. Captain Avilov," asked Pushkin plaintively, "can even you get us out of here? The odds are not good."

"Then we will have to be extra clever, won't we?"

Pushkin smiled. "I suppose we will."

"Hand me the headphones. I want to listen for a while."

Avilov put on the phones and settled back in the chair. He and the *Star* were two blind men of war with only their ears to listen to the sounds of the sea. He heard the steady *thrumm* of the destroyers, the low throb of the subs. They were there, all right. He cast his hearing further. Here were the sounds of the sea itself, the bass rumbling of shifting undersea mountains so big they dwarfed anything on land, the hiss of sulfurous eruptions thousands of feet below that fed alien-looking creatures, the whoosh of stealthy sharks, playful dolphins, and beyond that, in the distance . . . It was almost as if his mind wanted to break the physical link that held him to the ship. For a moment he was part of the sea. It could have been hours or minutes that he spent in that dreamlike state. He didn't know. When he returned to the familiar sonar room Pachenko and Pushkin were staring at him. It didn't matter.

He knew what to do now.

Avilov turned toward Pushkin's odor, one he had never noticed before, a clean scent, cool like mint. "Isolate that contact."

"Yes, sir." Together they eliminated frequency after frequency, filtering out all the ambient noise until the single contact Avilov had chosen was isolated on the sonar "waterfall."

"That's the one."

Pushkin listened closer, checked his gauges. "It's closing."

"I know," said Avilov happily. "Come, Yuri."

Avilov stepped into the control room, counted three steps, and mounted the periscope landing. The railing was a reassuring guide. "Gentlemen, I am ready to depart this place. Is there anyone who wishes to stay?"

"The Americans invited us for lunch?" asked Stepov.

"Not yet. Now, listen to me. For four days we have been sitting quietly, and for four days the Americans have been wondering if we are here. The slightest error on our part and they will be certain, and then they'll be on us at once. It is even possible they will launch a torpedo at us."

"How do we get off this ledge?" asked Mishkin.

Avilov said with calm assurance, "An escort's coming."

Mishkin looked blank. "Captain, we have no ships in the area."

"Nevertheless. Sonar, range to contact."

"Two thousand meters and closing."

"Weapons Officer Vashovsky, contact course and speed."

Vashovsky was a quiet man with the soul of a poet and the mind of a warrior. He spent his time reading Yevtushenko and listening to music that sounded like automobiles crashing. No one completely understood the laconic Georgian, but on a sub, as long as you didn't crowd others, every man was given his space.

"Contact closing on course two seven zero, depth seventy meters, speed three knots, Captain."

"Sonar, put the contact on the speaker."

There was a burst of static, and then the compartment was filled with high-pitched squealing sounds. Everyone stopped to listen. The voices circled the earth with long, lonely cries. From the farthest deep they were tinged with the icy chill of the Arctic and touched by the warmth of the tropics.

"Whales!" exclaimed Pachenko.

"Proof there is a God," said Avilov contentedly, "who likes poor fools like us." His fingers found the intercom. "Engine room. We will be using the emergency propulsion motor only. No noise at all. Keep the reactor off line. No pumps."

"Captain, it will take time to start it back up if you need power."

"If those destroyers hear us, all the power in the world won't help. I want everything shut down whose frequencies on the line would give us away. Now follow orders."

"Yes, Captain."

"Mr. Pachenko, rig for silent running and pass the word

verbally to prepare to get underway. Man battle stations silently."

"Yes, sir." Pachenko left the control room.

The mournful sounds of the approaching whales filled the conn. "Sonar, range."

"Eight hundred meters. Course two seven zero."

Avilov's blood stirred hotly to the challenge. He felt a pulse beat within him come to life. Even blinded, this was where he had to be. Despite the danger, this was where he was most alive. "Helm, prepare to steer course two seven zero. Navigator, I'll need constant course corrections to stay in the herd. Be alert."

"Ready, Captain."

"Contact closing at five hundred meters."

Avilov turned half-blind eyes to his crew. "Blow main ballast, four second blow. Two degree up angle. Make your depth seventy meters. Engine ahead slow on EPM only. Helm, come right to two seven zero."

The *Northern Star* rose off the ledge to join the whales.

"Captain, Sonar. Biologics one hundred meters and closing . . . fifty meters . . . Computers identify them as blue whales. At least ten. Maybe more."

It was easy to imagine the whales around the ship, hearing them through the hull rather than over the speaker. Avilov pictured the huge, beautiful creatures, graceful and supple and almost a third as big as the sub itself moving aside to let a great new dark cousin swim among them.

"We are in the herd," said Pushkin, awe in his voice.

"Depth seventy meters," said Mishkin.

"Suggest you come right ten degrees, Captain."

"Helm, right ten degrees rudder, steady two eight zero," Avilov ordered.

Suddenly the *Star* lurched precariously and a low scraping sound filled the control room. "Collision," said Mishkin quietly.

"Perhaps they think we're another whale, and an attractive one at that," Stepov remarked innocently.

"Suggest coming right an additional ten degrees, Captain," said Vashovsky sternly, indicating what he thought of levity at this moment.

Avilov figured if he could stay in the herd for another two hours or so they would be far enough away to go deep and proceed at low speed. It would be pure luck if they found him again.

"Captain, Sonar. The whales are turning north."

"Acknowledged. Helm, right ten degrees rudder."

"Steer new course three five zero," said Stepov, and he added as an afterthought, "Captain, what if they want to mate?"

Chapter Nine

Atlantic Ocean

JUSTINE'S STOMACH DROPPED AS THE CARRIER CAME UP AT THEM. It might look big up close, but from the hold of the descending helo it looked like a flyspeck in the ocean. In fact, she hadn't been able to see it at all until they were only a quarter mile away. At night you couldn't see much, and the few light configurations she *could* see could have been miles away or right in her face. Without depth contrast she couldn't tell.

"How can you see what's going on down there?" she asked the crewman who was riding with her.

"We can't. LSO has to tell you on the radio."

Justine looked skeptical.

The man grinned. "Can't make it too easy for us, ma'am, can they?"

"God forbid."

"You ought to see it when there's real weather. Like trying to hump a moving . . . er, sorry, ma'am."

"I understand completely."

The helo banked steeply. Justine smothered a curse.

She still had Mac on her mind. This assignment was forcing him to accept a change in status that affected his

76

whole life. The warrior had to become a teacher, and he was having a hard time. Could he come to terms with it? She wanted so much to be able to help him. They'd both learned how important it was to depend on each other. You couldn't go it alone. God, how they'd learned *that*.

"We're cleared to land, ma'am."

"Ducky."

The pilot knew his job. They touched down with barely a shudder, and the crewman disengaged her harness. "You can stop strangling your chair any time, ma'am."

"So you say." Justine's hands were white-knuckled on the armrests. She was getting too old for this.

The night sky was dazzling out on deck, vast and clear. There was noise everywhere, rotors turning, jet engines flashing. The carrier was coming around, its wide white wake curling like a tail. The command island was an oasis of light on the vast deck. She started for it, figuring it was the logical place to meet Ben Garver, but the crewman caught her arm.

"Right, ma'am. Over there." He pointed.

The F-14 Tomcat sat on the deck, a twin-engined missile with swept-back wings. Justine shook her head firmly. "No. I refuse. You tell that heartless sonofabitch—"

"I don't think I could tell him that, ma'am."

"Coward." Justine thought about climbing back into the helo and hiding, but Garver wouldn't have gotten her here without good reason, and if a ride in an F-14 was a part of it . . . She shrugged. They'd be damn careful with an *admiral's* friend.

It took longer than she would have thought to get her into a torso harness, G-suit, helmet, and oxygen mask. The F-14's pilot had his canopy up and was attending to his preflight checks. He gave her a casual wave, which she returned, muttering darkly.

"Not as nice as that black suit with the short skirt, but you wear it well," said Garver, looking devilishly pleased that anything could disturb her equanimity.

"Most men send cars, Ben," she said peevishly. "What the hell is this?"

"It has style, don't you think?"

One of Garver's great pleasures in life, she knew, was to be a part of her world. The two were so dissimilar. He was the only son of a naval family that went back to colonial America, a veteran of battleships, a distant fighter. She was an aristocrat turned guerrilla warrior who could cripple a man with her hands and had been at war since she was eight. He had no children, and the father/daughter relationship suited both. They usually hid their deep affection for each other behind impertinence and dry needling.

"Okay, Ben. Give."

"We have a problem with a Russian submarine called the *Northern Star*," he began.

The professional part of her mind absorbed the facts about Avilov and the plot to sell his sub. ". . . so I want you to take a ride. A personal look-see is better than a hundred aerial photos if the subs miss Avilov and we have to go in. At this point you'd best assume we will."

"I spoke to Arthur Winestock," Justine said. "He told me you asked for me personally to lead the strike."

"He wanted to be the one to tell you. It was fortunate you were here and this is your specialty, but I'd have asked for you anyway. You're the last offensive weapon I've got if my ships don't stop the *Northern Star*. You don't mind?"

"Would it matter if I did?"

"To me it would."

Justine shrugged. "This is what I do. Like you. Like Mac. If it's time to go again, I'd better get started."

"You're about to earn your wings. Take care."

Justine had never experienced a carrier takeoff. She could have lived without it. They were hurled along the deck and fell off the edge. Her stomach dropped into her sneakers like she'd been sucker-punched. They roared into the dark sky and she tried to breathe evenly. It was an eerie feeling being isolated inside the big plexiglass bubble with the stars blazing overhead.

"Sabaña Key in ten minutes," Binze announced.

They roared through the night, but her mind was elsewhere. She'd been taken on an emotional journey by the little plastic object that hung from Binze's control panel. A blond stallion. His good luck charm, probably.

Justine uncapped the thermos and sipped her coffee slowly. She'd won a horse like that once, in a fight in the desert. She still thought about a man there named Kemal, chief of the tribe, whose dark eyes and flashing smile had made it a close thing, a journey to the edge of an abyss of deceit from which she and Mac might never have recovered. She came close to crumbling on the desert sand, hurt and broken . . . but she had pulled back. Here, now, she was glad of it. Marriage takes you strange places, she thought. Stranger still are the ones it takes you to keep you together.

They raced toward a tiny cluster of lights. She'd have only seconds to make a visual ID, but it was something else she was trained for. Let it all come in, sort things out later. Get the whole picture, the total impression. The aerial photos taken by the tactical air reconnaissance photography system (TARPS) pod under the plane would provide details later.

The island swept by almost too quickly, but the eye works fast. One picture. She saw the main house and the long pier, the outlying work buildings. She estimated the distances in all directions, enough to build up an internal map.

Will this be the place I don't walk away from? she wondered.

Then it was gone.

Augusta

Scotti pulled the headphones off and tossed them back on the sonar console. "Whales," he said bitterly. "A school of goddamn blue whales. Where the hell are the Russians?"

"It's been four days, skipper. Maybe they're not there." XO Lane resettled his wire-rim glasses on his thin nose.

"They are, Paul. It's still a waiting game. He's gonna make his move sooner or later. I thought he'd go for the destroyer."

Scotti had used a destroyer as a ruse, hoping Avilov would try and make a break for it underneath, using its sound for cover. At several points he had it turn hard and had the helos dip their sonar pods to check for the sub. Nothing. But the plan was sound. Sound. Avilov still needed sound to cover his run. Sound . . . like in whales!

"I'll be a son of a . . . I'll bet he's using the whales as cover."

"We'd hear his engines," said Jake Connors, sonar officer.

"Not if he had his reactor shut down and was using his EPM. What speed are those whales making?"

Connors checked his panel. "Three knots."

"He could do that with his EPM," said Scotti, more convinced than ever. "But he can't do any more than that."

"We have no target if he's in the herd," said Connors.

"Unless we want to blow up a few million pounds of whale," amended Lane. "You like whale steak, Jake?"

"Had it once, sir. Like eating fishy liver."

"We'll drive him out of the herd," said Scotti. "No EPM in existence can make five knots, and that's what those big blue mothers are going to be doing in about five minutes if I have anything to say about it."

He strode back into the conn. "Countermeasures, prepare to fire noisemakers."

"Countermeasures, aye."

"Fire control, where's that herd?"

"They've turned, sir. Heading north. Range two thousand yards."

"All ahead flank. Narrow that range to five hundred yards."

Not too close, thought Scotti as *Augusta* surged ahead. Don't want to run into his props if he's in there. "Fire control, prepare a constant solution on that herd. You'll have a target soon enough. Should be the straggler if this works."

"Fire control, aye."

"Torpedo room, status of all tubes."

"All tubes flooded and ready, Captain."

"Set noisemakers and torpedoes to enable in the shallow zone. Open outer doors tubes one and two."

"Set for shallow stratum. Outer doors open."

"Launch noisemakers. Prepare to fire tubes one and two."

Northern Star

Avilov held onto the steel railing. Another bump pushed the *Star* like she weighed no more than a passenger car. The hull popped and groaned. Things happen quickly on a submarine. One moment Avilov expected a few more minutes of undetected sailing, the next he was fighting not to drown as a small hull fitting broke in the sail and cold water cascaded in, showering the control room.

"Chief of the watch, direct damage control to locate and isolate that flooding," Avilov yelled, unable to see the source himself.

Suddenly the full impact of being blind hit him, and it was a frightening thing. He couldn't see where the water was coming from. He held onto the railing for dear life. The water hit him like sharp slaps, driving home to him that in any kind of real emergency he was useless.

Pachenko scrambled up the sail ladder to attempt to shut the manual hull valve. Stepov was only a half second behind.

Avilov stood stooped under the cascade. He could smell

the hot, wet arc of electric circuits in danger of short-circuiting if the flooding continued. But the water abated.

"Hull fittings secured, Captain."

"Check the status boards and replace fuses as necessary."

The suddenness of sonar's cry shook everybody. "Captain, noisemakers!"

The sounds came over the conn speaker, a loud string of firecracker noises intended to divert an enemy torpedo. Avilov realized at once what was happening.

"Yuri, they think we're in the herd. They're trying to drive the whales too fast for us to keep up."

Sure enough, almost echoing his words, "Captain, sonar. The herd has increased its speed to five knots. They're diving deeper and pulling ahead."

He could picture the American commander. Probably on the *Star*'s flank with a good solution on the herd. He'd be ready to fire as soon as the *Star* fell behind. Avilov had to keep up with the herd, but three knots was as much as he was going to get out of the EPM. For more speed he'd have to restart the power plant, and the noise would make them a perfect target.

Damned if he did, damned if he didn't. They had only seconds. Unless . . . north, they were heading north. He tried to remember the charts on these waters. Yes, it could work. If it wasn't too deep. If he could find it in time . . .

"Twenty degree down angle," he ordered. "Make our depth two hundred meters."

"Pari?" It was Pachenko. "What about a high-speed turn to starboard and go deep, launch back on their track?"

"He'd love that," said Avilov flatly. "All the noise in the world to fix on. Attack center, what is our speed?"

"Three knots, Captain."

Avilov fumed. It had to be here somewhere. "Drop us fifty meters," he ordered. Where the hell was it?

"Depth two hundred fifty meters."

"Speed three knots, Captain." There was an edge in

Vashovsky's voice. Avilov heard it plainly. Vashovsky was wondering if the captain had finally lost his touch. He wasn't the only one, to judge from the muttering. Avilov wondered if he would have heard it before. Seconds passed.

"Speed three knots, Captain. Just as before."

"Drop us another fifty meters," Avilov ordered.

"Speed still three knots, Captain . . . wait . . . wait! Captain? Three point five knots. Four. Four knots . . . four point five!"

There it was. Avilov could have shouted with relief. But not yet, not if they'd lost the whales. "Sonar, where is the herd?"

"Ahead of us, Captain. Steady at five knots." There was a sudden bump. "Disregard that. They're right alongside."

There was cheering in the control room. The Hawk had done it again. But how?

"What the hell is going on?" asked Pachenko.

"The Gulf Stream, Yuri," said Avilov happily. "The glorious, beautiful Gulf Stream. I knew it ran north, I just didn't remember the exact depth. We're in its current. That's where the extra speed is coming from. We can keep up with them all day if necessary and never restart the power plant. Let them try to find us now."

"Remarkable."

"You have command. We'll follow the whales for a full day, then break off and resume our run. I'll be in my cabin drying off."

"Yes, sir."

Avilov heard the pride in Pachenko's voice. He accepted the congratulations of every crewman he met as he counted his way back to his cabin, one step at a time.

Augusta

"Conn, sonar. No additional contacts. The entire herd ran to five knots. There aren't any stragglers, Skipper."

Scotti had a bad feeling about it, but no EPM could do five knots. They'd have heard the reactor plant start up at this distance. The *Northern Star* had to be somewhere else. He broke off the attack and doubled back to the patrol zone, angry and defeated.

"Radio, send this. *Augusta* to COMSUBLANT. Unsure of enemy position. Alert the battle group. High degree of probability *Northern Star* is headed their way."

Chapter Ten

Jacksonville

MACKENZIE READ *AUGUSTA'S* COMMUNICATION. AVILOV HAD made it past her. The *Northern Star* was believed headed this way. Given the time pressure on him, he couldn't do much else. He had to go for it.

The tension in the conn rose another notch when he told the PCOs. The hours of stress were wearing on them. The preparations to kill. That harsh reality changed them. MacKenzie felt for them. For his new captains, war had come too soon.

"I know Captain Scotti," he said. "If Avilov got past him, it shows how good he is. It says here he may have used a school of whales to evade detection."

"Whales?" said Flynn. "That's a new one on me."

"Let's hope we're a new one on him," said Jessica.

"Conn, sonar, new surface contact."

"Identify," said MacKenzie.

"Computer says she's the *Caron,* Spruance-class destroyer out of Norfolk. Moving fast, Skipper. Thirty knots. Looks like she's heading for the battle group."

The *Caron* was out of Norfolk. She carried two Lamps Mk

1 ASW helos. MacKenzie figured Garver wanted to add them to the group. It was also a perfect opportunity to turn command over to Jessica Moran.

"Mr. Bell, I intend for you to retake the conn to implement your plan, but Miss Moran is going to initiate it by taking us into the group under cover of the *Caron*. Miss Moran, you have the conn. Mr. Bell, shift to fire control."

"Aye, sir."

It was a historic moment. Jessica stepped up onto the scope platform and responded, "Sir, I have the conn. Mr. Springfield, plot me an intercept course for the *Caron*."

"Aye, ma'am."

Jessica hit the all-ship intercom. "Good morning, *Jacksonville*. This is Captain Moran speaking. I know some of you have heard the ugly rumor that a woman was going to be in command of this ship. Let me deny it categorically. A *naval officer* is in charge of this ship. I am certain all of us will continue to function with the professionalism that is the *Jacksonville*'s hallmark. I know I can count on you all to make me proud."

"Engineering, prepare to answer all bells," Jessica ordered.

"Engineering, aye."

"Sonar, range to contact."

"Ten thousand yards and closing."

"Acknowledged."

"What's your plan?" asked MacKenzie.

"Sir, I'm going to put us in a hover and wait for the *Caron*, then come in under her when she passes."

"All right. Go ahead."

She took a deep breath and jumped in. "Mr. Randall, make your depth three hundred feet."

"Three hundred feet, aye."

"Mr. Flynn, rig for ultra-quiet."

"Ultra-quiet, aye."

"Sonar, keep me informed of range to target."

"Sonar, aye . . . seven thousand yards . . . closing."

For the next hour Jessica continued to move the *Jacksonville* toward the *Caron*, but was it her imagination, or did the crew seem lethargic and slow to respond? She refused to let it get to her, but after half an hour more she felt she had to take MacKenzie aside.

"Sir, are they deliberately being sluggish?"

MacKenzie had noticed it, too. He didn't want to think anyone was deliberately obstructing Jessica Moran because she was a woman, but it was clear they weren't working at top form. "This kind of tension is debilitating," he said. "It's an enclosed world. No relief. They're feeling it. Keep going, Jessica. You're doing fine."

"Okay." Jessica appreciated MacKenzie's support. But still, it just didn't seem like the same crew that operated under him or Bell. It didn't have the same snappiness. What was the matter? The nagging thought kept coming back that there was something, but it wouldn't come to her, so she turned back to the task at hand.

"We're at ordered depth, ma'am." Randall informed her.

"Acknowledged. Right ten degrees rudder."

"Ten degrees rudder, aye."

"*Right* ten degrees rudder," Jessica insisted. "Repeat my order correctly."

"Yes, ma'am. Sorry," said the helmsman.

In so many ways the sub was like the DSRVs she was used to. Ballast, trim, six degrees of motion, things second nature to her. It began to feel more like home. Familiar. The conviction "I *can* do this" solidified in her guts.

"All stop. Prepare to hover."

MacKenzie went into a lengthy explanation of the things she could and should be doing at this moment, and she took it all in like an attentive sponge. MacKenzie was a good teacher. His love of what he did came through clearly. She sensed that he would rather be doing than teaching. Maybe that wasn't so bad. Great teachers often came from the ranks of great doers. He was patient and supportive and a great role model, and she couldn't ask for more on her first run.

She saw him swipe at his temple. "Headache, sir? You, too?"

"Little bit," he confided. "Not to worry."

"Range three thousand yards and closing," said Bell.

"Navigation, I need a course."

"I suggest one eight . . . zero."

"Very well, lay it in."

"One eight zero, aye."

Jessica took them up to two hundred feet and slid in ahead of the cruiser. It took longer than she would have liked, damn it, but still no one seemed to be deliberately stalling.

"Chief, what's wrong?"

He was holding his neck the way one feels for swollen glands. "Feel weak, ma'am. A little dizzy."

"Call for a replacement and go see the doc, okay? Can't have you reading gauges dizzy when we're this close, right?"

He smiled. "Right, ma'am. Thanks."

It took a moment for the new man to make his way up from the torpedo room, where he was having a smoke. It struck Jessica as humorous that one of the few places on board you could smoke was the torpedo room, like the old cartoon where someone holds up a match in the darkness and illuminates the TNT sign.

"Damnedest thing," she heard the new chief of the watch mutter to the Randall as he slid into his seat at his console. "Couldn't even get a decent smoke. My cigarette kept going out."

It was the final clue. It hit Jessica all at once. The lethargy, the headaches, the cigarette. Of course! A problem they faced constantly in the limited confines of the DSRV. "Jamie, run a check on the oxygen content in the atmosphere."

"Why?" MacKenzie broke in.

"Sir, we have headaches breaking out, and this man just reported his cigarette wouldn't stay lit. I already commented about the lethargy. I have to watch our atmosphere on the DSRV real close with all the matings and such. I think we have a drop in the O_2 level that the gauges haven't picked up."

"Proceed with the check, Mr. Flynn," MacKenzie agreed at once.

"*Caron* one hundred yards astern," reported sonar.

"Continue your approach, Miss Moran."

"Aye, sir. All ahead two thirds . . . steady . . . maintain speed," Jessica ordered.

The noise increased as the *Caron* sailed overhead. When it increased to a maximum Jessica grabbed the moment. "Mr. Randall, make our depth one hundred feet. All ahead flank."

"One hundred feet, all ahead flank, aye."

The *Jacksonville* slid under the *Caron,* matching her course and speed.

"Sir, we've hitched a ride," Jessica said to MacKenzie.

MacKenzie's approval was quick and vocal. "Handled like a pro, Captain. Well done. And you were right about the oxygen level, too. It was down two percent, enough to produce lethargy and some more serious problems if we hadn't known. We're pumping extra oxygen to compensate for it now."

"I'm glad." Jessica was feeling better herself. And the slight excess oxygen charge would produce a little euphoria till it balanced out.

"Fine work, Miss Moran. Take us into the battle group."

"Yes, sir."

News spreads quickly in a three-hundred-foot tube. Heads turned, long ingrained ideas changed. The new CO might have tits, but man, she was cool.

Mail call on a sub is one of the only diversions men have. Due to time and space restrictions it isn't received in an envelope on sheets of paper; it's a brief electronic transmission separated into component parts, much like telegrams. Families often use codes to communicate larger ideas. "5-OK" can mean all five members of the family are well, or ILY a familiar "I love you."

When Carter took the conn, MacKenzie detailed Flynn and Jessica to oversee the mail delivery. It might seem a simple duty to assign to such senior officers, but it was taken very seriously. Other than during the brief mail transmissions, men on submarines had to think of themselves as dead to the world. Mail was a critical part of keeping up morale.

"Nothing for you, Jamie?" said Jessica as they worked in the small ship's office by the chief's quarters.

"No. Not my style, Jess. I don't see how a lot of guys do it. I have a friend has seven kids. He's never been home for the birth of one. They call him 'mister' when he gets back."

"We who serve," Jessica agreed.

"Nothing from husband or kids for you, either," observed Flynn.

"Tough to promise a guy you'll be home for a while, then get the *Gray Lady Down* call and run right off for time unspecified."

"What about kids? I keep hearing about biological clocks ticking."

She made a wry face. "Mine may be ticking, but I haven't heard the alarm ring yet."

Flynn grew serious. "I never wanted to miss anybody, you know? Life on shore's over when you get on your boat. Six weeks or six months. If I'm here, I wanna be here. At least that's what I always thought. Suddenly I find things changing. And I'm a little off balance."

Jessica was skeptical. "The original one-night man talking like he's ready to settle down and play with the brats around the fire?"

"You never know, lass."

"I know your reputation."

"You don't think I can change?"

"Maybe. Some guys grow out of it. But women for you are like—well, merit badges. It's your way of measuring things, the way you know you've still got it. I don't mean it unkindly. Sometimes women need to measure things, too."

"Maybe this commanding officer stuff is getting to me, Jess. It's different when you're in charge. Responsibility's all on you. I'm getting to the point lately where I wince when they say the starting pitcher's twenty-three. Hard to get over that."

"You worry too much. Age isn't so important."

Flynn met her eyes. "Maybe some things are more important than others."

Jessica patted his arm. "Listen, Jamie. I was pretty worried about the other PCOs. I mean, if you guys got together and gave me a hard time, there was no way I was gonna sail through this. But Mark and Reg and especially you have been good guys. You're all tops in my book."

"Anything I can do, Jess. Just ask."

"I'll do better. I'll tell *you* something," She chucked him under the chin and winked. "You ask me, you still got it, Jamie. You'll get over whatever's bothering you. There. We're done. Can I take the mail? I want to interact more with the men."

"Sure. Go ahead."

She picked up the paperwork and left.

Flynn got up to wash printer ink off his hands and looked at his reflection in the mirror over the sink. The lines were deeper. The skin was just a little more slack. His hairline was definitely receding. An aging idol still gathering merit badges. It wasn't a pleasant thought. "You figure I'll get over it?" he asked his reflection.

She didn't see how he felt about her. She treated him like a brother. Nothing more. Flynn could spot surrender in a woman farther away than fire control could spot an upcoming target. He didn't see it in Jessica Moran, despite his having shared his innermost thoughts.

You'll get over whatever's bothering you, she'd said.

"What if I can't?" he wondered.

Chapter Eleven

AUTEC Cafeteria

JUSTINE AND GARVER ATE DINNER IN THE BIG AUTEC CAFETE-ria. The recon photos were being processed, and a hot meal was in order after the wild flight over Sabaña Key.

"Mac called in. Jessica's doing well."

"I wasn't worried," Justine said. "She's tough and smart. In a just world she probably would have been a sub captain by now."

"You seen any just worlds?" Garver asked.

Justine snorted derisively. "Not in this life." A thought occurred to her. "While we eat, Ben, take me through the training. I don't really know a watch station from a train station in spite of listening to Mac all these years."

Garver had to smile. "You want the whole nickel tour? The way we make sub captains?"

"Sure."

"An officer's first tour at sea trains him for several different jobs. Taking care of the reactor, maintaining trim and ballast, being in charge of the control room and the safety and operation of the entire boat. He learns how to position his sub and how to fix it when it breaks.

You're a senior lieutenant by now. Then you spend six months at the Submarine Officer's Advanced Course to become a department head. You're trained in the tactical deployment of the ship. Putting it into action, in other words."

"What are department heads?"

"Primary assistants to the captain. The navigations/ operations officer, the engineering officer, and the weapons/ combat systems officer. It lets him . . . what is it?"

"Him or her," corrected Justine.

Garver looked skyward. "Him or her. This is where we examine leadership and organizational skills. They get to see why the captain makes the decisions he does. The real business of command starts when the department head qualifies for executive officer. An XO can run the ship. He's second in command. He executes policy."

"The captain's shadow?"

"No. He's figuring out how *he'd* do things. A lot of it's about making your rep. Mac has always had just the right blend of boldness, aggression, and practicality. We'd make him an admiral if he'd ever fully accept the change from op status."

"It's hard for him, Ben. You know that."

"Justine, guys my age won't be around forever. Mac's got to take over eventually."

"He's struggling, Ben. Teaching's so . . . passive."

"Well, maybe I've changed that a little." Garver twinkled. "You should have seen him try to convince me I should let him teach the PCOs on the *Jacksonville* and go after the *Northern Star*. Like it wasn't what I wanted in the first place." He hesitated. "You mind if I ask how you and he are doing?"

She touched his hand affectionately. "The *Kentucky* helped us both, Ben. We know more than we used to. We talk more. If we have to change, I think we can handle it."

"You know if you ever need me . . ."

She smiled. "I know. You're a dear friend. Now take me the last mile, Ben. How does an exec make it to command?"

"Any exec's technically good enough, but how does he react under pressure? What will he do when the shooting starts? That's something we can't know till he's in it. That's why the PCOs are here. Submarine qualification is a knowledge of the ship's capabilities. Command qualification is the ability to take those capabilities into battle." He changed the subject. "How are your preparations coming?"

"I'm working on the logistics. It may have to be an underwater demo team."

"I hate using you, Justine. But the president won't send a large military force into Cuban waters without visible provocation."

"A stolen nuclear sub isn't provocation?" she said contemptuously. "You'll forgive me if I don't always love how easily politicians draw lines, Ben. This is okay. This isn't. This we can defend. This we can't. I'm more primitive. I'd drop lots of bombs on the damn thing from the A-6s and be done with it. Let Castro scream his ass off. Who cares?"

"We'd have an even bigger image problem down there."

"I'd like our image to be that we have some balls for a change." She sighed. "But I don't make policy. Is Jackson or Greene still on active duty? I've worked with them before. It'll save time."

"Jackson's still in," said Garver. "He's in charge of SEAL Team Five. I'll bring him here."

"And his top man." Justine finished her coffee. She was distant now, evolving as the mission drew nearer.

The change in her was something he had witnessed once or twice before. There was a cold light in her eyes now, and she seemed charged with a deadly energy. People swerved out of her way, not knowing why. Garver did. The part of her shaped in the Nicaraguan jungles had come alive again. Anticipating danger brought out the killer in her. He knew he would never possess this deadly and provocative woman, and he envied Mac that, because at this moment she was more beautiful than he had ever seen her.

"I've got work to do," she said, and she was gone.

Chapter Twelve

Jacksonville

"MR. RANDALL, MAKE OUR DEPTH THREE HUNDRED FEET. Ahead slow. Sir, we're in position closing on the battle group."

"Well done, Mr. Carter," MacKenzie said warmly. He handled the sub like he did everything else, meticulously, never an issue unattended. If anything, a little too careful. This wasn't the family car. He made a note to talk to Carter. He seemed a little anxious still. It was MacKenzie's job as a teacher to find out if anything was actually bothering him or if he was just adjusting to the pressure of the training-turned-real. Mac realized he should speak more with his PCOs. Being more of a tend-to-your-own-problems kind of person, he'd have to get over feeling that asking personal questions was an invasion of privacy. He knew better. No one did it alone.

"Return to plot coordinator. Miss Moran, XO. Mr. Bell, take fire control. Mr. Flynn, the conn is yours. Take us to the *Mahan*. Time is running short. He's feeling that, too, you can bet on it. Only a week left. Maybe he'll get careless."

"I have the conn. Mr. Randall, make your depth six zero feet."

"Six zero feet, aye."

Flynn raised their masts to listen to the radio chatter. The destroyers were on heavy alert. Colby's squadron of ASW helos were in the air looking for the *Northern Star*. There was plenty of chatter between the pilots and the ASW coordinator on the carrier, whose call sign was "X-ray," working in his compartment behind the combat information center. It came over the conn speaker fast and furious.

"X-ray, 610."

"Go ahead, 610."

"Request clearance inside five miles to make a wake check."

"Roger, 610. You're cleared."

This was a request to "dip" a sonar dome into the carrier's huge wake, where sound and water conditions made it difficult to spot a submarine.

"610 making dip."

"Roger."

"X-ray, Red Lion 610. Next dip on Mother's 237 for 6."

"Roger, 612."

"Colby's got them well trained," said MacKenzie.

"It'll be a cold day in hell when a pack of damn rotorheads beats us to Avilov," said Flynn smugly.

MacKenzie smiled. Flynn was supremely confident, the kind other men called a born warrior. If he couldn't outfox the opposition, he'd ram right through it. But he knew the rancor in Flynn's tone wasn't real. Pride made it normal that everyone felt his job was the most important, the most glamorous, the most essential. It was amazing how quickly a downed pilot or sailor's animosity for the "helo pukes" changed to deep and sincere regard after a difficult rescue on the high seas.

Flynn looked at the sonar screen in the conn. There was a

new tracing in the center band. "Sonar, have you identified that contact?"

"Contact is identified as biologics."

Fish. "Acknowledged. Mr. Springfield, plot a course to get ahead of them and get close to the bottom. I want to come in on their flank."

Springfield chewed his pencil for a moment. "Aye, sir. Can do."

Flynn punched up the MC. "This is the captain speaking. We are approaching the carrier battle group and will be attempting to insert ourselves within its destroyer screen over the next few hours. Maintain ultra-quiet. This is not a drill. Captain out."

Inwardly MacKenzie wondered if he could work up a better plan than the PCOs and decided he couldn't. It was creative and clever. Bell had spotted a hole in the battle group's defenses and figured Avilov might make for it. A new generation was running his sub. The future generation. All he'd gotten was a reprieve. The urgency of Avilov's Atlantic run was the only thing keeping him in command, and he knew it. Damn it, you didn't remove a pitcher with a no-hitter in the ninth inning, did you? Why him, now?

"Keep up the good work, Jamie," MacKenzie heard himself say.

"Why, thank you, Captain," said Flynn, switching his Irish brogue on happily. "'Tis a pleasure huntin' with the likes of ya."

"Jamie, I'd like to get some food," Carter said.

"Sure, Reg. Mr. Springfield, take over."

Carter made himself a sandwich in the wardroom. He was deeply worried, off balance. Irritability and ill temper were so unlike him. He knew MacKenzie saw it in the conn. Maybe he should tell him. MacKenzie could be trusted. But what could even he do? Bigger fish than MacKenzie or Reggie Carter had been sacrificed to an admiral's ambition before.

"Shit," he said.

"Sir?"

He'd forgotten about the steward. "Mind your own business," he snapped. The man ducked back into the galley like he'd been slapped. Christ, I'm losing it, Carter thought.

Carter was a religious man. The human soul was something very real to him. So was the idea that costing another man his soul could cost him his own. Was there a way to destroy Mark's career and not destroy the man? He began to ponder a way to serve Ransom and Mark both. To remove him from Ransom's reach, yet finish him at the same time. The choice even had a name.

The Devil's alternative.

AUTEC Control

Red Cado checked his clipboard. "Sir, *Jacksonville*'s at the search area. Mac still has the PCOs handling the conn."

"Good." Garver spat out a piece of cigar that had been clinging stubbornly to his lip.

"May I speak honestly, sir?"

"Shoot."

"We've got us a hell of a situation out there. Why not use Mac one more time? Why cling to a decision that may make no sense in light of the present emergency?"

"Because there will *always* be another emergency. Another next time. You think just because the Soviet Union split up we've seen an end to conflict? China's selling weapons like they're going out of style. North Korea's working on an atomic bomb. Japan's fielding a real army. *That's why we need teachers.* To make new captains. That's what'll keep us the best navy in the world into the next century. It's why I've drawn the line. No matter how good a man is, there comes a time when he has to move on. A fool fights it. A wise man accepts it and grows."

"Will Mac?"

"He has no choice." Garver glanced at the date clock on the wall. A week to stop Avilov.

One week.

Chapter Thirteen

Red Lion 610

For LCDR Frankie Rico it was a matter of pride.

Rico was from Detroit, "when it was livable," he always added. As well as: "You learned one rule: Take no shit." That was both heritage and gospel. He hovered his helo forty feet above the ocean, trailing his sonar dome into the carrier's long white wake. Subs liked to hide there if they could. It was Rico's job to see they couldn't. The ultra-sensitive AQS-13E dipping sonar could be let down by cable as deep as four hundred fifty feet and transmit signals to the helo's sonar operator. If a target was acquired, Rico would drop his Mk-46 torpedoes. He had failed to detect very few subs over the course of his career and wasn't about to let this Avilov character get past him. Or worse, let some snot-nosed PCOs sink the Russian sub first. Especially a *female* snot-nosed PCO. He shuddered at the thought. Colby would have his ass on a plate. Besides, he didn't like this bunch. Who did that bastard Flynn think he was, insulting the skipper like that?

Rico got back to business. The area was clear. "Sonar, pilot. Stand by to raise the dome."

"Roger . . . cable is within angular limits."

The copilot switched the coupler to Doppler mode. "On Doppler."

"Up dome," Rico ordered.

"Roger. Up dome. Leaving 350 feet." When the dome had cleared the water the crewman reported, "Dome clear."

Now Rico could move the helo. Any sooner and he would either pull the dome off the cable or pop it out of the water to where it might strike the aircraft. There was a moment of intercom silence as the reeling machine retracted the dome to the trail position, six to ten feet below the helo, then shut itself off.

"Pilot, dome is at trail."

Colby called in to X-ray, the ASW coordinator on the carrier. "X-ray, 610. Breaking dip. Next dip station Mother's 180 for 3"—he identified his next position, three miles from Mother, the carrier, on course one eight zero.

"Roger, 610."

"Widen your brickwork, Racer."

That was Colby in 615, using Rico's personal call sign to tell him to increase his sonobuoy field by dropping more sound locators into the water.

"I'm on it, Stogie," radioed Rico. "For sure, they're buying tonight."

"Glad to hear it, Racer."

Rico was close to the dip point, downwind about three quarters of a mile. "X-ray, 610. Mark dip."

"Roger, 610."

Rico often wondered what it would be like to be in a sub making its attack run on the battle group, how the tactical picture would look from below the scene rather than above it. As far as he was concerned, he had the advantage. There were only so many places a sub could take a shot from. Finding the right one was often a process of elimination. What would I do if I were the sub CO? he always asked himself. Sound was usually the answer. Noise was the submariner's ultimate paradox, loved and hated. It could mask their movements or betray them.

It was a sunny day with high wispy clouds. The wind was rising somewhat, but the ocean was still fairly calm. Of course, it could change quickly. Rico wanted to make Colby happy. His balling outs were legendary in their ferocity. Rico worked extra hard to avoid them.

The vista ahead grew unexpectedly beautiful. A few times Rico had had moments driving on a highway when suddenly, for no apparent reason, all the cars and trucks seemed to be going the same speed, and it felt like the road was moving underneath the cars rather than the cars over the road. It was like that now. The other helos in the squadron were poised over the gleaming quicksilver sea, cables trailing down like tethers. The carrier was ahead, a huge city of a ship plowing through the waves. Aft and abeam were the cruisers. Destroyers sliced sharply through the water on both sides of the triangular formation. An oiler and a supply ship darted about like playful dolphins. For a long moment all were in stasis. All had the same rhythmic curve and movement. Rico took in the scene like a flash picture. One perfect liquid hill of ships and aircraft. Then random motion broke the scene apart, and it returned to its individual components.

Rico stabilized the hover. "Sonar, pilot. Down dome."

"Roger, pilot. Down dome . . . dome submerged."

"Roger." Rico waited till he heard, "Pilot, sonar . . . dome is at 300 feet. Commencing passive search," then he radioed X-ray that he was continuing to look for the enemy sub.

Jacksonville

Carter was holding the *Jacksonville* at four hundred feet, stabilizing the ship using only the EPM and the trim tanks.

The neat maneuver let him maintain his position silently. Those in the conn were extremely tense now. Curt commands were issued from tight faces. At any time sonar might call out "torpedo in the water," and it would be a real war shot, not some fancy electronic tube with a pinger in it.

Carter was back in command taking *Jacksonville* into the next phase of their hunt.

"Destroyer's coming on fast, Reg," said Jessica from the fire control station. "Closing three thousand yards."

Bell said, "Suggest you take us north a few hundred yards."

"Speed twenty knots," said Jessica. "Two thousand yards and closing."

"Flood all torpedo tubes," ordered Carter.

"Flood all tubes, aye."

"Stay alert for that burst of speed," MacKenzie reminded them.

"One thousand yards and closing," said Bell.

"Conn, sonar. There she goes, sir. Sharp increase in speed. Closing at thirty knots."

This was it. The destroyer was making up distance, heading right for them with her engines running at maximum.

"Mr. Bell, you have the conn. Fine job, Mr. Carter. Take the navigation station. Miss Moran, XO. Mr. Flynn, shift back to fire control."

"I have the conn," said Bell. He had an adrenaline rush stronger than anything he had ever felt before. No moment on the football field was ever like this. The football games of his youth paled into insignificance, a foolish little squad of ants on the grass tossing around a silly-looking object for indecipherable reasons. How could this have held meaning for him? He wanted to get the *Northern Star* more than anything he had ever wanted, and, he guessed, maybe more than anything he might ever want again.

"Mr. Randall, make your depth two hundred feet. Five degree up bubble."

"Two hundred feet, five degree up bubble, aye."

"She's over us," said Flynn.

"All ahead flank," Bell ordered.

"All ahead flank, aye."

There wasn't any room for error. The sound of the big screws penetrated the cabin, at first a dull throb, rising to a loud and constant crashing as the *Jacksonville* rose.

"Watch your ears, sonar," Bell warned.

They had to get closer to the *Mahan* than they had to the *Caron*, and the shaft noise was enough to rattle bones. Depth was always measured from the keel to the surface, or from the keel to the bottom of the ocean. The ship's height had to be subtracted from the distance-to-hull figures, so the hundred-foot figure left only forty feet from the bottom of the *Mahan* to the top of the *Jacksonville*.

Bell took the intercom. "This the captain. We are maneuvering into our required position. There is no danger. Do your best to ignore the noise."

"They're zigzagging," said Flynn.

Carter was ready. "Suggest left ten degrees rudder, Captain . . . no, fifteen."

"Left fifteen degrees rudder," ordered Bell. He didn't want to think about all that water outside. All the things *in* the water. Several times now he had felt the fear, the weakness, but he concentrated on his task and it went away. So far nobody had noticed. He had to continue to command. Everything depended on it.

"They're looking for Avilov," said MacKenzie. "That change was to let that helo clear the *Mahan*'s wake."

"I'm going in tighter," said Bell. "Make your depth nine zero feet."

"Any closer and we'll be able to reach out and touch her," said Jessica.

"Nine zero feet, Captain," said Randall calmly.

"They're zagging," said Flynn.

"Suggest right ten degrees rudder, Captain."

"Right ten degrees rudder," ordered Bell.

The propeller noise was incessant. Men covered their ears or stuck cotton wadding in them. "Shift your rudder. Steady as she goes," ordered Bell.

MacKenzie watched the team work. He had tried different combinations now, and he felt this was the configuration that worked best. Bell was their natural leader. MacKenzie was handed a communication from the radio officer. He addressed the PCOs. "Seems we've had some contact with the *Star*. The carrier thinks she's close."

Jessica was watching Flynn's screens over his shoulder, and she beckoned to Bell, leaning close so she could be heard above the noise. "The cruisers have moved up. They're shortening the inner zone for the helo squadrons."

Flynn put his head near theirs. "Helos are moving again. Tenacious mothers."

The tension in the conn was palpable. The steady pulse beat of excitement matched the beat of the giant props overhead. It was dangerous being this close to the *Mahan*. A few feet up or a sudden shift in undersea currents and there would be a collision.

The *Northern Star* was somewhere out there.

"Come to Papa," Bell whispered.

Chapter Fourteen

Northern Star

THE CONN WAS AVILOV'S LAIR NOW. HE LEFT IT RARELY EXCEPT for a few hours' sleep or a meal in his cabin. He had come to understand his ship now in ways he never had. Listening to the world the same way the *Star* did, feeling its isolation, he realized it wasn't a thing of steel and wire at all, it was an idea. Progress unimpeded by external reality. What sublime and wonderful arrogance! Was any force on earth stronger than man's ego? Seal ourselves in fragile shells and run without eyes through the depths, as free as gods, dwarfing the pressures. Blindness had opened his eyes.

What did he miss seeing, anyway? There was no beautiful scenery to gaze at, not even his wife's lovely face to feast upon. He wondered where Katcha was now. Sitting by the beach on Sabaña Key feeding the children, probably, waiting for him as she had so many times, unaware of the danger. He had never let her down in their twenty-year marriage. He wasn't about to start now. He'd get to Sabaña Key if he had to carry the *Star* there himself.

The Americans were making it hard. At some point the numbers took over, and you could not defeat them no matter how good you were. Avilov had used trick after trick just to get them this far. He needed more. In this way his blindness helped him. He understood as never before how clever the weak must be to survive.

Pachenko was shaking his head in amazement. "They must have half the fleet up there, Pari."

Avilov heard them. "We try and run by them, there will be more torpedoes in the water than even we can evade. But we need to move quickly. We're running out of time. Only five days left."

"They'll hear us," said Pachenko flatly.

"Maybe. How big are your balls, Yuri?"

"Excuse me?"

"Tell me. What do you think they expect us to do?"

Pachenko thought it over. "Run deep and silent and try to sneak past them."

"Right. They probably have their submarines lying deep, waiting for us. The surface ships are like beaters pushing the tiger through the brush right into the hunter's blind. So what does the poor tiger do? Stupid creature, he rushes right into their sights and gets his head blown off. Well, I am not a stupid tiger."

It occurred to Pachenko that Avilov was actually enjoying himself. "How does all this fit in with your anatomical question?"

"If the tiger were smarter, he would realize that the only safe place for him is in the blind itself, *with the hunters.*"

Pachenko blanched. "You're not going to—"

"Who better to play blindman's buff? Flash silent battle stations. Rig for ultra-quiet. Sonar, locate that carrier."

Red Lion 610

Rico wanted to fire his torpedoes so badly his bowels hurt. He had dropped his dome three more times and come up empty. Three other helos were on station, results the same.

Bart Davis

The destroyers were steaming alongside the carrier like faithful hounds. The *Forestal* surged on, a city afloat. She was his responsibility, and he wasn't about to let her down. He radioed, "X-ray, 610 request clearance in the inner zone for another wake check."

"Roger, 610."

Rico was a good pilot with a real feel for his aircraft. He reviewed the tactical situation. Think like a sub captain, he reminded himself, concentrating on the problem. You had to look at where tactical operations were limited. Subs hid in noise or in rough water to hide their own sound.

He keyed in his radio. "Stogie, Racer. Got an idea."

"Go common," Colby radioed back. "Let's keep it private."

Rico switched his radio to the squadron frequency. "Skipper, what do think of letting Rooster clear the wake and Kelly take the point while the whole group suddenly increases speed and makes a hard turn to the right? You and I hover and wait. If he's in here somewhere, we might just flush him."

"Let me see what X-ray says."

Rico was taking a risk volunteering a plan of action. From now on events would be his responsibility. But damn, those PCOs had annoyed the hell out of him.

"Racer, Stogie. You're having a creative day. The plan's a go. It's on your head now. Don't come back without a sub on your plate."

Vintage Colby. He was like those ancient Spartans: come back *with* your shield or *on* it. If Rico's plan worked, he would get credit for it; if not—well, shit, he didn't even want to think about *that*. "Roger that, Stogie. He's dead meat. Sonar, pilot. Up dome. Breaking dip."

"Roger, pilot. Up dome, leaving three hundred feet."

For the next fifteen minutes X-ray moved the pilots. "That look like what you had in mind, 610?"

110

"Roger, X-ray."

They boxed in the big carrier, helos in front and back, Colby on the port side and Rico on the starboard. Rooster and Kelly had already lowered their domes into the water. It was time to catch the sub napping.

Jacksonville

"Carrier's turning," said Flynn excitedly.

"Let's see what they flush," said MacKenzie. "Mr. Bell, from here on in it's all yours."

Bell had to work to keep his voice professionally neutral. "Aye, sir."

The carrier group was turning fast. He was in a perfect position to make his run if they exposed the Russian sub. One perfect Atlantic run. That wasn't much to ask for, was it, God?

"Conn, sonar. Increase in speed from all contacts."

"Acknowledged. Maneuvering, prepare to answer maximum bells. We'll be running hard, then coming to a sudden stop to shoot our torpedoes. Watch our pressure transient when we slow."

"Maneuvering, aye. We're ready, skipper."

"Helm, prepare to come around smartly."

"Helm ready, sir."

"Mr. Flynn, be ready to plot a firing solution." *If* he's there, sang doubts in Bell's head. "This will be a passive sonar shoot. I do not intend to go active."

Suddenly sonar's excited voice rang out, "Contact, Skipper. Bearing . . . almost got it . . . there! Computers are working on it . . . Bearing . . . zero nine zero. Range . . . one thousand yards. Course is . . . two seven zero. Prop noises, sir. It's a Russian sub!"

Bell could have danced a jig. It was under the carrier. It was there!

"Maneuvering, all ahead flank," ordered Bell.

111

The *Jacksonville* surged into the inner zone. The throb of the *Mahan*'s engines, so long a companion, died abruptly as they left her protection.

"Helm, hard right rudder to new course two nine five," ordered Bell.

Carter was saying something about the ship movement but Bell couldn't concentrate on it right then. Moran was reporting the carrier's increased speed and something about helos close in. How could anyone think in all this racket? He felt it start in his head. *The water. The things in it.* His mind was reeling. He had to concentrate.

"Firing point procedures. Helm, come left to two six five degrees. Set angle on the bow port twenty," he ordered.

"Sir, angle on the bow does not check," said Carter almost at once.

Bell had screwed up. He'd gotten confused and had the target going in the wrong direction. Christ, his head was pounding. He saw other times, other places. He fought it off. He thought, Don't let it be happening again!

"Only surface is truth," said MacKenzie quietly behind him.

The teacher was standing by his pupil, Bell realized. It calmed him. He began to see. MacKenzie was reminding him that everything in sub-versus-sub warfare was guesswork. Educated guesswork. Only sight, meaning surface, was objective. Bell had to build his case. Range, speed, course and bearing. These were the elements he needed for a solution.

"Correction, starboard twenty. Zero bubble. Torpedo room, open outer doors."

"Open outer doors. Torpedo room, aye."

"Solution ready," reported Flynn.

MacKenzie said, "They've got to go deep to run, Mark. Set below limits stratum to protect the carrier, too."

"Set below limits, aye."

"Standby to fire tubes one and two," Bell ordered. Moran said something he couldn't hear, about tracking the rest of the ships. What the hell was sonar saying? Helos where? Who could think with all this racket going on? Oh, God, don't let me miss!

Flynn said, "Ship ready; Solution ready; Torpedo Room ready."

"Maneuvering, all stop."

Jacksonville slowed. Bell hoped the angle on the bow was correct, hoped the torpedoes would stay on course, hoped no one had outthought or outguessed him. He said firmly, *"'Thunder is good, thunder is impressive; but it's lightning that does the work.'* Shoot tubes one and two."

"Set—Standby—Fire."

"Tube one unit away."

"Set—Standby—Fire."

"Tube four unit away."

Northern Star

"Captain, we're losing speed!"

"We can't," Avilov warned. They had to keep up with the carrier's turn or they would be exposed to the open sea. Already the noise was fading. "Engine room, report!"

"Problem in the secondary plant . . . no, wait . . . I think . . . full power, Captain. Frozen valve . . . rerouted. We'll have it in a minute."

Avilov slammed the mike back. Too late. Somebody must have heard them.

"Captain, torpedoes in the water. High-speed motors. Two contacts. An American submarine closing on our port side."

A sub? Where the hell had *he* been? It came to him all at once. Under the *destroyer!* Another fox in the flock. He wasn't the only one. Avilov had only seconds to make the right decision or he was dead along with all the men on his ship—and his family died with them.

"Captain, torpedoes closing . . . They have acquired us. Five hundred yards.

"Countermeasures, launch decoys."

"Decoys away."

"Fire control, do we have a solution on that sub?"

"Partial . . . still partial," said Vashovsky. "The rest of the group is scattering. It's a madhouse up there."

"Torpedo four hundred yards and closing."

"Snap shot tube one and three," ordered Avilov. "Firing point procedures. Open outer doors and fire tubes one and three."

"Tube one . . . away. Tube three . . . away."

"Three hundred yards and closing . . . Captain!?"

Twin torpedoes coming. He had to dive deep to get out of their way. The order to dive the ship was on his tongue when he had the sudden thought of how clever the American had been to hide under the destroyer. Maybe he was even clever enough to try to flush him deep. Avilov made the biggest bet of his life.

"Yuri, emergency surface."

"But we are still under the carrier!" Pachenko cried.

"Do as I say!"

Pachenko hit the emergency blow lever, and a ten-second burst of compressed air blew water out of the main tanks all at once. *Northern Star* shot up the last twenty feet and hit the carrier's hull. There was a huge crack as they collided. Seals ruptured and water burst in from the piping overhead. The hull groaned and electrical circuits shorted out with acrid smoke as the water hit the consoles.

"Torpedo twenty yards . . . ten . . . Captain, the torpedoes passed under us!"

Avilov banged a triumphant fist. "They couldn't shoot too

high for fear of hitting the carrier. Quickly, Pari, into the overhead. Secure that flooding."

Pachenko shot a look of pride and awe at Avilov as he scrambled into the overhead. "The Hawk wins again."

"Not yet, Yuri. First we must get out of here. Stepov, take us very deep. Six hundred meters. Shift to the EPM only. With all the noise up there no one will hear us leaving the party now."

Jacksonville

"Conn, Sonar. Torpedoes in the water! Closing on us."

MacKenzie stepped up at once. "I have the conn. Emergency deep. Twenty degree down bubble. All ahead flank."

Bell's attention was split between the race to elude the Russian torpedo and the hope that his own units had run true.

"Conn, sonar, high-speed motors trailing away. We've outrun his torpedoes, skipper."

"What about our units?" asked Bell.

"No contact, sir."

Bell said to MacKenzie, "He guessed, didn't he?"

"He must have." There was nothing but respect in MacKenzie's voice. "I was patched into sonar. Just before the torpedoes got to him there was a loud crunching sound. Crazy as it sounds, I think he surfaced under the carrier and the fish blew by underneath."

"Surfaced under . . . ?"

MacKenzie nodded. "They'll be beginning to say nobody can beat this guy," he said, reaching under his cap to run a hand through his hair tiredly. "Maybe they're right."

"I'm sorry I failed you, sir."

MacKenzie put a hand on his shoulder. "Mark, I was never even close to relieving you. This guy's one of a kind."

"What do we do now, sir?" Jessica Moran asked.

"We try for another shot at him," said MacKenzie. "Mr. Bell, take us back in."

Red Lion 610

Rico's first thought was, Colby's gonna kill me! He couldn't believe it when he heard X-ray yell over his helmet phones, "Torpedoes in the water! Sub's under the carrier." He gave out with a string of oaths that carried all the way back to the sonar crew.

It hadn't been the wake after all. The son of a bitch had been under the carrier. The turn flushed it, but the PCO sub had gotten there first. Rico hit the throttle hard. He was more than five hundred yards aft. His face was hot and flushed following the action on the voice channels. He didn't like being outmaneuvered. The PCOs might have gotten to the Russian first, but they missed. His turn now.

The fleet was in disarray. Ships were steaming all over the place in evasion tactics. If the Russian got deep they'd lose him for sure.

"X-ray, 610, permission to freelance."

"You are authorized to freelance, 610."

Rico told his sonar crew to keep their heads down and roared low over the water, now authorized to pick dip sites on his own. The enemy sub had made a snapshot and broken away. Which way? West.

"Sonar, pilot. Down dome."

"Roger, down dome."

Rico scanned his board. Nothing. Colby was going to ream his ass over this one. It had happened on his watch, in the middle of Rico's plan. He could see that big ugly face curled around his stogie delivering a dressing down in front of the others. "Great plan, Rico, next time you wanna keep your mouth shut?" Typical Colby.

Rico ordered the dome up and almost moved the helo before it had cleared the water. He was moving too fast, desperate to find the sub, getting careless with procedures. It was dangerous. Men died that way. The chief sonar man's voice burst angrily over Rico's headphones.

"What the hell are you doing, Skipper?" he yelled.

"Finding that Russian sub. You got a problem with that?"

"Not if you do it the right way."

"Just get that dome back down."

"The reeler can't . . ." The sonar man bit back a curse and shut up. "Sonar, aye."

Finally Rico saw it. There, was that a flicker? "X-ray, 610. Target acquired. Request clearance for weapons release." His hand hovered over the release switch for his torpedoes, waiting for the command "Weapons free" to fire.

"610, X-ray. We are terminating. Return to Mother."

"I'm close, X-ray. I swear it."

"We can't verify that, 610. Sorry. Bring it back to the barn."

"X-ray, just let me—"

"Negative, negative, negative. Close your array."

Rico fiddled with his radio switch sending static over the line, then cut it off completely. "Not just yet," he muttered.

One final time he drew the dome up and sped over the water.

"Sonar, pilot. Down dome."

"Skipper, I don't . . . Damn. Sonar, aye."

Jacksonville

MacKenzie had to hand it to Avilov. A genius, that's what the Russian captain was. And he was on the loose again.

"Conn, Sonar. We're still getting helo noise. Close by."

"Helm, right ten degrees rudder," Bell ordered. "Mr. Randall, make our depth two zero zero feet."

"Two zero zero feet, aye."

A sudden scraping noise stopped them all. It wasn't a noise anyone had ever heard before.

"What the hell is that?" Flynn wondered aloud.

Later Bell could not say how he knew, or why, just that a sudden assemblage of clues in his subconscious slipped into his mind. He reacted without thinking, certain of only one thing: that any delay would kill the pilot.

"Belay that dive order! Emergency surface," he yelled. "Emergency blow main ballast tanks. Ten-second blow." Bell reached out to pull the "chicken switches," but Mac-Kenzie stopped him.

"Explain yourself."

"Sir, I think that pilot's got his sonar cable snagged on us. If we go down we'll take him and his ship with us."

"Up scope." Galvanized, MacKenzie swung the scope around with his arms hunched around the handles. "He's right. The helo is snagged. Emergency surface. Mark, Jamie, Jessica, get on deck with tools to cut that line. Mr. Carter, take the conn."

MacKenzie grabbed the radio. "Helo streamer is tangled in our sail plane. We need an SAR team in the air *now.*"

Red Lion 610

Rico felt the snag and cursed his luck. He had decided to call it quits five minutes too late, and it was going to cost him his dome. All around, a shit day. He hated to use his jettison capability. He'd be lucky to escape all this without charges.

"Sonar, pilot. Jettison dome."

"Pilot, jettison malfunction. The reeler's jammed, Skipper. Maybe all that up-and-down crap."

"Cut it," said Rico, fighting a crosswind.

"Fine," glowered the sonar chief. "Except we got no cutters. Some bright boy left them home."

The first glimmering of fear touched Rico's mind. The wind was rising quickly, and he had no maneuverability tethered to the sub. Controls were getting sticky. He fought to keep flying.

"X-ray, 610. Tangled streamer. Mayday! Mayday!"

He almost lost control trying to play the sub like a fish on a line. Maybe if he just jerked it a little, somebody would wise up to him up here. Just when he thought it might work there was pull on the line from below that almost yanked him out of the air. The helo dipped wrenchingly. He fought it back up, scrambling for every inch of altitude.

"Yank the damn assembly out of the deck if you have to," he shouted into his mike. "Disengage us." The winds were gusting wildly now. He had to get clear. One more jerk like that from the submarine and he'd be pulled into the sea.

Rico's sainted mother once told him she'd had a vision of the Virgin. At that moment Rico was sure it didn't compare to the sight of the sub surfacing below him. They must have figured it out. An SAR helo was on its way. They might have made it. Rico would never know. He felt the craft kick to the right, then to the left suddenly, and barely had time to wonder what was causing the wiggle when the tail rotor failed. The helo yawed hard to the right and its nose dropped ten degrees. Rico knew he was in deep trouble. Maybe even a malfunction in the gear box on top of the tail. The helo spun out of control. They dropped fast, yawing hard. He desperately bottomed the collective, the control that varied the pitch of the rotor blades, to lessen the wild swings. It was the only thing he could do besides pray.

The helo hit the water hard and flipped over.

Jacksonville

Bell followed Flynn and Jessica onto the bridge. Flynn had their big cutters. It was a choppy sea and the wind was howling. The helo's sonar dome was wedged under the starboard plane, jamming it. Bell and Jessica had to balance precariously to hook the cable and pull it close enough for Flynn to cut. But just as Flynn got it between the cutter jaws it went slack.

"He's going down," shouted Bell, realizing what it meant.

A hundred yards away the helo hit the water and seemed to fold in on itself. The blades crumpled and stuck up like giant crab legs.

Jessica grabbed the sail mike. "Captain, helo down. Steer right ten degrees rudder. All ahead slow. Men in the water three hundred feet off the starboard bow."

"Stay up there and give us our heading, Miss Moran," came back MacKenzie's voice.

"Right, sir. Steady as she goes."

The crew had made it out of the helo. All but one had their heads up, waving. The other man's face was in the water. He'd drown if someone didn't reach him soon. Bell panicked. The sea laughed at him. It was happening again. Bile rose in his throat. The SAR helo was still a mile off. It would be too late. Bell climbed onto the sail plane to dive off, and froze.

He remembered the warm wind and the smell of sizzling meat from the barbecues on the beaches around Sydney harbor. The Aussies were celebrating the return of the fleet with a show that rivaled the Fourth of July. The carrier had already steamed out to sea to take back its planes. Bell's sub was lying a mile out, letting the locals and their fleet of small boats get a last look at her.

He was up in the sail on watch, enjoying the school of dolphins playing in their bow wake when the little family power boat capsized.

"Mark," Jessica yelled, "what's wrong?"

With a start Bell realized he was clinging to the sail ladder with both arms. His hands wouldn't release.

"Somebody better get to that guy before he drowns," Flynn yelled, struggling to disengage the dome.

MacKenzie appeared on the bridge. Bell looked up to him, eyes pleading. MacKenzie came down the ladder and pulled at Bell's hands. Bell lost his grip and plunged off the sail. The sea closed over his head, and the wispy voice that had haunted his dreams spoke to him again: *How silent and good. Sink down. Forget. No more faces. How easy. Forget the bodies in the water . . . the bodies in the water . . .*

The life at stake brought him back. Bell struck out for the downed airman. MacKenzie was swimming, too. They reached the pilot and pulled his head back. A jagged white shaft of collarbone protruded from his puckered flesh and had speared into the safety vest, pinning his face in the water. Bell vomited into the sea.

MacKenzie pushed the bone back. Bell got his nausea under control and held the pilot's head up, using his fingers to clear the pilot's mouth. The pilot's eyes were closed tightly. Bell couldn't tell for sure whether he was alive or dead.

The throb of the search and rescue helos reached them, and the prop wash set the water rippling wildly around them. Divers dropped into the water and got the pilot into a harness, and the helo winched him from the sea.

Bell watched the pilot ride up. One of the helo crewmen sat on the edge of the hatch with an automatic rifle cocked and ready, on the lookout for sharks. Bell grew conscious of his own dangling legs, so tasty, so vulnerable. . . .

He called in a course change to the capsized boat and went over the side. The children wouldn't last long in the water. He remembered the silence of the long, slow dive underwater that brought him close to the boat. A dolphin flashed by, unmindful of the emergency. The man was clinging to the hull and to his wife and daughter, yelling for the boy as he tried to keep the girl from slipping under.

Bell dived down into the clear green water. After a while the pressure in his ears matched the burning in his lungs, but he was determined not to come up without the child. Somewhere behind him he fancied he could feel the throb of his sub's engines. Were they tracking them like some enemy contact? Was the boy near? He surfaced and dived again. He felt that big presence looming nearby. Comforting. Ready to pull him out when he had the boy. There. A glint of something metallic. Bell never knew where the air came from to make such a dive. He had to clear his ears before the pressure nearly crushed his skull, but his fingers clasped around that little wrist, so frail and small, like a twig in his big hand. His lungs were on fire in that desperate quiet under the water. The surface was a shining plane of light that lay just a few more strokes away. . . .

Bell had been hit by some of the best tackles in the game, but never with such ferocity and power. He thought he'd been rammed from behind by the sub. . . .

He wrenched himself back to the present. A diver slipped a flotation vest around him and snapped him into a harness. Bell rode up into the sky, and strong hands pulled him into the helo bay.

He sprawled on the deck in an exhausted heap, watching the remaining helo crewmen being reeled up through a rainbow haze of whipped-up spray like puppets on strings.

Chapter Fifteen

AUTEC

FATIGUE WAS CLOSING MACKENZIE'S EYES AS HE AND BELL walked to the Q from the helo pad. They were wet and exhausted and hadn't slept in over twenty hours. He was worried about Bell. He'd been deadly silent since being hauled into the SAR helo. Finally he opened up.

"Captain MacKenzie?"

"Yes?"

"I froze. If you hadn't—"

"You went in after a downed flier," MacKenzie said. "That's my report. They all might have died if you hadn't realized what was happening."

"That sub got away because of me, too," Bell said, believing it. *If I had been able to concentrate,* he thought. "It's the truth, sir." *You don't know what's going on inside me.*

"Lieutenant, that sub got away because it was captained by a wizard." The look on MacKenzie's face was as fierce as it was sudden. "Nobody could have beaten Avilov today. You understand? Not you or me or anyone. It was his day. Next time maybe it'll be ours. Maybe not. Either way you live with it. Mark, come inside. It's time we talked."

MacKenzie had a comfortable set of rooms furnished cleanly and simply. The one really nice touch was a balcony with some rattan furniture and a splendid view of the ocean beyond the palm trees. Mac took a phone call and responded with a quick "Right, we'll be there" and hung up.

"Scotch?" he asked Bell.

"I'd settle for rubbing alcohol," Bell said, hanging his shirt over the railing to dry. The sun felt good.

MacKenzie filled their glasses. "This relates directly to your fitness to command. I want to know what happened in Australia."

Bell stiffened. "Sir, that matter is closed."

"The files are. Judging from today, I don't think you've closed it."

"The board of inquiry found—"

"Sure. I know," MacKenzie said, "single traumatic episode. Insufficient grounds to disqualify. But I saw what happened on the sail plane today. It's still alive in you. Keep it there and it'll consume you. Believe me, I know."

"Sir. Yes, sir," said Bell tightly.

"Don't sir me."

"This is something I have to work through alone."

"Why? There's no goddamned virtue in going it alone. I used to think there was, and it almost cost me my career, my marriage, and myself. Let me help, son."

Bell put his glass down. "Thanks for the drink, sir."

MacKenzie sighed. He saw his own youthful enthusiasm in Bell. It was frustrating to see his stubborn pride, too. "Very well. They've scheduled a hot wash after-action review in twenty minutes. Word is we're not leaving till somebody comes up with a way to get this guy."

They assembled in the control center. A glaring Colby led his squadron in, and they sat in a cold, tight little group in back.

Every aspect of the operation was evaluated by two senior

admirals: Vernon Tucker, Deputy Commander for Submarines, a crisp, gray haired man with a tan, wizened face; and Joe Gentille, Deputy Commander for Surface Warfare, a bandy-legged man with powerful arms and a sad face. With them was the officer in charge of the AUTEC base, Commander Brady Roving; and Jeff Staffey, the AUTEC program manager, a good-looking young engineer in a polo shirt, chinos, and loafers. He carried a thick computer printout that he put on the conference table in the front of the room.

"First we're going to run through a real-time record of what happened out there," Staffey announced. "You'll be seeing a multicomputer analysis of the air, surface, and subsurface action made from the carrier's combat analysis center's engagement tapes, X-ray's, and the *Jacksonville's*. If you have questions, we can stop and focus on a particular aspect."

It took over an hour to sort through the components of the engagement. Watching it this way, as omniscient observers, there were murmurs of appreciation for Avilov's brilliant tactics. Tucker and Gentille were fair men. There was no attempt to fix blame for losing the *Northern Star*. Near the end Tucker said, "Let's hold it there, Jeff. Commander Moran, this has been your first introduction to submarine warfare. I'd like to take this opportunity to welcome you to the service."

"Thank you, sir. Proud to be here."

"Mac, your PCOs probably made the best try. Anything to add?"

"Yes, sir. They behaved as warriors. A fine, aggressive approach team. Avilov just did the unexpected."

Tucker nodded and looked them over. "Anyone who could have guessed Avilov would surface under the carrier is smarter than me. Good try."

"Recommendations?"

MacKenzie made a technical analysis that surprised Bell

in its detail. Tucker made notes, nodding from time to time. When MacKenzie was done, he said, "Anything else? Anyone?"

"Sir?"

"Yes, Commander Colby?"

"Sir, we had an incident today in which we almost lost a helo crew. The PCOs are responsible."

Flynn spoke before thinking. "Hey, we didn't—"

Tucker cut him off. "Mr, Flynn, please restrain that well-known Irish temper. I'd like to hear Commander Colby."

"A personal failing, sir. Sorry."

Colby continued smugly. "Admiral, if they had done proper sonar surface sweeps, they would've heard Red Lion 610 and avoided the sonar cable. Instead they snagged it, forcing the helo into a crash."

Tucker frowned. "Mac?"

MacKenzie spoke calmly. "Mr. Bell was responsible for saving Helo 610's crew."

"I'd like to know how," said Colby.

"Run the analysis back. It shows X-ray had given the 'close your array' command," said MacKenzie. "Helo 610 had no business making a sonar dip at that point."

"He had a communications failure," said Colby angrily. "Your PCOs ran into him and yanked him out of the sky."

Bell looked sick. Jessica put a hand on his shoulder. "Easy, Mark. Colby's just being a bastard."

Bell whispered worriedly. "His lies are on my record now. I can't afford that." *'One of the most striking differences between a cat and a lie is that a cat has only nine lives.'* But Bell saw another one of the qualities that made MacKenzie the most respected submarine captain in the fleet. He was relentless.

"The order to descend that *would* have sunk the helo was countermanded by Lieutenant Bell," continued MacKenzie coolly. "Mr. Bell—I repeat, Mr. Bell—correctly surmised the sonar cable was snagged. He ordered emergency surface and emergency blow of all ballast tanks. My periscope sweep proved Mr. Bell right, and I surfaced the ship."

Colby looked like he was going to explode. He jammed his cap back on and clamped his hands on the armrests like they were MacKenzie's neck.

"Commander Colby, how is your pilot?" asked Tucker.

"He'll live," Colby said, "no thanks to that submarine. Sir, I don't care who was in charge. My man went down because of it."

MacKenzie said, "You might be interested to know Mr. Bell went into the water after your pilot."

Colby pointed his cigar like an accusing finger. "He put him there. That's all I know."

Tucker took stock of the dissenting voices and came to a decision. "I'm sorry, Mr. Bell," said Tucker. "I'm going to have to convene a formal inquiry. "We'll review the tapes first thing tomorrow. All right, that's it for now. Get some boats out to sea. We're right back on the *Northern Star.* We're down to days, ladies and gentlemen. I expect maximum effort. Mac, can I see you?"

"Yes, sir."

Colby pulled his men out with an "I'll see *you* later" look.

Bell shoved his hands into his pockets and left the room, angry and depressed. Flynn and Jessica caught up to him outside.

"Don't worry, Mark. MacKenzie backed us a hundred percent," said Flynn.

"Then why the inquiry?" asked Bell.

"Just a formality," Jessica assured him.

"I hope so."

"You gonna be okay?"

"Yeah. You're probably gonna run again," he said. Her energy level was amazing. All he wanted to do was sleep.

She grinned. "Tough to do many miles on that sub. See you guys later."

"See you, Jess," said Flynn. He watched her go admiringly. "Christ, that's some woman. Did you see her today? She was great."

"She might be tough to add to your list, Jamie," said Bell. He meant it sympathetically, but Flynn turned on him angrily.

"I didn't mean it that way. She's different."

"Hey, okay. Sorry."

"All right," said Flynn, mollified.

Bell was surprised. So Flynn had a thing for Jessica Moran. Even though Bell had seen him with a lot of women, this choice took him by surprise. Flynn's conquests were a legion of adoring women of surprisingly varied types who saw in him a charming pirate/poet they found irresistible. But Jessica seemed older, tougher, and more mature than most. Also, she didn't seem to return his interest. He wondered if Flynn might be hurt by that more than most men. Rejection would be new to him.

The sun was low in the sky. Some sailors were sunning themselves on the beach. A volleyball game was underway. Flynn got them cold beers, and they sat in the sun.

"I feel crummy about losing that sub. I don't think I'll ever be good enough," Bell said soberly.

Flynn traced the condensation sliding down the glass bottle thoughtfully. "Mark, I mean this seriously. Reg and I are good, maybe even better than most. But you could be in another league."

"You're just trying to make me feel better."

Flynn shook his head, suddenly solemn. "Not so, bucko. In time the only man might be better is Captain Mac himself, and we think you'll give *him* a run for his money someday. It's like this, Baby Bell. A lot of men learn to be COs, but it's like a suit of clothes they put on. The suit fits exceedingly well in Reg's and my cases. Jess's too, I admit."

Bell grinned. "With all due modesty."

"As always. But you—well, it feels like you're meant to be

in charge. Like we were supposed to be working for you. That's a freaky feeling."

Bell thought it over. It *had* felt good. Like his father had said it did. And Twain: *"Your true pilot cares nothing about anything on earth but the river, and his pride in his occupation surpasses the pride of kings."*

Bell said, "I'm gonna walk for a while, Jamie. Thanks."

"Sure."

"And with Jess, good luck."

Jamie started for a moment. "It's that obvious?"

"To a friend. I just hope . . . you don't get hurt."

Flynn looked at him with sad eyes. "Too late, my friend. But O'Flynn appreciates your concern. Go heal. We've all had a long day."

Carter dropped back from the others. He saw Flynn put a fatherly arm around Bell and knew he should have been supporting him, too. Instead he could barely hide his relief that Tucker had called for a hearing. If Bell washed out, it would take Ransom off his back. But he knew the tapes would back Bell up.

Unless they didn't . . .

Jeff Staffey was the last to leave. Carter ducked into the range safety room until he passed and then went back into the control room. The user section behind the glass wall had computers and communications consoles, but the range section with the big video screens held the original data. He opened the first of several cabinets in the carpeted room, looking for where Staffey had stored the master engagement tape.

He ran a hand over the bright blue cases. They were filed by date . . . there. He had the means to scuttle Bell with just a little judicious editing. He turned a computer on.

Had he sunk this far? His fingers hovered over the keyboard. Whatever he was doing was better than the alternative he was considering. The disk was still loading.

He fought his internal war listening to the tiny whirs and beeps, like the wheels of his mind turning. *There are a hundred men who would swear you were their lover* . . . Visions of Washington postings. A knot in his stomach reminding him of his honor and duty. Ransom . . . Bell . . . back and forth. Branded all his life. Unable to disprove a lie. *There are a hundred men who would swear* . . .

"Reg? A little extra homework?"

Carter jumped. It was Jeff Staffey. He must have come back for something.

"Can't be too prepared," he lied feebly.

"And maybe you'd go a long way to help a friend?" Staffey suggested, eyeing him thoughtfully.

Christ, Staffey thought he was here to *help* Bell. "Look, I only wanted to make sure—well . . . we gotta stick together." He tried to sound earnest.

"Colby's a prick." Staffey winked. "But you don't have to worry. I know what the tape says. Bell did the right thing." He hit the eject button. "I gotta put this away, you understand?"

"Sure." Carter was sweating. "You won't say anything?"

"Nope. You're the kind of friend I'd like to have if I ever get into trouble, Reg. Not to worry. Matter closed."

"Thanks, Jeff. Thanks a lot."

Staffey replaced the tape and locked the cabinet. Carter masked his lost and sinking feeling and hid his hands in his pocket so he wouldn't see their trembling.

Chapter Sixteen

Andros Island

BELL WAS EMBARRASSED AND BITTER. IF THE HEARING WENT against him, he would resign, that was all. Things seemed to be spiraling downward for him. He had missed the *Star*. His personal demons were still haunting him. The pressure on the *Jacksonville* was making it worse. Twain wrote that courage was resistance and mastery of fear, not absence of it. What if you couldn't master it?

Jessica Moran was standing in the shallow water. She'd changed into a loose purple tank top over neon-green spandex running shorts. Her running shoes dangled from her hand by their laces.

"Hi," he said.

"Oh. Hi, Mark. Just cooling my feet. Feel any better?"

"Long walk helped."

"That's the way I feel about running."

"Everybody's got to have something," he agreed.

"So who loved Mark Twain in your family? Reg told me you're named after him."

"My dad."

"He navy, too?"

Bell hesitated for a second. "He was the last CO of the *Thornton.*"

"The sub that . . . oh, Mark. I'm sorry."

"'*Warm summer sun shine kindly here,*'" he said softly. "'*Warm southern wind, blow softly here; Green sod above, lie light, lie light.*' That was Twain's epitaph for his daughter. We had it carved into his headstone. He was a good guy. What about your folks?"

"Still in the city. My dad's a Teamster. Drives a truck. He says the suburbs are for pussies."

"Tough guy, huh?"

"Nah." Her voice grew warm. "A puppy. Just talks tough. My mom got MS when she was thirty. He spent a year working over our house so she could get around. Pulleys, cables, ramps. Special windows and doors and appliances. She'd never leave. Says it would kill her. Most everybody knows them. One gang leader even took tennis lessons from my dad in this program he runs. Scared the shit out of the little suburban brats when he walked onto the court. They thought he'd knife them if he lost." She grinned at the memory. "He was good, too. My dad got him a scholarship till they saw his police record. He never forgot Dad tried. Two of his homeys guard our house all the time."

"You like football?" he asked.

"I can't follow it. What the hell is a nose tackle? Can't be what it says."

"It isn't."

"I like movies," she said. "The older the better. I went through this big stage where I tried to be Loretta Young."

"Can I tell you a secret?"

"Is it deep and dark?"

He nodded. "I actually got a projector once and showed a Deanna Durbin movie in my dorm."

"What happened?"

"They taped me to my bed and shaved my head. Athletes aren't known for their cultural appreciation."

"Mark, about today. When the helo went down—"

"Skip it, Jess."

"But I—"

"I said skip it. Just something I'm working out. Now how about dinner? There's a restaurant off base that's supposed to make a mean fried conch. And I have Flynn's report on the local bars. We can meet him and Reg there later." He saw her hesitate. "PCO buddies," he declared, holding up two fingers. "Scout's honor."

"In that case," she said, "I buy the program."

Skinny's was crowded with men and women at the bar and dancing. "Well, if it isn't our other halves," Carter said, sighting Bell and Jessica.

Flynn looked sort of quiet and sober and shot back his Irish whiskey as though it quenched some inner burning. Carter thought it was an odd reaction. Unless . . . Could the legendary Jamie Flynn finally have been struck by real love? Carter accepted love at first sight. One look had been all *he* had needed when he met his future wife. The newness of it was evident on Flynn's face. Carter had been his classmate long enough to know that Flynn considered himself quite lucky never to have fallen for longer than a night. This was having a major impact on him.

Bell and Jessica plunged through the crowd to them.

"Top of the evenin', mates," said Flynn softly.

"You know, sir," Jessica said to MacKenzie, "I forgot I promised Luke Johnson I'd say hey to you."

MacKenzie acknowledged the name warmly. "We had a lot of great rides together. Luke saved my hide more than once."

"He said it was the other way around, sir."

"Just like him to distort the facts. Drink?"

"Beer will be fine."

"Me, too, said Bell.

"A beer for a quote, Mark," offered MacKenzie, holding it back.

"Very well, sir. How about *'Soap and education are not as sudden as a massacre, but they are more deadly in the long run.'* Or *'If you pick up a starving dog and make him prosperous, he will not bite you. This is the principal difference between a dog and a man.'*"

MacKenzie slid it over. "More than earned."

Flynn turned to Jessica with an intensity that startled her. "You did a fine job today, Jessica. Really great, considering everything."

"Why, thank you, Jamie."

"I mean it."

"I know you do."

He walked away, and she looked after him strangely. She was prevented further wonder by Skinny sidling over. Nightly the physical and philosophical giant, born Wendal Moxey, stood watch over his realm with his eldest boy, the only man in the place bigger than he was, Tiny. Skinny was holding a bottle without a label containing some strange-looking plant life in the liquid.

"How 'bout some root juice, Cap'n Mac? Guaranteed to cure what ails ya."

Jessica grimaced. "Looks evil."

"Might be," said MacKenzie with a grin. "If you're here long enough, Skinny always pours some. Tradition."

Skinny got into a conversation with Jessica about "the power and the glory," and MacKenzie used the opportunity to take Carter aside.

"How are you feeling, Reg? Everything all right?"

"Fine, sir. I mean, there's lots of tension and all, but everybody's going through it, right?"

"I don't know. A few times you've looked like you have something extra on your mind. I've never heard you snap at anyone before. Something you want to share?"

"No, sir." *You can't help me, he thought. No one can. I'm trapped.*

"Be bold on the sub, then. Don't hold back. You've got the talent. Don't worry about failing." He talked for a while, and Carter seemed to take it all to heart.

As he spoke Carter was thinking, *Maybe I can tell him. Maybe he's the one to fight for me.* It was time to tell him.

"Teaching is pretty new to me," MacKenzie went on. "If there *is* anything, come to me. It will go no further. You've got a great rep, Reg. I wouldn't want anything to damage it."

That froze Carter. *There are a hundred men who would swear you were their lover.* It sickened him. MacKenzie had made up his mind for him. Bold he would be. Bold enough to solve his problem alone.

"Sir, I can handle it."

"Very well. Let's head back."

Rather than going home right away, MacKenzie drove down to the beach after dropping the PCOs. An AUTEC cable-laying ship was coming in. Water glistened past its prow. Being with the COs was difficult. He felt off balance. He felt unsatisfied with his conversation with Carter. The man was carrying something, but he couldn't get him to open up. How did he teach them? What did they expect? He still wasn't at peace. Why the hell had he offered to take them on *Jacksonville?* Because they were his only way back to command. But was that all? Or did he have something to give, something he didn't yet understand? It was time to take his own advice. Talk to someone. He couldn't solve his problems alone.

Justine had changed into running shorts and put her hair in a bun. Jessica was waiting for her outside.

"I'm glad you called, Mrs. MacKenzie. I had too much energy to sleep anyway."

"Me, too. Mac wasn't home yet. I figured it was a good time to talk before you got underway again. How are you doing?"

"Okay. The pressure's on. Only four days left to get this guy. By the way, you can set the pace if you want."

"Just let me put my cane away."

"Hey, I didn't mean—"

Justine took off. After twenty yards or so Jessica came up beside her. Justine resisted the impulse to run the girl off the road or set a killing pace. She was more mature than that, right?

Jessica backpedaled. "You okay, Mrs. MacKenzie? I mean, if you don't usually run this far, we could stop."

Justine kicked in the afterburners.

"Where'd you learn to fight like that?" Jessica asked when she caught up. "You're Spanish, right?"

"My early training was in guerrilla warfare and insurgency in Nicaragua. We're an old family. My grandfather was once president. When Somoza came to power we joined the revolution. That's where I learned."

"Wow."

Justine felt something behind her, but there was nobody. What am I running from? she wondered. Why am I competing with this child? Pain was creeping up her shins. Jessica ran effortlessly. So young. Justine felt a stab of pain. I am at the middle of my life. The *middle* of my life. However fast I run, I can't outrun that. Age. That's what I feel behind me.

They padded down the highway, two lithe shadows.

"Am I allowed to ask what you are?" Jessica said. "I mean what you do exactly? That was a helluva lesson you taught on the ship. In a tight skirt to boot."

Justine focused on the big silver moon ahead. She would not, could not give up. "Not very ladylike, eh? Flashing my pantyhose for the entire crew." She ran onto the sandy shoulder, easier on her legs. "I'm a senior operations

136

director in the Central Intelligence Agency. On occasion I run operations in the field."

"Mrs. MacKenzie, can I ask something personal?"

"Justine. Sure."

It came out in a rush. "What's it like to look like you? I mean, I'm sorry if I . . . Jesus, I don't want to get personal, but you're so beautiful. And talented. Were you always?"

"Yes." Justine said it so matter-of-factly that Jessica knew she was simply answering honestly. "My father was a concert pianist. So was I, for a time. Even when I was very young men came to look at me when I played. It wasn't nice feeling their eyes on my breasts and belly. It . . . embarrassed me. But my father wanted the border guards to listen so that he and my brothers could kill them."

Jessica stumbled, then came back with a burst of speed. She wasn't sure at first she'd heard right. "Kill them?"

"So we could get weapons and ammunition over the border. I rarely play now."

"I'm sorry."

Justine shrugged. "I only told you as a lesson. Balance in all things. No one has everything."

"I'll remember."

"Run," Justine said, moving ahead.

Runners call it the spike. Your body sweats itself free of accumulated poisons and begins making endorphins, natural painkillers. There's a high attached to it, a freedom from yourself that feels like your spirit is propelled by the wind. Justine caught the spike, and it lifted her along the dark road. Pain subsided. She *flew.*

Beside her Jessica said, "God, you're lucky."

It was Justine's turn to stumble. *Lucky?* All the pain of her childhood, the endless combat. Always feeling like she was singled out for special agonies. Then she saw herself as Jessica must. Running down the moonlit highway with the wind streaming past her face and her legs feeling like they could pump forever, she felt for the first time the richness of her life—Mac's, too—in spite of their trials. Suddenly she knew what to give her husband.

"You're good for me, Jessica Moran," she called out happily.

"Me, why?"

"Why's the sky?" Justine laughed into the wind. There was a purity to the night. Whatever was behind her fled. Was this what coming of age meant?

"C'mon. I'm a sweaty mess, and that water looks great."

"We don't have suits," Jessica balked.

Justine felt fresh, like a kid. "Who's gonna see?" She ran to the beach and pulled off her clothes. "Race you to that sandbar."

"Yes, but—"

Naked but for a pair of bikini briefs Justine dived into the water. She swam with swift, clean strokes, breathing every fourth one like a racer.

Jessica marveled at Justine's boldness as she stripped off her clothes, too. Normally body shy, it was kind of erotic. Her nipples crinkled. She felt enormously free being almost naked in the moonlight on the deserted beach, as if she could do anything she pleased. She swam out to the sandbar and the silently beautiful Justine MacKenzie.

"A sub on night maneuvers could get an eyeful," she joked.

Justine laughed. "Let 'em look. Tell me how you got to the navy."

Jessica stretched. "This guy in my neighborhood wanted me to marry him. Hell, for a while I thought I would. Stay home and make babies. Shop. Talk to the girls about the sex you weren't getting, get beat up once in while when he came home drunk. It was what everybody did where I grew up.

"One day I was in the Laundromat doing my boyfriend's clothes, sort of half listening to these two other women. One of them had just taken her kids to Disneyland and talked to Goofy. They've got the characters live there, you know. She said hello to him and told the kids to say hi, but a little while later she couldn't remember whether it was Goofy or Pluto she'd said hello to. Maybe she even said "Hello, Goofy" to Pluto. It was really embarrassing. She just didn't know *what* to tell her kids. It suddenly hit me that my life would be just like theirs if I married this guy. Sooner or later I'd be sitting somewhere worried about the difference between Goofy and Pluto and whether or not I had fucked it up. I had to get out. This Navy recruiter told me I could join up or try for the Academy. My grades were good. I was an athlete. My dad knew the congressman from my district because he ran programs for the city. They accepted me. I went. They wouldn't let me near submarines, and for a while that made me mad. Then I got the DSRV job. I learned to like it."

"And now this."

Jessica sighed. "Yeah. But what *you* do. No one ever tells you about a thing like that. It must be fascinating. A whole different kind of life. All they tell you in school is you can be a secretary, a teacher, or a nurse, and the boys can be doctors and lawyers."

"Most of us are an odd combination of abilities and backgrounds."

Jessica looked interested. "Sort of like me."

"Yes, well, I suppose. But you have what you wanted."

"I felt good today," Jessica admitted. "But I'm beginning to see it's a bigger world than I thought. I don't think I'll ever forget the way you looked when I first saw you. Not only the clothes. The way you carry yourself. It made a big impression on me. I'd like to be like that."

"In many ways you already are."

Pleased, Jessica lay back in the sand. "You know what, Justine?"

"What?"

"Fuck Goofy *and* Pluto."

The naval officer and the high-ranking government operative high-fived and dissolved into giggling laughter.

The light was on when MacKenzie got back to his suite. "Just?"

"Mac? In here."

She was sitting in bed in one of her oversized T-shirts, reading.

"I'm glad to see you," he said.

She leaned up to kiss him. "I just got back. I went running with Jessica."

He gave her a quick peck and said, pacing, "I gotta talk to you. I'm having trouble with this whole PCO deal. What do you think?"

She put the book down and tried not to smile. It was just like him. No preamble, no lead-in. He had a problem to work out, and he couldn't let it go until he had the solution. The change in their relationship was including each other in their inner worlds. Some people called it communication.

"You hate not commanding a sub," she said.

He looked genuinely surprised. "You knew?"

"I figured. You're an operations man. Teaching might seem awfully tame."

He got a beer, dropped into a chair, and propped his feet up.

"Chips."

Sheepishly, she brought the bag out from under the covers. "I know I agreed not to eat in bed, but a bag of chips and a good book . . . that's heaven."

"I'm probably lucky. Some women want diamonds." He munched thoughtfully. "When Ben gave me the higher goals speech I bought it. But now that I'm in it, all I can think of is those who can, do; those who can't . . ."

"You've demonstrated that you can do. Better than anyone. It's more than that."

"I'm listening."

"You're not ready to move on to a new stage of life."

He looked annoyed. "Nonsense."

She said calmly, "Good. *That's* not defensive."

He bit back an angry retort.

She put the book down. "When I ran with Jessica before—"

"She's doing fine, by the way."

"I've heard. She thinks you're cute."

"I'm appalled."

She smiled. "No, you're pleased. Anyway, we went running, and I kept trying to keep up with her, you know, not wanting to appear old or slow in front of her. I kept feeling this nagging thing at my back, like something was after me. After a while I realized what it was."

"What?"

"I was terrified of getting old and having to change, being too fat or too slow or whatever comes with it, but that's not the important part. What was important is that I realized that I had to accept it for two very good reasons."

"It's inevitable," supplied MacKenzie. "Right?"

She nodded. "That was first. The second was the kicker."

He looked interested. She tried to find the right words to give it the same impact it had had on her tonight. "Mac, I'm *better*. Everything that's happened in my life—or yours, for that matter—from my father to you to now, has made me better. Richer. I wouldn't want to be a kid again. That's for—well . . . *kids.*"

Something in his eyes changed. Recognition, maybe? The hard lines eased a bit. She'd hit home. She let him absorb it for a while, try it on for size.

"I'm going out to the ship," he said finally.

"Oh?"

"We're running out of time. We'll be underway early. Why wake you?"

"All right."

He went into the living room. She heard the front door open and close. As much as she would have liked him to stay, she knew he had to work this out on his own. His coming to her at all was an indication of the strides they'd made in their marriage. It was all right for him to be alone now. She'd given what she could. He would work over what she'd said, looking for the truth in it, just as he did in the conn. Bits and pieces of a puzzle, then a leap to understanding. He would find what was true for him.

She had faith.

Chapter Seventeen

Northern Star

PACHENKO REPAIRED THE DAMAGE CAUSED BY SURFACING UNDER the carrier as best he could. They had no attack scope now, and the radio mast was partially disabled. And there was seepage from the ruptured seals, but so far the bilge pumps were handling it.

"Sonar, conn," said Avilov. "Is our friend still there?"

"The same as before, Captain. I can't hear him, but if you say he is there, I will not argue."

"Pass the sound in here."

The conn speaker crackled. There. Just at the fringe Avilov heard the destroyer that had been chasing them for two days.

"Pavel, make your depth twenty meters. All stop."

Pachenko had never seen Avilov better. Since evading the battle group they had been picked up by three other ships, but he had managed to lose them all. In spite of his blindness he moved the *Star* like it was a bubble in the sea. A thermal here, a quick run there. He had picked up this destroyer fully ten minutes before the sonar operator did.

They were just a few hundred miles from the Bahamas, still in deep water. Pachenko moved to the chart table.

Avilov asked him softly, "How close are we to the fire point?"

"Ten miles. Make your turn now."

The words "up scope" were out of Avilov's mouth before he could stop them. It slid up with a harsh grinding noise. "Make the sweep, Yuri," he covered. "Good practice for you."

Avilov saw only the dimmest outlines of things now, the sharpest contrasts. Everything else was a blur. This at a time when the run for Sabaña Key would be most dangerous. The waters would grow shallow, the passages tight. It was his constant worry that the time bomb in his skull would explode and Pachenko would have to take the *Star* in alone. The clock was ticking, too. Only four days left. Four days left. Four days left . . .

"I'll be in engineering," said Pachenko.

Pachenko had cleverly created little bombs that would deliver smell and smoke but very little damage. Planted in the fan room, it wouldn't take long for them to make the ship almost uninhabitable. After the "fire" went off as planned he would bring the *Star* close to Sabaña Key and find where their families were. How many soldiers guarded them? Where were their weapons? When did they sleep? Then they'd attack. He'd drop Stepov and Pushkin on the other side of the island with Pachenko while he sailed into the harbor with Mishkin and destroyed the boats and seaplanes as a diversion. If they timed it right and the force on the island wasn't too large, they might get away with it.

Pachenko came back in and put a hand on Avilov's shoulder. "Ten minutes. Be careful."

Avilov felt for the intercom. The water temperature was seventy-eight degrees, and there were ten hours of daylight left. He'd carefully put enough sound in the water to keep the destroyer close. It would make right for the *Star* as soon as it heard the SOS. His personal breathing unit was in a compartment overhead. Any time now.

"Captain, this is Pachenko. Fire! Fire in the engine room! Fire! Fire in the engine room!"

"Captain, torpedo room. Acrid smell. We have an acrid smell. Possible fire."

The fire alarm rang stridently. Smoke poured out of every ventilating grill. Few things are more terrifying on a sub than fire. It can race through an entire ship and incinerate everything in its path in minutes. Men held their stations only by rigorous training.

"Captain, we can't contain it. The reactor is in danger of an automatic shutdown."

Avilov hit the intercom. "This is the captain speaking. Surface the ship and prepare to abandon ship. Prepare to abandon ship. There is no danger if you don your personal breathing units." He turned to those around him. "Listen to me, all of you. Remain at your posts. We are removing the crew as a precaution only. Mr. Pachenko will have the fire under control in minutes."

There was some grumbling, but this was Avilov, the Hawk, and he had seen them through a hundred crises over the years. They stayed.

"Captain, sonar, there is a contact . . . a destroyer! You were right," Pushkin said happily. "They are responding to our distress signal."

"See? I told you not to worry," Avilov said through the smoke. "Mr. Stepov, take over the radio and keep sending the SOS. Abandon ship."

Pachenko helped men out the escape hatch and gave orders to launch the life rafts. It took less than fifteen minutes to get the crew into the water. Smoke was still pouring out of the hatches. Overhead Pachenko heard the sound of aircraft, no doubt taking pictures. Good, those were the pictures they wanted.

When the last raft went overboard Pachenko went to the fan room and replaced the circuit breakers that allowed the fans to restart. In a matter of minutes the smoke cleared from the corridors and was vented out of the ship. He secured the hatches and made his way forward. It was an eerie feeling walking deserted corridors. Half-eaten meals sat on the tables in the crew's mess. A videotape was still playing to an empty room. He shut it off. He made his way aft to the engine room and transferred control of the reactor to the local that was close to the control room. The same with the torpedo room after he released oil and debris through them, more evidence of sinking. He cleaned them and reloaded torpedoes in all tubes, flooded them, and then transferred control to the mimic board in the control room. For almost all purposes they could now control the ship from there alone.

He returned to the control room. Stepov was there, and Mishkin and Vashovsky and Pushkin. The old reliable ones. "The fire is out, Captain. The reactor is safe and operating normally in local control."

"Remove your masks," ordered Avilov. "Pavel, submerge the ship and make our depth five hundred meters."

"Five hundred . . . But why, Captain? Shouldn't we pick up our men now?" questioned Vashovsky.

"Not if we are to follow orders," said Avilov. He heard confusion in their voices. "Pavel, confirm our depth. Yuri, bring me our operations orders from my safe. Quickly."

Yuri fetched them, and Avilov fixed Mishkin by the sound of his scuffling feet, Pushkin by his rustling clothes, Vashovsky by the way he flicked his fingernails together, Stepov by the wet sniffle that had afflicted him lately.

"How many of you want to see this ship become the property of Ukraine?" Avilov knew them well. They were all ethnic Russians. They all shook their heads. "Good, that is what we are about. Ukraine cannot claim what was destroyed by fire, can they? We will change the *Star*'s appearance at a secret base in Cuba. Then she can go to her new home in Kola Bay, and the Russian fleet is one sub larger with no one the wiser. Here. Because this is an unusual situation you may read the orders from Admiral Rushkov himself."

They passed the orders from hand to hand, nodding slyly. So the Great Russian Bear was not dead yet, not if he could be so clever.

"Are you with me?" demanded Avilov.

"We are, Captain," said Stepov.

"All right. Now we must be very quiet and sneak out from under all the attention our fire has caused."

"We are at five hundred meters, Captain," reported Mishkin. "I'll take the helm."

"Good. Steer to course two one five. EPM only."

For an hour they moved slowly from the "disaster." In the deep warm waters they were as noiseless as a shadow. They worked together, doubling up on jobs. Mishkin handled the helm. Pachenko handled trim and the ballast control panel. Vashovsky was on fire control, Pushkin on sonar; Stepov navigated.

The Hawk stood with his raised arms clasping the overhead railing like powerful wings. He was not going to let his wife and children die. Not with deck of the *Star* under him and her weapons at his command.

The unexpected sound of the underwater telephone ringing almost gave Avilov a heart attack.

"Yuri?"

It was all the more shocking because the instrument was only used for ship-to-ship communication at short distances.

Pachenko lifted the receiver and listened. "Yes?" he said. Then "Yes" again. "I understand." He replaced the phone.

"Who the hell is out there, Yuri?" demanded Avilov.

"It is the captain of the Libyian submarine *Adri*," said Pachenko softly, wonderingly. "A Kilo class diesel-electric boat. He congratulates you on a perfect performance and informs us he will be our escort to Sabaña Key. He says his name is Captain Zilah, and he hopes you remember him from the Academy. He also advises you that he has a perfect firing solution on us should we display any notion of a change in plans."

Avilov saw it. Virtually silent, the *Adri* must have been waiting here on station for days, perhaps weeks. Once again he had been outmaneuvered.

"Lerner's fences," he said bitterly. "It seems we've run into one more."

Chapter Eighteen

Jacksonville

MACKENZIE SAID, "MAKE YOUR RUN, MR. FLYNN."

"Aye, sir. Time to put the brigands to flight."

MacKenzie had to admit James Grady Flynn was as audacious as a eighteenth-century pirate, and every bit as bold in handling his ship. The kill order still held on the *Northern Star* despite reports of her sinking. No one was standing down till the deep-diving robot search subs found a ruptured hull or enough debris to convince the skeptics.

MacKenzie wanted to sharpen the PCOs' skills and their level of concentration, so he put Bell and Carter on board Scotti's *Augusta* and set them against Flynn and Jessica on *Jacksonville* as they continued the search.

"I think I have him," said Flynn.

Almost in response, sonar's voice rang out. "Conn, torpedo in the water. Bearing one eight zero. It's heading due south."

"Well, that's fine," said Flynn, "considering we're heading west. Did you get a fix on *Augusta?*"

"Yes, sir. Same bearing . . . range three thousand yards."

"I have a solution, sir," said Jessica Moran at fire control station. It was clear she admired the way he handled his ship.

"Acknowledged. Helm, turn to one eight zero, ahead one third," Flynn ordered.

"One eight zero, ahead one third, aye."

Flynn moved swiftly. Commanders had their own styles, like artists or athletes. Bell moved his ship gracefully, sliding it through the sea with a dolphin's ease. Flynn moved it like a sword, slash here, thrust there. Take the enemy through the heart.

"Range one thousand yards."

"Flood tubes one and three." Flynn looked to MacKenzie. "Permission to fire, sir."

"You are cleared to fire, Captain."

Flynn had Bell dead to rights, but it wasn't enough. He executed a maneuver called "riding inside his baffles." Baffles were cone-shaped areas from thirty to sixty degrees off the sub's main stern line where sonar couldn't detect an enemy's presence. But you had to be very close. That made it dangerous. A thousand yards or less was a very short distance to stop a sub, so there was the constant danger of collision. Flynn worked without the slightest fear.

"Range eight hundred yards," reported sonar.

"Being in this close doesn't bother you?" MacKenzie asked.

Flynn's quizzical look was answer enough.

"Solution ready," reported Jessica.

"Very well," acknowledged Flynn. "Standby tubes one and two."

"Ship ready; Solution ready; Torpedo ready."

"Shoot tubes one and two."

"Set—Standby—Fire. Tube one . . . away."

"Set—Standby—Fire. Tube three . . . away."

MacKenzie pictured Bell in his control room looking south for Flynn, only to find him sitting in his baffles. Even without reviewing the tapes he knew Flynn's dead-on shot up *Augusta*'s stern would have crippled her.

"Well done, Mr. Flynn."

"Thank you, sir. Nice work, Jess," he added warmly.

"Miss Moran, take the conn."

"I have the conn, sir," she responded crisply.

MacKenzie radioed *Augusta* that Reggie Carter was to take command, and the duel commenced again.

"Make our depth one four zero zero feet, five degree down bubble," Jessica ordered, taking them deep. She threw a quick look of pride and gratitude to MacKenzie before commencing work with Flynn at the chart table planning strategy.

Jessica's fiery enthusiasm was catching. The crew responded well to her. MacKenzie found himself enjoying it, too. Lots of people found it fulfilling to raise others to do what they couldn't anymore, even claimed the rewards were as great. Well, he supposed if his PCOs needed a father, he might as well be the best father he could be. They were children he had to bring to adulthood, a new kind of life for him. And with that thought a window opened. Something he had previously ignored suggested itself, a challenge as vast as the professional goals he had set for himself years before.

"Sir?" She was flushed with pride. "I did what you said, and I think we might have a fix on *Augusta.*"

He felt a seed of hope grow inside him, tentative, still unsure, but there nonetheless.

He said, "Let's talk about it."

Phoenix

Bell was exhausted. He had never figured Flynn to be in his baffles. He could do better if he could concentrate. The headaches were getting worse. Sometimes the water beckoned so sweetly. *Just sink down . . .* He had to get a hold of himself. Could he continue to command if this kept up?

"I think I've got what you're looking for, Reg," said Bell, trying to clear his head.

Carter was out to restore their wounded pride. He studied the flat-bottomed cliff on the chart table. The best way to expose an enemy is to go quiet and have a place to hold your ship. Shut everything down and wait and let him drift into your sights.

"Looks fine, Mark. Lay in a course. Rig for ultra-quiet."

Carter bottomed *Augusta* on the cliff. "Secure every piece of machinery except the oxygen generator. We'll sit and wait. Countermeasures, put out a pair of those new radio-controlled noisemakers. Low pressure. I want them on this ridge when we leave it."

"Countermeasures, aye."

The dogfight between him and Jessica Moran became a battle of patience. When Jessica poked her head out first, Carter copied a move he'd learned from MacKenzie and set off noisemakers to cover the sound of his coming off the ridge.

"Torpedo heading away, Skipper. Right into the cliff."

"All ahead flank. Helm, hard right rudder. Maximum cavitation. Captain, permission to fire."

"You are cleared to fire, Mr. Carter," Scotti responded. MacKenzie was one of his oldest and closest friends. During their distinguished careers the two had shared a friendly rivalry in which neither could claim absolute victory, although both did. These PCOs are damn good, he thought.

Carter executed a high-speed pivot to fool Jessica's sonar and get her to launch on bogus noise. The sound from the immense cavitation of the propeller, called a "knuckle," showed up on sonar the same way a target did. Jessica fell for it. Carter's shot "hit" the *Jacksonville,* while Jessica's torpedo only burst bubbles.

"Well done, Reg," congratulated Bell.

"Sir, message from *Jacksonville.*"

Scotti took it and read it. "They developed reactor problems on that last run. Have to go back to Andros for repairs. They want you both back, too, right away. Mr. Bell, lay in a course."

Chapter Nineteen

Andros Island

THE DAMAGED *JACKSONVILLE* DOCKED SHORTLY AFTER *Augusta*. AUTEC personnel swarmed over the ship under the direction of the chief engineer. Everyone was anxious to get back to sea. Time pressed. Every hour brought Avilov closer to his goal. Three days now. Three days left to stop him.

MacKenzie saw Bell coming down the pier wearing the same haunted look as when the helo went down. It confirmed a hunch of his. He made sure the chief engineer had things under control and caught up to him. "It's time we talked, Mark. Mind if I join you?"

"Up to you, sir. How's the ship?"

The beach was empty. "Steam leak in the secondary. We need new valves. I'm hoping we can get out to sea again by dawn. What did you think of your runs today?"

"I lost. Again."

"You lost because Flynn caught you napping. Since when does a commander of your abilities forget to clear his baffles?"

"I don't know."

MacKenzie put a hand on Bell's shoulder. "Whatever's

inside is killing you. I see it when you think no one's looking. Like on the sail the day the helo went down. Today maybe it affected your performance. Why not tell me? I'm a good ear."

"Forget it, sir."

How could he reach him? MacKenzie wondered. What could he say? He tried to let his honest feelings rise up and, when they did, spoke them simply.

"Mark, this PCOI billet is hard for me. I wish I was where *you* are, trying to make it to command, wanting it so badly. Going through it all again. But they took it away from me. The thing I was the best at. So what's left is trying to do the best job I can for you, and I'm not sure I know how. I'm trying to be your friend. Maybe we can get each other through this. Let me be a teacher for once, Mark. Let me help."

Bell stopped. "Can you, sir?" Slowly and deliberately he took off his shirt. "Can you, after seeing this?"

"Dear God." MacKenzie had seen plenty of scars, but nothing like these. A jagged row of deep triangular cuts ran the length of Bell's left arm, inside and out and down his back. "Mark, what did this?"

Bell looked out to sea, isolated again.

"Let it go, son," MacKenzie said softly.

Bell's voice seemed to come from a million miles away. There was something ghostly about it, frightening. "We were in Australia for a port visit. A mile or two offshore I saw a family boat capsize. There was a bunch of dolphins in the water bounding in and out of the pressure wave, and the guy was probably watching them and not concentrating. I was officer of the deck up in the sail bridge. The guy was holding on to his wife and little boy in the water. I called for the small boat to be launched, gave a course correction, and turned the conn over. As soon as we got close enough I went over the side. A wave swamped the boat just as I got there. I dived for the kid, and I can't tell you how deep I went, but I got him. Sir, I got my hand on that little arm, and I didn't let go. I could see the surface. It was so close. So close . . .

"I felt something hit me from behind, and at first I thought it had to be my ship, 'cause only something that big could've knocked me around that way. I must have been real near the surface, 'cause I broke through and got air into my lungs. I still had the kid's arm. You understand? I still had him. My back and shoulder felt like they'd invented pain, but I held him out of the water so he could breathe. That's when I saw it, a big gray blade slicing through the water and I knew it wasn't the sub that had hit me. They told me later it was a Great White shark, and that one of the guys on deck who had been in these waters before brought an M-16 out with him and put ten or fifteen rounds into that thirty-foot monster and didn't even turn its head."

MacKenzie heard his fear come back like a recurring fever. His voice came faster. "I was so scared. There was nowhere to go. The sub was too far. And I had this kid. I had to protect him. I heard the parents screaming and the guys on deck shouting, and the dolphins were leaping around like mad, and all I could do was face this thing coming at me, and I didn't have anything to fight it with. I never saw jaws like that, like a big ugly cave with teeth coming at me. He had a bow wave breaking in front of him like a sub's. I did the only thing I could. Maybe it was years of football reflexes and reacting to crazed tackles coming at you on a blitz, but all I could think to do was to put my arms around the kid and hug him to me, and maybe the hardest thing I've ever done in my life was to turn my back on that *thing* and hope that it would get me and forget about the kid."

Bell was back there now. MacKenzie could see that. He was white-faced in the moonlight, and every muscle was locked with terror. MacKenzie put a hand on his arm. It was like stone. Tears ran freely down his face, and he made no move to staunch the flow.

"I never felt pain like that. They said it was like watching a man bite into an apple the way that shark sank its teeth into me. But that wasn't the worst. The shark . . . it knew. It was evil, sir. I believe that. A devil lived in that shark, because it didn't want me. It chewed me up and tossed me aside. I was in shock, my body wouldn't respond. The kid was slipping out of my hands. I held on to him with every ounce of will I had, and suddenly the shark was there again. I must have been under the surface, maybe close to drowning, I don't know. I opened my eyes, and I was looking right into its eye. That's when I knew it was evil. I saw. The way it looked at me, and then . . . and then . . . then it took the boy. It was almost delicate the way it opened those massive jaws and took him. There was a crunch, and suddenly I was . . . holding . . . an arm. All I had was an arm that ended in a jagged spike of bone, and I hated that thing like I never knew I could hate before. I don't know where I got the strength, but that grinning monster was right in front of me, and the water was filled with blood and bits of things, and through it all I could see that great gleaming evil eye looking at me to see what I thought of my own helplessness and to relish what it could do to me. Maybe there is a God. I don't know. Something gave me the strength to lift that jagged piece of bone, and I drove it right into that eye with all my might.

"Don't let them tell you sharks have no voice, because I'll hear that scream in my mind till the day I die. He reared up in pain, and that huge silver body flashed by, and the tail whipped up so hard it drove me to the surface and saved my life. He came back and could have killed me, should have killed me, but a dolphin flashed in and rammed him in the side like a torpedo. Then another. The shark kept thrashing in the water, and the dolphins kept ramming him, and there was more blood. Over and over again they drove their hard, bony noses into his sides till he must have been in agony."

Bell saw the final pictures in his mind, the nightmare from which he could never escape. It wasn't the dolphins that turned him, he knew. The shark was so close that one bite would have been all it needed to finish him off. It wanted the broken and bleeding human to remember, wanted him to live with it, the hardest thing of all. And the last image, the one he would never forget, just before he lost consciousness from the shock and the pain, just before the deep silence took him, was of that evil, arrogant monster flashing by one last time with the arm bone of that little boy jammed into its eye and the hand still attached, waving to him, waving as the monster swam back to hell.

Bell broke, sobbing in huge spasms that racked his body. MacKenzie put an arm around him. "Mark, listen. It was an animal. Not evil. Only an animal."

Bell shook his head. "I thought so, too, for while. But don't you see, sir? It wasn't hungry. If it was, it would have taken me. That kid wasn't enough to keep that killing machine full for an hour. It took the kid because I was protecting him. It ate for hatred. So I hated back.

"They got me on board, and the ship's doc did what he could. He operated on the wardroom table and saved my arm. When I woke up I remembered everything. They had pumped me so full of painkiller I could have walked if the shark had eaten both my legs. I waited till they left me alone, and I made it to the armory and got a .45. The guys in the control room thought they were seeing a ghost. I must have been a sight, full of blood and bandages, wild-eyed. I took the conn by force and made them go after the shark. I dived the ship and had sonar scan for biologics. We went past crush depth. I didn't care. I would have dived to hell to get that bastard. I even got a torpedo tube loaded before they jumped me and wrestled the gun out of my hand."

"You were out of your head. No one could blame you."

"Sure. And lots of good people told me so when I got back. But it took almost a year of physical and emotional therapy for me to believe it. In the end the shrinks called it what you read, a one-shot deal, Trauma-Induced Single Event. No reason to remove me. But there were the snickers for a long time after I got back.

"I've heard all the jokes about Bell's Great White, sir, and the XO's Moby Dick. I don't blame them. Would you want to sail under a guy who might flip out again and take everybody to the bottom? Somebody put a picture of a coffin on the wall. Somebody else ripped it off, but I saw it.

"I took it. I had no choice. I spent six months on the sub without incident. My CO and the screening board certified me for command if I could qualify. That's why I have to prove I can make it all the way," he said. "If I don't, I'll never be rid of it. But still when I'm in the conn I think maybe I'm going to lose it and take us down. It makes me afraid to command. You were right about today. Flynn never should have caught me. I couldn't concentrate. Did you know I dream of sinking under the water sometimes and just letting go?"

"It's just a dream, Mark. You're the least quitting man I know."

Bell rubbed the tired muscles of his face. "Now you know, sir. Can you still trust me to run the team?"

"I trust you, Mark. It's you who has to find his faith again."

"What do you mean?"

"A few years ago I had an . . . accident," MacKenzie said. "A girl was killed. It took me a long time to get over it. To believe life had something to offer me again. I found it did."

"How?" Bell asked.

"It won't matter to you how I did it. You have to find your own way back. It has to be your own absolution. But letting it go is the first part."

Bell's shoulders slumped. "It's too hard."

"Despair makes you feel that way. Care to hear what a friend taught me?"

"Yes."

"He said that despair is our partner from birth, and any day it does not come for you is a day to be grateful for."

"So what do I do now?"

"Forgive yourself. It's tougher than it sounds. Treat every day like a gift, because it is. But I don't want to stand here spouting platitudes. I think what you need is on the *Jacksonville*. You can count on me to help you find it. I still have faith in you."

"I don't see why." Bell slipped his shirt on. "But thanks, Captain. I hope I don't let you down."

"Good night, Mark."

"Good night, sir."

BOQ

Mac went and checked that repairs were almost complete and then headed home. He wanted to see Justine. She was on a balcony chair, feet propped up on the railing.

"I want to talk," he said.

"Okay."

He folded himself into the other chair. Justine's dark eyes showed only the briefest of disturbances to indicate she was anything but peaceful.

"I left the other night because I knew you were right," he began.

"Ahh."

"I needed time to think. I didn't want this change. I still don't."

"Do you have a choice?"

"I don't care about choices," he said angrily. "I don't care about logic. I want my sub back. I deserve it, too. Just, most men never find anything they're great at. But I did. Sure, I can be a teacher, or a policy maker, or a candlestick maker for all that it matters. But greatness? When I'm commanding a submarine I'm the best Peter MacKenzie God ever created. You know it, and so do I. If we're honest."

"You are truly yourself there. I agree. And you can do what nobody else can. So?"

"So why not let me go? When the time comes I can't do it anymore, just show me the door. I'll go easy. But not till then. Why put me out before that?"

"To save you," Justine said simply. "That's what Ben's asking you to see. To let you age gracefully, no mean feat for any man, or woman. I'm not as fast as I used to be, and I don't love the lines I see in the mirror either, Mac. I'm coming to my own changes, and I don't like it any more than you do. Ben's trying to get you to understand that it's time to move on, that the creation of new Peter MacKenzies is more important than just letting one man have his selfish way and burn out on board his sub and be no good to anyone after. He's asking you to do what you signed on for, Mac. Act for the good of the service."

"God, it hurts," he said.

"My darling, I know how that feels."

He nodded slowly. "I know you do." He let the sun warm him for a while, trying to find a way to express what he felt. "I'll do my job. I never quit on anything before, and this is no exception. But inside, that's where I know I've got to change, and that's the hardest. See, I always thought there were two stages to life. First, as a kid, you're dependent on your family. Call it the environmental support stage. You grow toward self-support. That's stage two. You find your own way. Move out. Become something. I was always an independent kid. I'll never forget how proud I was the first time I took my parents to dinner and paid the check. Or when I got command. It was perfect for me, Just. I set my goals, and I accomplished them. Till Garver changed it all.

"After we talked the other night I got to thinking maybe you're right. Maybe it's time for me to move on. To another stage. I get glimmerings of it when what I say to the PCOs gives them confidence. Or when I see how much they depend on me. I'm starting to realize there's a third stage, one I never suspected."

"Which is?"

"The one where you support others."

"What does that mean, exactly?"

"It means being PCOI *has* taught me something. Something I'm coming to value. Nurture and you get it back. Life returns life. I think it's the way out of my dilemma. It's what I'm trying to give Mark and Jessica and Reg and Jamie."

"You're sounding suspiciously like a father."

"Am I?"

"It's always interesting to me, Mac," Justine said thoughtfully, "how you seem to find a logical way to your emotions. It makes them less frightening, more accessible."

"I think I think too much."

"No," she said. "You are probably the most complete person I've ever known. Karate players call it *Ki*. Power from balance."

"I don't feel so balanced right now."

"Here's what I think." She went inward for a few moments, then continued. "You remember I told you about being in the desert after the *Kentucky* last year. All that death. That Russian general Karansky seemed used to it. For Kemal it was like the desert itself; I don't think he could imagine life without it. But I swear I'll never get used to it. When I was sure I was going to die that last day, I thought that if I ever got out of there I might like to have a child. It was kind of an affirmation. Now I hear you talk. Could we both be saying the same thing? That maybe the time has come for us both to move on, as you say, to the next stage of life?"

"Maybe."

She hesitated, knowing what she was about to say was an irrevocable decision if they made it. "Mac, what do you think about having kids?"

"See? That's what I mean. I thought we were fixed, but

actually there's a whole additional set of choices. Sure, I've thought about it. What man hasn't? It's interesting. Could be great, maybe."

She sipped her drink thoughtfully. "But are you sure? I'm not. It seems so . . . permanent."

"Sure? No. Every parent I know seems tired or worried or both. And that's on good days."

"We'll have to trade in the light of your life, the '78 Porsche, for a station wagon."

"Not the Porsche!"

"And there would come a time when sex was out of the question," she said.

"Not the Porsche!"

She threw a pillow at him.

He leaned over and kissed her. "So what's the verdict? Are we willing to move on to a new life together?"

"Do we have to say yes or no now?"

"We have to settle a lot of questions about where duty and family intersect. I'd like to know."

She walked inside, pulled off her T-shirt, and tossed her briefs away. Her nipples crinkled in the cool air. Her hands slid over her belly and thighs. She said, "Maybe we should start work on it before I get scared and change my mind."

He came in and put his hands on her, a sensation he never failed to relish. He said softly, "You're serious about this kid thing?"

She showed him.

BOQ

Carter paced his room angrily. A call home to his wife, Susan, hadn't made him feel any better. After twelve years of marriage she sensed something was wrong and pressed him about it. Unable to tell her, he turned gruff in defense. It ended in a fight.

There were times you were called on to take a stand. He had managed to avoid racial conflicts by substituting competence and control for rage. He wasn't interested in changing the dumb bastards, simply in outdistancing them. Now, at the beginning of what should be his most fruitful years, when he thought he'd put all conflicts behind him, he faced his biggest challenge.

What had he been thinking that he could countenance hurting Bell? He knew what was right. He would go to MacKenzie before they sailed. Better yet, he'd call him right now. Waiting would only reduce his nerve. He was halfway through MacKenzie's number when something on the dresser caught his eye. A packet of photos. Polaroids. He put the phone down and leafed through them. His face got hot. His guts twisted.

He and Susan had gotten bold one night, and she'd dressed up in the revealing nightie and posed for him. She was a shy girl. It was a private thing between a married couple, less sexy than half the stuff on MTV, but it added a little spice to a long and faithful marriage, so who was to know or care? He taped the packet of photos under his nightstand drawer as he'd seen in a detective movie and forgot about them. Till now. The blood rushed to his face as he thought about Ransom and whoever had searched his house seeing them. Had they been passed around to others who laughed and made comments about her breasts? He twisted the pictures till they tore.

The phone rang. He wrenched it off the hook. "Carter."

Ransom's voice, as wispy and dry as old wheat. "She's a very pretty girl, Reginald."

Carter had never hated anyone as much as he hated Ransom for his sexual blackmail. "I'll kill you, you corrupt old bastard."

"No, you won't. I can just as easily arrange a car accident. They happen all the time to women driving their kids to school."

Carter's impotence choked him. How could he fight this?

"I thought you might be considering alternatives to obeying me," said Ransom's raspy voice. "I hope you see there aren't any. Have a good voyage, Reginald. Come back a winner."

It was hot in Ransom's house, and dry like he was. There were no plants; they wilted within hours. He put the receiver down and settled back in his high-backed chair. Carter would do as he was told. The pictures were such a nice touch.

"I've got to do it now, son. You see that, don't you?" he said.

Father, I know you want the best for me. Waiting all these years just because I asked. Won't you wait a while longer?

Equality of damage was a firm principle with him, surely his son understood that. "You do, don't you, son?"

Yes, Father. But destruction doesn't balance death. You taught me that. Forget the boy.

Ransom twisted uncomfortably. Forget him? He got close to doing Bell when he was a star quarterback. The poetry of a crushed arm or a severed Achilles tendon, all the lovely little injuries that would have destroyed his career appealed to him. But his son wouldn't let him. So moral. He was the best part of Ransom; he knew that. So he waited. His reward came on the day Bell announced to the world that he wanted to follow in his father's footsteps and be a submarine captain. That's when Ransom saw what his true revenge had to be. He also understood that his son's making him wait had made it better, so he waited again. When Australia happened to Mark Bell, Ransom knew fate had delivered the perfect weapon into his hands. It all fit. All of it.

Father, talk to me. Father?

He shut out the voice. His son would understand. In the end, they had both run out of time.

Base Permanent Housing

Flynn looked down at the girl's milky thighs and felt something stir inside him. Self-contempt. He caught a glimpse of himself in the mirror sitting on his knees between her naked legs. He looked haggard in the lamplight. It made his skin the same greenish color as the shades that shut out the afternoon sun.

She reached up for him with a whine, "C'mon, Jamie. Do it again. You promised."

He mumbled something and staggered off the bed. The girl rolled over and lit a cigarette without bothering to pull the covers over her. She had an appetite like a bulimic teenager—as soon as she was done she was ready to start again.

Flynn sprawled into a chair. The smell of smoke, liquor, and sex gave her bedroom a swampy, miasmic feel. His mouth felt like the Russian army had passed through. His head felt just plain heavy. Her white nurse's cap drooped from the mirror over her dresser. The bed was a shambles from their sexual gymnastics. He pulled her panties out from underneath him. They were big and white with a stain in the crotch. Her bra looked like an industrial-strength truss. All of a sudden Flynn longed for the clean air outside. He reached for his pants.

"Oh, no, you don't," she said coquettishly, bounding off the bed to him. She was all over him, rubbing, sucking. Her wet mouth sought his, and her hand reached low, insistently stroking.

He caught her hands behind her back and clamped the wrists together in one of his big hands. "What is it you want, girl? Tell me." There was a sudden darkness in him that was screaming to be let out.

She saw it, and a light went on in her eyes. It excited her, he could see that. She thrust her breasts forward, big floppy sacs that all of a sudden disgusted Flynn. "I want it hard, Jamie. You know . . . *there.*"

Now Flynn felt his manhood grow. He turned her around so she was facing away from him on his lap and impaled her from behind. She screamed as he bent her over, her face almost touching his knees.

"Oh, God," she yelled. "Yes . . . yes!"

He yanked her up and down, ramming into her, never releasing her wrists. He cupped one pendulous breast, mauling it angrily. When he came it was a gurgling, choking thing with his face pressed wetly against her back, straining in time with her spasms and shouts. He collapsed back in the chair and pushed her off him. She crumpled to the floor, rolled over, and lay there breathing hard.

"God, Jamie, that was great. Except my name isn't Jessica. You didn't forget it, did you?"

"I didn't say—"

"Yes, you did, Jamie-poo."

Flynn knew who his anger was for. The instant he discharged his sexual tension he felt the old familiar self-loathing. What the hell am I doing here? he asked himself, as he'd asked himself so many times lately. The quivering flesh on the floor didn't answer. She was snoring. What did I want her for?

He knew the one he wanted. The one with the bright eyes and quick mouth he had first met on the beach. Jessica Moran. Fellow PCO. Competent and bright and smart. Love, finally, at his age? He didn't know why she awakened it in him, but why did anybody care for anybody? The irony of it was he couldn't have her. He could spot surrender in a woman at fifty yards, just as he could spot rejection. He had been kinder to her than to any woman ever, and she still didn't want him. Damn it. He *knew*.

He grabbed the bottle of whiskey by the throat and walked onto the terrace. He wished the girl had a cat. He needed to kick something besides himself. A blast of liquor eased the pain in his stomach and started a new one in his head. He stood up on a chair by the railing. "The king is dead. Long live the king!" he yelled unsteadily. He got up on the corner of the railing, steadying himself on the planter. Space yawned before him. The concrete walkway swayed below. Cable dish antennas on the roof were oddly beautiful against the night sky.

"We're the four Musketeers, damn it!" Bitter tears came to his eyes. "The goddamned Musketeers!"

Windows were opening. The girl appeared in the doorway, kneading her red eyes. "Flynn, what are you doing? Stop shouting. I've got to live with these people. Get your naked ass back in here. Flynn!"

What did MacKenzie call them? Yeah, the best approach team he'd ever seen. He drank to that, lifting the bottle high. He almost fell. His guts hurt. You're an asshole, Flynn. An old asshole, and there's no worse kind.

"Flynn. Come down. You're going to fall!"

Flynn smiled drunkenly.

"Flynn!"

He never felt the ground come up and crunch him.

Chapter Twenty

MAC AND JUSTINE MET THE PCOs FOR DINNER. *JACKSONVILLE* would be fully repaired and able to sail within the hour. AUTEC crews had worked overtime to get her in shape. The time factor was weighing heavily on everybody's mind. Three days left. *Augusta* had already put back to sea.

Bell felt close to breaking. They had trained him to fight external enemies. How did you fight the internal ones? "Sir, did Admiral Tucker say anything about the hearing?" he asked during dinner.

"There won't be one. The tapes told the story."

"Congratulations, Mark," said Justine.

"I'm sure relieved, ma'am."

"Told you," said Jess.

Flynn dissolved into a coughing fit.

"What's wrong?" MacKenzie asked. Flynn was holding his side and cradling his left arm.

"Nothing a little Old Bushmills won't cure, sir."

"Sorry, we're underway too soon. Try aspirin."

For Carter, the clock was ticking. With Bell cleared he would have to act. Could he?

"You all look ragged as hell," MacKenzie observed unhappily. His continued examination might have unearthed something, but he was cut off when Colby stepped up with four of his men and pointed his stogie accusingly at Bell.

"Time we settled this. I heard what you had to say the other day, Lieutenant. The captain here talked fine, too, but you still got to answer to me for Rico going down, boy."

Carter smiled without humor. "Gee, that's certainly one of *my* favorite expressions. Yours, too, Jamie?"

"Maybe he'll let us quote him, Reg."

"I tried to do my best for your man, sir," said Bell.

"Don't give him the satisfaction, Mark," said Jessica.

"Move off, Colby," said MacKenzie firmly. "That's an order."

"Somebody's got to pay for Rico. You willing? *Sir?*"

MacKenzie's temper flared. Damn, he didn't need *this* right now. "Colby, you know who's to blame, and so do I. If your pilot was less afraid of what you'd do if he failed, if you weren't such a tough guy for a change, he would have broken off when he was supposed to and not risked himself and everyone else trying to get a sub he'd already lost. Men face danger for a certain kind of commander, they throw themselves into it recklessly for another kind. Your kind."

"You son of a bitch," stuttered Colby. "You're lucky you've got rank and women here to hide behind."

"Colby, don't," warned MacKenzie, but it was too late.

Colby touched Justine. She did something too fast to follow, and he was suddenly doubled over with his arm locked in hers. She rammed him into a tree, and the crack could be heard ten feet away. MacKenzie tried to stop it, but the pilots jumped in. A wild roundhouse connected with Flynn's side, and he cried out in agony, doubling over. He would have been crippled by the pilot's next blow, but Jessica stepped in and landed a right cross that spun the man around and drove him to the sand.

Ben Garver's voice boomed out like a cannon shot. "Everybody up, *now!*"

Bodies froze.

Garver said, "Somebody with a real talent for creative writing better explain this."

"Admiral?" A sailor was kneeling over Colby. "Sir, I'm a medic. This man needs attention."

"See to it."

MacKenzie said, "It's over, sir. I'd like to forget it."

Justine brushed sand off her dress. Standing behind Garver was a well-groomed middle-aged man wearing a gray business suit.

"Hello, Arthur," she said.

"Justine. Party?"

"Discussion group."

"You're all damn lucky I have no time for nonsense," said Garver. "The rest of you get back to your squadron. Mac, you and Justine with me. Bring the PCOs."

The big screens in the control room were lit. Surface ships were indicated by green lights with bearing numbers underneath. Course tracks elongated on the screen as they were updated. In the northeast corner of the range a small red circle flashed on and off.

"So that's the *Northern Star*," said MacKenzie. "The fire was a trick."

"*'The reports of my death have been greatly exaggerated,'*" said Bell.

"He's got nerve," Garver said. "We try for weeks to blow him out of the water, and suddenly he just waltzes into our range like we invited him. Forget nerve. This guy's got industrial-sized balls."

"He came in the Northeast Providence Channel about three hours ago," said Winestock.

"He's got to know he's in the range. That we can hear him," said MacKenzie.

"We agree. It has led to some interesting speculation."

Arthur Winestock of the Central Intelligence Agency was

Justine's boss. A ramrod-straight, controlled man, he was one of the most agile thinkers MacKenzie had ever known. He was well read in an astounding variety of areas, and—by virtue of his position as CIA Director of Operations, which included covert operations—one of the most dangerous men in the world.

"He represents, ultimately, two choices," said Winestock. "Blast him out of the water, something we have been trying to do all across the Atlantic without success. Or go out there and find out what the hell he wants. We hope he has a simple trade in mind. His family for the *Northern Star*. We have the resources, he has the sub."

"He has no way of knowing we're aware of the hostage situation," said Justine.

"True," said Winestock. "But why else appear in the range after going to such lengths to pull off a disappearing act other than to tell us and offer an exchange? Justine, can you get them out?"

"It changes things. It's not just underwater demolition work. We'd have to put a party ashore with weapons. Stage a raid."

MacKenzie said, "Getting ashore's tougher than you think. The Cuban navy isn't a serious contender on the high seas, but it's hell on wheels with coastal defense. Any submarine within five miles of Sabaña Key stands a good chance of being detected."

Winestock frowned. "It's either in and out fast with no noise, or no go."

"You could use an SDV," MacKenzie suggested. "Swimmer Delivery Vehicles were built for just this kind of circumstance. Single-man units are launched through torpedo tubes. Larger ones carry eight bodies and mate to the hull just like a DSRV."

"Admiral Garver?" It was Jessica Moran.

"Yes, Commander?"

"Sir, I'd like to drive that SDV. I've seen the specs. Same controls as the ones I'm used to."

Garver looked to MacKenzie. "Mac?"

"She's got more experience than anyone here. *Augusta* could drop the SDV, hide, and double back for the pickup."

"Fine. You'll tell Avilov we're willing to make a deal."

"Yes, sir."

Across the room, Bell felt a chill. Another run at Avilov. Was he up to it? He had beaten them once. What would this encounter bring?

"Sir, he's leaving the range," said Carter.

The computer image moved slowly off the map while each person silently contemplated the danger that had just changed the course of his or her life.

AUTEC Base Hospital

Colby hated the way they fixed his face. It made him look like he was practicing to be a goddamned ventriloquist when he spoke. And worse, a goddamned *woman* had done it to him. He tried not to think about it. The doctor told him basically if he just shut up and let it heal, he'd be fine in a day or two.

He didn't know why he should be so hesitant to see Rico, but now that he was just down the hall he couldn't put it off any longer. According to the doc, Rico's collarbone was healing nicely, and the damage from exposure wasn't severe. The busted ribs would knit in due time, although they were painful. It could have been a lot worse. Colby simmered. If only the silly son of a bitch had broken off when X-ray told him to, none of this would have happened. The radio failure was bullshit, Colby knew that. He had done it himself enough times. But that sub should have been more careful, too. It was the sub's fault Rico was here.

Wasn't it?

He peered into Rico's tidy little hospital room. Rico's eyes were both black, and his face was heavily bruised from hitting the windscreen. He was resting quietly with bandages all around his upper body, strapped into a shoulder harness holding him immobile. Colby knew his legs had been cut up pretty bad, too, but the sheets covered them.

Colby tried to make his tone dry and humorous as he walked in. "Listen, I got this brother-in-law's a lawyer. Real ambulance chaser. Could be big money in it for you if you sue."

Rico's eyes narrowed. Colby had hoped he'd look pleased at the visit. Instead he looked worried. But he bantered back anyway. "Shit, why not? Everybody else does."

"How the hell are you, Rico?" Colby asked.

"Not bad, Skipper. Hey, how come you sound like a fucking stockbroker?"

"Little disagreement with a lady."

"Must have been some lady."

Colby let it pass. "Doc says you'll be ready to come back in a month. Wanna go home? I can swing it."

Rico tried to shrug, but the brace prevented it. "Just as soon stay with the squadron."

"Whatever you say."

There was an awkward moment. Then Rico asked, "Sub got away?"

Colby nodded. "Yeah."

"That's life, huh?"

"Sure. Look, you wanna tell me what happened out there, Rico? This isn't for publication. Officially it was an accident caused by communications failure."

Rico sighed. "Well, that's bullshit."

"Yeah, I figured. How come you didn't break off?"

"I was *this* close, Skipper." Rico winced, lifting his thumb and forefinger held almost together. "I heard the break order, but I had some noise, and I figured maybe I could get a shot off. I didn't want the PCOs to get him either. You made it real clear. My plan, my ass on the line, remember?"

"Yeah, I remember."

"I shoulda pulled up my dome in that close. Maybe even X-ray saw it on his screens and tried to radio me, but of course I couldn't hear him either. At least nobody got hurt."

"You already checked?"

Rico nodded. "First thing."

Colby was silent for a while. "You shouldn't have risked yourself, Rico. You know that. It was a lost cause."

"Not to you, boss. I know that. On your shield and all that. I'm just sorry I fucked up. Look, I'll do the buying. And about the other bet . . ."

"That isn't important, Rico. Not any of it." Colby stood. "Look, you just get better. You're back in the air as soon as you're fit. Okay?"

"Thanks, sir. But if you wanna replace me—"

"Shut up, asshole," Colby growled. "I wish I had ten more like you." Rico looked surprised. Colby thought, *He should've looked pleased.* "Look, I gotta go. The rest of the guys are coming over later."

"Be good to see them."

"You need anything, you call me, hear?"

"Skipper, there is one thing. The Bubbleheads. That guy Bell. The one that made the bet. And the PCOI, MacKenzie. I think maybe they saved my ass out there in the water. You see them, you thank them for me, huh?"

Colby felt his face get hot. "Sure, kid. I'll do that. See ya."

Rico stopped him. "I'm real sorry, Skipper."

"Just get better, Rico. And come on back."

"I will. Thanks for coming by."

"Yeah. Sure."

Chapter Twenty-one

Northern Star

PACHENKO LOOKED UP FROM STUDYING THE BOTTOM CHARTS and shook his head. "Nowhere to run, nowhere to hide. Not yet, at least, Pari."

"Captain, sonar. The *Adri* is still with us."

Avilov was boxed in. He was furious with himself. Was it the bump on his head that was making him so stupid? He had been outthought by Lerner at every turn. First he had paralyzed Avilov by taking his family hostage. And then he guessed correctly that Avilov would betray him after the "fire" and stationed a second sub here to intercept him and shepherd them to Sabaña Key.

He was powerless to do anything about the *Adri*. Sonar heard their outer doors open. It had a perfect firing solution on them, and Captain Zilah was cleverly staying aft of the *Star*. The *Adri*'s torpedo tubes were forward-mounted. Avilov would have to turn to launch, a doubtful move given their respective tactical positions.

Time. Time. Time. It preyed on him. Less than two days left to make Sabaña Key.

"Sounding."

"Two thousand meters, Captain."

176

Deep water. More than enough. He played the only card he had.

Pachenko picked up the underwater telephone when it buzzed. "Pari, Captain Zilah says that regardless of whether our inertial guidance problems resulting from the fire have been fixed, he's setting a new course out of these waters and must respectfully request we comply. He warns of American hydrophones in the test range."

"What course?"

"Out the Northwest Providence Channel, then south through the Florida Straits. Deep water all the way."

"Confirm his order and steer to new course three three zero."

"Yes, sir."

That was it, then. Zilah was nobody's fool. He wasn't about to let them dawdle here. Avilov could only hope that the Americans had indeed extended the range to the larger dimensions Russian intelligence reported they were planning, and that the *Star* had appeared, however briefly, on their screens.

Avilov remembered Zilah from when he had taught the Libyan at the Academy. Those were good days, at home with his family for a long stretch. Katcha happy all the time. Zilah was a big, coarse man who made his thick, black, rubber-soled boots a mark of style. Bushy eyebrows and a shaved skull gave him a look of a fierce desert chieftain rather than a naval officer. He was reputed to be a rider and hunter of some repute in his native town, whose name he carried. Avilov had no doubt he would fire a torpedo at him without a second thought if he guessed Avilov was up to something.

"Pytor," he told Stepov, the navigator, "you have the conn."

Avilov made the familiar trip into sonar. Two steps down and one across, grab the lip of the hatchway and draw the curtain aside, duck your head and feel for the seat.

"Hello, Captain," said Pushkin. "Still nothing."

The visual displays were useless to him. "Give me the headphones, Ivan."

He sat in the darkness, listening. The eight other sonar screens were blurred blotches of light arrayed around him. This was a dangerous game for an old blind man to be playing. If it worked, a lot of people were going to die. He thought long and hard about it. What choice did he have?

He sat in the darkness and the sounds of the sea came to him clearly through the *Star*'s hydrophones. He could hear the different biologics: fish, dolphins, whales. He had even begun to distinguish between the upper and lower angles, sounds derived from above and below the plane of the ship. It was remarkable, really. It was starting to be indistinguishable where the sub left off and he began. Maybe it was always like this and he had just never fully appreciated it before, blinded by his sight. His mind reached deeper into the sea, casting outward on a line of sound waves, farther and farther, waiting for the sound he had bet everything on, waiting for it to come to him.

In the control room, what remained of the *Northern Star*'s crew tended to her systems and continued her course. Pachenko thought about his family and the fact that he had placed their fate in the hands of a blind captain he still trusted more than any man on earth. He knew what Avilov had in mind, and it smacked of his usual audacity, even brilliance. He was sorry for the lives it would cost, but as they said, you can't have it both ways.

He checked the reactor, then made sure the settings on the torpedoes were correct. He went back to studying the charts. The crucial piece was still missing. He went to the old maps, drawn by hand before the days of electronic cartography, painstakingly made. It was in one he finally found what he was looking for. A formation in the Florida Straits just might make it possible. *If* it was still there, *if* no undersea quake had reduced it to rubble. *If* they fit. A lot of ifs. It would require a terrific feat of piloting. Funny how events conspired. Ironically, Avilov might be the only one who could bring it off. He gathered the charts and took them to the wardroom, leaving word for the captain to come there when he was done.

All the while Avilov sat in the sonar compartment listening in the darkness.

Chapter Twenty-two

Sabaña Key

EPSTEIN HATED BEING CUT OFF LIKE THIS. FOR TWENTY YEARS HE had been told not to risk himself. The information he provided to Israeli intelligence was too important. Their knowing where the money went meant knowing where the weapons went and, in turn, who the terrorists were. But he'd waited as long as he could. Still no contact had been made. Nor could he count on the Americans. Word was Avilov was still coming despite the navy's search for him. So he had to act, and act alone. That was always dangerous.

At this hour most of the men on the island were eating in the hacienda-style main house where Lerner, al-Zawi, Sayid, and his security men were housed. A quarter of a mile away were barracks for the welders and electricians who would be flown over from Havana when the subs arrived. The Russian families were living in the workmen's cottages. They mostly kept to themselves. The beach was beautiful, and food was plentiful. Avilov's boy liked to fish. They all waited patiently for the *Star* to arrive. Epstein knew they would be killed as soon as Captain Avilov delivered his ship. They had been taken hostage to keep the captain in line, still living only in case he demanded to see them before turning over the *Star*.

Sabaña Key had changed the rules he had always worked under. It was one thing for Epstein not to let a shoulder-fired missile or two go. The *Star* was a state-of-the-art submarine carrying nuclear cruise missiles. He knew his people. If a cruise missile landed in Israel, the Middle East would go up in flames.

Epstein shed his ornate colonel's uniform for a pair of loose khaki shorts, an old T-shirt, and a pair of sandals and sat out on the pier. He scratched his hairy legs, staring out across the clear green water. The pier extended out five hundred feet into a channel dredged out by Cuban engineers. The explosives were still stored in the work buildings. Piles of camouflage netting were stacked every few yards on the pier, to be stretched to new pilings driven into the sea bed. Then the alterations would commence.

Epstein had a Jew's respect for any man who made something out of nothing. In the end, however, Lerner was just a black marketeer on a grand scale. Epstein had long ago stopped hoping that God would come down and enforce His moral law. Experience had taught him that He left that to man.

Sayid was coming along the pier. He took out his pocket Dictaphone and began a letter.

"So, banker, not much like the grand hotels you usually stay in, but it'll do," Sayid said, coming up on him.

"People pay thousands a day for a beach like this, Sayid. If only you had the foresight to bring some women along . . ."

"That's the truth." Sayid frowned. "But you know how Fasah is during an operation. It's bullshit, if you ask me. Women keep everybody loose."

"Maybe he didn't want the American to think we'd resort to anything so savage."

"Fucking?" Sayid laughed heartily. "If he thinks that, who's the savage?"

Hamed abu Sharif laughed in turn. "What about the Avilov woman and her friend?" He pointed to where the

181

two women and the teenage boy and girl were playing in the surf.

"In due time," said Sayid, unable to hide a wolfish leer. "We'll get to them after the husbands are gone."

The women would be used by Sayid and his men, then killed. Like the desert, Sayid had been hardened by inhumanly harsh conditions, baked into an obdurate insensitivity by the fires of the region. Epstein sighed. Sooner or later somebody was going to have to break the endless cycle.

"What are you doing out here?" Sayid asked.

Epstein showed him the Dictaphone. "Letters. Beats working inside."

"You eat?" asked Sayid.

"Enough. What's the word on the *Star?*"

"Get your wire transfers ready, or however it is you pay out the exorbitant sums of money you're trusted with," said Sayid. "Avilov will be here on time according to Fasah."

"We're reaching big now, aren't we? A nuclear sub. I thought out leader had given up trying to beat the Americans at their own game. Next time he might be *in* his tent when they send their smart bombs in."

Sayid was unamused. "It's a new era. Desert Storm taught us one thing."

"How to get Arab asses kicked?"

Sayid's face hardened. "Start and don't stop. If Hussein had taken Riyadh, we'd be telling half the world what to do now."

Epstein shrugged. "Mohammed preached peace. The greatest negotiator the world has ever known. He never said bomb New York."

"He'd never been to Times Square," said Sayid.

"You have a point. Sayid, do we have any scuba gear? Diving ought to be great here."

"We have rigs for the divers who'll be working on the subs. Masks, fins, snorkels, the whole works. I'll have one of my men fill some tanks and bring them to you."

"Thank you."

The dim beginnings of a plan were forming in Epstein's mind. After Sayid went back to the main house he sat for a while and tried to refine it. The trouble was, without help he was going to be hard pressed to get out of here alive.

"Excuse me, sir?"

"Hmm?" The woman's voice startled him.

Katcha Avilov was a handsome woman in her late forties. She must have been a stunner as a young girl. Her shoulder-length auburn hair had a silver streak in it running from her forehead back, the kind he always pictured a witch as having. It gave her an ethereal quality, enchanting. Her skin had a pink glow from the tropical sun. In spite of having borne two children her figure was trim and athletic. She wore white canvas shorts, a blue blouse, and sneakers. Strong. Sharp. Able to take care of herself. She could have been a sabra.

For a moment he envied Avilov his woman. Her eyes held a twinkle of the secrets she knew. He felt a strong sexual urge, but this one would be a one-man woman. She would be sparing with her joy, making it all the more precious. It made him jealous, and that made him sad.

"Do you speak Russian?" she asked.

"A little," Epstein answered. "But no one can pronounce Russian, and no one cares to learn Arabic, so English is my usual language."

She laughed at that. "English, good."

"Can I help you?" he asked.

"That boat there. The little one? Can we use it? My son wants to explore. You know how boys are."

"I don't," said Epstein. "I have no children."

"I'm sorry," she said.

It made him sad the way she said it, as if he had missed out on something really good. He found himself wanting to explain his life to her, and that troubled him even more deeply. What's wrong with you? he asked himself. But he

183

knew. He was picturing himself with a woman like this and a family and a small plot of ground they were the reason for.

"Your husband will be here soon, Mrs. Avilov."

She immediately brightened. "Really? Oh, that's so good to hear. Call me Katcha, please. I'm anxious to get back to Havana."

"I'm Hamed abu Sharif."

She held out her hand. "Pleased to meet you . . ."

"Hamed," he said, helping her out.

"Hamed." She smiled.

Half-formed ideas locked together, and Epstein came to a sudden decision. "Look, I was thinking of doing some scuba diving. Would you like me to take you out? We could bring a mask and snorkel for the boy."

Katcha Avilov's eyes narrowed for a moment. Epstein knew what she was thinking, what all good-looking women have to think. Watch a really pretty woman walk down the street. Stares straight ahead, never makes eye contact with any man for fear he'll think it's an invitation. But Katcha gave a little snort as if unhappy with herself for thinking such things and smiled warmly. "Yes, of course. Misha would like that. You're very kind."

Epstein wanted to be thought of as a lion, a warrior. This was really too much, he told himself, even while wondering if she would wear a one-piece bathing suit or a bikini. That pleasant thought was suddenly marred by the specter of Sayid and his men coming for her. In the end she would want to die because all she had saved for Avilov alone, including her precious dignity, would have been destroyed. He kept his face carefully closed. Could he allow that to happen? Could he allow her to matter when the stakes were this high? His throat felt tight. Katcha's eyes narrowed again as if she saw past his veil to his inner conflicts, then she was up and walking back down the pier calling for Misha to come and get on the boat with the nice man who was going to take them snorkeling.

184

Chapter Twenty-three

Jacksonville

BELL KNEW HE DIDN'T HAVE IT. IN SPITE OF THE CAPTAIN'S faith in him, letting him remain approach officer, he had lost his confidence. The battle was over. As soon as he got back to Andros he was resigning. Better for all. He dived the ship to four hundred feet, ahead flank, one hundred percent reactor power, but he was only going through the motions, and he knew it.

Carter took over as navigator, Flynn as fire control boss. The strain in the conn was palpable. Flynn was pale and shaken. From the fight on Andros, Bell suspected. Carter was withdrawn.

Bell envied MacKenzie. He was as focused as a hunter stalking prey, yet as serene as a fisherman on a mountain lake. Their progress seemed to be inextricably linked to the power of his personality. It might be the reactor amidships that physically drove the *Jacksonville*, but MacKenzie was its motive heart. Bell realized something watching him. Over the years he'd heard a hundred different definitions of being a commanding officer, but as far as he was concerned only one really nailed it. The captain was the most confident man on board.

"What's the latest plot on the *Star?*" MacKenzie asked.

"If he holds steady, we'll reach him within the hour," Flynn responded.

MacKenzie knew the rest of the battle group was steaming toward Cuba as a diversion for Justine's rescue mission. They had orders not to penetrate Cuban waters, but the Cubans didn't know that. If a dangerous situation developed, presence might be enough to get Justine's team out. For force projection, nothing beat a carrier full of A-6 Intruders loaded with smart bombs sitting off your coast.

Avilov was keeping a straight course, easy to follow. They picked him up on sonar every hour for about ten seconds running his reactor and pumps at maximum, an intentional "I'm still here" signal. At that moment, however, MacKenzie was less concerned with Avilov than with the problems in his own conn. How much longer could he go with Bell? The man looked positively haunted. Flynn looked medically unfit, and Carter had just reprimanded his quartermaster again.

"Patience, Mr. Carter. Mr. Bell, see to your weapons. Mr. Flynn, do you need to see the doc?"

"I'm fine, sir."

Definitely not. MacKenzie decided he'd had it. "Mr. Flynn, you are not fine. Nor are you, Mr. Carter. Or you, Mr. Bell. The wardroom. Now. Mr. Randall, take the conn."

"Aye, sir."

As soon as they were in the wardroom MacKenzie slammed the door and turned on them angrily. "We are closing on the best captain in the Russian navy. This whole thing might well be another of his tricks. We have to be ready for anything, and not one of you is performing up to his ability. Somebody better tell me what the hell is going on with this team, and they better tell me now."

He was met with stony silence. Carter looked inward. Bell stared at the floor. Flynn looked pained. No one spoke.

"In that case," said MacKenzie, "you leave me no choice. I can't go into battle with men I have no confidence in. Your PCO status is revoked. All three of you are relieved of duty."

"Sir?"

"Yes, Mr. Carter."

"I . . . nothing, sir."

The phone by the CO's chair chose that moment to ring. MacKenzie yanked it out from under the table. "Captain."

"Sir, we're closing on the *Northern Star.* Five miles."

"On my way." He turned to the PCOs. "You know where to find me."

MacKenzie strode into the conn. He had to put the PCOs and their problems out of his mind. *Unless you relieved them so you could take full command,* his mind interjected. He had to wonder. Was it true? Had he taken back what was his, in spite of Garver's orders? It had been so easy to push them aside. . . .

He couldn't deal with it now. Avilov was his priority. He was the greatest tactician MacKenzie had ever faced, almost prescient in his moves. The man had defied incredible odds to get this far. There was no way to talk to him by radio or underwater telephone. Their systems were incompatible. They'd have to get close in, surface, and actually meet face-to-face.

He tried to put Justine out of his mind, but those were crack security troops on Sabaña Key. How many times could she risk her life before the odds caught up with her? Was this the time one of them wouldn't come home? The thought of having a child made him fear for their mortality as never before.

"Mr. Randall, I need a fire control boss."

Randall thought for a moment. "Lt. Danvers, sir. He's in his rack."

"Wake him."

Ten minutes later Danvers appeared in the conn still rubbing the sleep out of his eyes. He had a round, fleshy face and a crew cut that showed a lot of pimply skin. "Sir."

"Where you from, Mr. Danvers?"

"Sioux City, Iowa, sir."

"Can you handle fire control?"

"Yes, sir. I won't let you down."

Good words, but MacKenzie wished he had Flynn in that seat.

"Conn, sonar. Captain, the *Northern Star* is signaling. Range five thousand yards."

MacKenzie didn't like surprises. "Maneuvering, all stop. Mr. Hill, rig for ultra-quiet."

"Conn, sonar. Contact bearing zero nine zero. Contact identified as Akula class submarine. Range four thousand yards, Skipper. Speed ten knots. Depth five hundred feet. Slowing rapidly . . ."

"Keep tracking. Torpedo room. Status of all tubes."

"Tubes one through four loaded with Mk-48 torpedoes."

"Flood all tubes and open outer doors. Mr. Danvers, firing point procedures. Maintain a solution at all times."

"Firing point procedures, aye."

MacKenzie glanced around the conn. "Let's look sharp, everybody."

Northern Star

Pachenko had been riveted to the fire control screen for over an hour. "He's close, Pari."

"Where's *Adri?*"

"Hiding deep. The diesel sub is noiseless. I don't think the American has them."

"But he has us."

Pachenko nodded. "As you wished. The noise brought them. They're alone."

Avilov peered into a darkness that was now complete. The

conn was quiet with only him, Pachenko, Stepov, Mishkin, and Vashovsky. Good men. They had not questioned him even once since the fire. He knew that after the carrier incident he had attained almost religious proportions in their minds. If they only knew how frightened he was. For his family, for the ship, even for himself.

"Weapons Officer Vashovsky, do you have solutions on the targets?"

"I have constant solutions plotted."

"Increase speed slowly to flank. No cavitation."

"We'll be deaf at that speed," advised Pachenko.

"I'll hear."

"Torpedo room, status on all tubes."

"All tubes flooded, Captain."

"Arm torpedoes." Avilov held his thought like a prayer: *I am truly sorry for what I must do now.* "Open outer doors."

"Outer doors opening."

"Answering all ahead flank," reported Mishkin.

"Captain," said Pachenko, "range to formation is ten thousand yards. Sonar standing by to go to active on your command."

"Very well. Attack center, prepare to fire all tubes."

Jacksonville

Hot and dizzy, Flynn fell into the metal door trying to get into the head. Down on his hands and knees by the commode he vomited. It was streaked with blood. The pain was monstrous. He tried to get up, but his legs wouldn't function. After he had fallen off the balcony the girl wanted to take him to the hospital. The bruises were discoloring even then. But the doctors would have made him stay, and the ship would have sailed without him. He made her patch him up as best she could. He thought he could hide his injuries. His ship needed him. Instead he was here.

He was glad Jessica wasn't here to see it.

God, how he hurt. . . .

Carter pedaled faster and faster on the Exercycle in the engineering compartment. The flywheel sang a high-pitched whine, around and around and around, going nowhere, like Carter himself. His career in the navy he loved was over. He could not stay after what he was about to do. All things considered, he had no choice. He would take the Devil's alternative. Destroy a man's body to save his soul.

Sweat coursed down his face. It was time.

The engineering watch were all involved elsewhere in the compartment. He had the console open and the damage done in a few seconds. He was committed now.

Bell lay in his rack in torment. Relieved of duty. He couldn't escape his past. Everything he had worked for was gone. He was unworthy of command, unable to handle its demands.

Destiny. That AUTEC pilot had warned him the first day. Well, he was right. His destiny was failure.

There was a knock at his door. "Sir, Mr. Carter needs you in engineering."

"Coming."

Bell slid off his bunk and went to meet his friend.

"What's up, Reg?"

Carter handed him a tool kit. "A malfunctioning sensor in the reactor. We need to go in and replace it. Give me a hand?"

"Sure." Bell was glad to be of some use to someone.

"Sir, the captain has authorized shutdown," Chief Engineer Fayette informed them.

"Very well. Commence reactor shutdown," ordered Carter. "Reactor operator, prepare to insert rods. Secure main coolant pumps."

"Main coolant pumps secure."

"Insert groups one, two, and three," Carter ordered.

When enough neutron-absorbing control rods were inserted into the nuclear pile the reactor dropped below critical mass, and the chain reaction stopped. After a brief period, radiation and heat stopped, too.

"Okay, Mark, all clear."

The reactor compartment was between the engineering space and the operations area, in the center of the ship. Access was from engineering's lower level. Bell cycled the big, lead-lined steel hatch and entered the compartment. Carter followed. It was a big compartment, no people or bunking, only sterile pipes and machines, everything covered with thick polyethylene shielding and all painted stark white.

They located the relay and replaced it.

"I'll recheck the console out there," Carter said. He was standing by the only communications equipment in the room, a "panic" phone hooked into the maneuvering area. He went out the hatch.

Bell made sure the relay was working properly and closed the console. A thought struck him, and he lifted the panic phone to tell Carter. It was dead.

"What the . . ."

The hatch was closed, too. Locked tight. What the hell was going on?

The unmistakable sounds of the reactor starting up came to him. He yelled, but no one could hear. Bell banged on the bulkhead. It was useless. Nothing carried through several inches of lead-lined steel.

Unless someone opened the hatch, there was no way out.

Chapter Twenty-four

AUTEC

THE SWIMMER DELIVERY VEHICLE WAS DELIVERED TO THE AUTEC helo pad underneath a big Sikorsky CH-53 Super Stallion helo. The same helo brought two SEALs, team leader Commander Lee Jackson and Lt. "Pepper" Torres. Jessica thought Jackson looked too much like a hippie musician with his shaggy haircut, and Torres too much like a model, to be SEALs. Until they took off their shirts and she could count their abdominal muscles one by one. Along with the bullet scars. She stopped counting those at ten.

The SDV was a miracle of compact engineering, lightweight alloys, and computerized design. It was shaped like a manta ray with a plexiglass window in its flared front. Commands from its airtight compartment were transmitted by radio signal to control surfaces, eliminating connecting rods.

"SDV-1 just won't do," she said. "You've got to have a real name." She ran a hand over its slick alloy surface. Its cousins were the DSRVs, *Avalon* and *Mystic*. It came to her.

"I christen thee . . . *Camelot.*"

* * *

In AUTEC control Justine clasped Lee Jackson's hand warmly.

"How are you, ma'am?" asked the sinewy Jackson with a big grin. "Haven't seen you since the hospital. You look great."

"You, too. Lee. Nothing shows."

"Not with this hair." He lifted it off his collar. The skin around his neck and ears was rough and mottled, as if it had been burned. It had been frostbitten. "The wolf scars and the missing toes were no big deal."

"I was most worried about my face," Justine confided. "But whatever it was that remarkable man put on me saved my skin. The doctor stateside said he'd never seen anything like it. Wanted to try to get a sample and patent it."

"He'd have to go find Stephan out there on the ice first," said Jackson.

They had been stranded on the polar ice cap some years before. Only the remarkable skills of a Russian ice specialist trained by the Inuit Eskimos had saved them.

"You've been briefed?" she asked.

"Noncombatant evacuation operation. I know the area. We can handle the terrain. There's four all together, right? Two women, a boy, and a girl."

"Won't be easy, this one."

"I figure working with you brings me luck."

"Thanks. Who's your number two?" she asked.

"Lt. Juan Pepito Torres. Out of L.A. We call him Pepper 'cause he's hot stuff. Almost as fast as you, maybe."

Justine sighed. "I'm not as fast as I used to be."

Jackson made a wry face. "Who is?"

Pepper Torres finished unloading their gear. He liked the hot sun, like Southern California's. But there was no brown here, only lush green. And you could breathe the air.

Torres used to say he owed his life to the movies. One time

his father took the family for a drive in their battered old Buick, and they broke down in Beverly Hills. This brought a policeman and a tow truck faster than crabs make your crotch itch, but the tow truck's whine startled a little girl's horse, and it bolted over the berm between her house and the road. If not for Juan's father, who had bred horses in Puerto Rico, making a perfect leap for the reins, the kid would have needed more plastic surgery than Cher.

The girl's father turned out to be a movie star and a good guy, an unusual combination. Suddenly Juan's family had a new place to live, and Juan's father had a job running a local stable—riding academy, they called it. Pepper worked craft services on the star's next picture. It was there he met the stuntmen. He loved what they did, and soon they began to teach him. He was a natural. Tough, smart, and fast. They said they lost a great one when he turned eighteen and joined the navy. The stuntmen's loss was the SEALs' gain. Like his father, over the years Pepper had made some great grabs.

"Commander Moran?"

"You found her."

He stuck out his hand. "Pepper Torres. I got our equipment off the helo. You tell me where it goes."

"Over here." The dark, well-built man with the thick wavy hair and engaging smile hefted a couple of duffel bags easily and walk them back over to *Camelot*. The sound when he put them in the hold told her they were anything but light.

"You're the SDV pilot?" he asked.

"I am."

He measured her, sensed her confidence. "Fine," he said.

"I hate this," Justine muttered, crawling into the SDV.

Crewmen made sure the tethers from the helo to the SDV were secure and gave the pilot the okay to go. They rose off the ground, and soon the ocean was flying past at dizzying speed. *Augusta* was already heading for their rendezvous in the Santeran Channel. An hour's flight time would see them there. Lying on their stomachs in the shaped "beds" of the *Camelot* swinging on the taut cable was like being in one of those rides at amusement parks that plaster you to the wall.

Jessica worked the controls, getting the feel. "I never thought I'd envy a sardine."

"Look at it this way," said Pepper brightly, his muscular frame confined even more than hers. "It's gonna make the sub feel roomy."

Actually, Jessica decided, being a sardine next to the handsome Pepper Torres might not be so bad a fate.

The water changed from crystal green to glassy navy blue. They passed over the shallow Grand Bahama Bank into the deep waters of the Santeran Channel. Less than fifty miles separated them from Cuba now.

"There," said Jackson. "To the left. See it?"

Augusta breached the surface to give the pilot a visual fix. A wake streamed out behind it as it slowed. Bright blue water from the props surged forward.

Jessica keyed in her radio. "Pilot, this is *Camelot*. We have them."

"Roger, *Camelot*. You ready to swim?"

"Roger," Jessica responded. "Do you copy, *Augusta*?"

"We copy. Come to Papa at sixty feet."

"Roger, *Augusta*. *Camelot* out."

Augusta submerged. The helo put a safe distance between them and released *Camelot* into the water. Jessica's board lit up. She was shaky for the first few moments. The craft rode like a light airplane, easily buffeted by strong currents, but soon she had the hang of it.

"Sadist," said Justine darkly. "You're enjoying this."

She was. Without the bitterness of having submarine command denied her, she could relax and enjoy the skills she had mastered over all those years. It was kind of like riding a tricycle after you had driven a race car, but she did it as well as she did everything else. She made one pass to add to her feel, then came about and settled over *Augusta*'s hatch as if she had been doing it all her life.

"I'd applaud if I could move my hands," said Justine.

"Feel free to whistle."

Scotti was waiting for them. "How did she handle, Commander?"

"Like a dream, sir."

"Good. Let's get you people suited up. We'll be at the takeoff point in thirty minutes."

Chapter Twenty-five

Jacksonville

CARTER IMAGINED HE COULD HEAR BELL POUNDING ON THE
bulkhead, but he knew that was impossible. It was too thick.
He readied himself. Timing was critical. He planned to take
the reactor almost to critical mass and hold it there for ten
seconds. Long enough for Bell to absorb too much radiation
ever to go near the reactor on a nuclear sub again. A lifetime
of radiation. Then Carter would "realize" Bell was in there
and get him out. The rules were absolute. As soon as his
dosimeter was developed the doc would take him off the
ship. Maxed out. His career would be over, as Ransom
wanted. It was Carter's way out. Destroy Bell's body to save
his soul. Both their souls.

Fayette handed him the clipboard to sign off that the
reactor compartment had been inspected and cleared. He
imagined himself saying later, "But I thought he was right
behind me!"

"It's clear," Carter said, "Commence reactor startup.
Reactor operator, commence withdrawing rods. Run main
coolant pumps slow speed."

"Commence withdrawing rods, aye. Run main coolant
pumps slow speed, aye."

Carter said, "Withdraw group one."

Northern Star

I am truly sorry for what I do now, thought Avilov.

"Do you still have a constant solution on the *Jacksonville?*" he asked.

"Yes, Captain," said Vashovsky. "She is making no effort to disguise her position."

"Range to the formation is five thousand yards," Pachenko informed him. "Active sonar ready on your command."

"Very well. Attack center, prepare to fire all tubes."

Avilov was as steady as a figurehead on the prow of a ship. Only Pachenko knew that the eyes that stared out from the Hawk's serene visage were now totally blind.

"One minute to deep dive mark, Captain," said Stepov.

"Attack center, do you have a solution on both targets, the *Adri* and the American sub?" asked Avilov.

"I do," said Vashovsky, "but I do not recommend firing with *Adri* still astern."

"I agree," said Avilov mildly.

"Thirty seconds to dive point, Captain. We have Morey Pass on the scope camera," said Pushkin from sonar.

"Put it on the screen," said Pachenko.

The image flickered and then held, gray and fuzzy at this depth. The Florida Straits ran between the American coast and Grand Bahama Bank, widening below the tip of Florida into a triangle of water bordered on the south by Cuba, the east by Andros Island, and the west by the Florida Keys. In the center, twenty miles off the Cuban coast, was Cay Sal. Eons of deposits laid down by ocean waters had built it into a towering undersea mountain rising from over a mile down. Only a small sandy spit showed above the ocean, but it was honeycombed with trenches and passages and caves below.

Morey Pass extended all the way through the undersea

mountain. It was originally thought of as a running route, a mapped-out road in the ocean into which a sub could sneak to outmaneuver an enemy, but it had proved too difficult for even the best computer-assisted steering to run. Rocks as sharp as knives lined the walls, and debris from undersea quakes often blocked narrow passages. It had been abandoned and, to Pachenko's knowledge, never tried since. But if you *could* make it through, if you *could* navigate the treacherous way, you would drop clear out of the Florida Straits, emerge in the Nicholas Channel, and sail straight to Sabaña Key.

Avilov said, "Is everyone with me today?"

No voice was raised against him.

"Very well. Yuri, all stop."

Avilov was running what the Americans called a Crazy Ivan, a full stop and reversal to clear your baffles. If anyone was behind you they had to turn or run right into your propellers.

"Prepare to come about with hard rudder, Mishkin. I want it fast when I give the order."

"Ready, Captain."

"Control room, sonar, *Adri* is slowing, slowing . . ."

The Libyan was too close behind the *Star*. He had to turn or ram them. "Which way is she turning?" demanded Avilov.

"Can't tell . . . can't . . . right, Captain! She's turning right."

"Hard right rudder. Now, Mishkin! Sonar, conn, go active."

Mishkin yanked the helm over to its stops, and the *Star* spun around on its axis like a top. It turned *inside* the *Adri's* circle, presenting Vashovsky with a perfect broadside shot.

"I have a solution on the *Adri,*" reported Vashovsky. "Range one thousand meters."

"Diving point . . . mark!" called out Stepov.

All roads led here. Morey Pass was directly below, both enemy ships were in his sights, and all the noise from the *Star* would conceal *Adri*'s presence from the Americans for the first critical minutes of the engagement. It was time to roll the dice a final time.

"Fire tubes one and two at the *Adri*. Fire tubes three and four at the *Jacksonville*. Secure active. Emergency deep. Ultra-quiet."

Jacksonville

"Conn, sonar. Torpedoes in the water. High-speed motors. Four, sir. Two headed into the shallow zone, two deep. We have been acquired only in the upper stratum."

"Emergency reactor startup," MacKenzie ordered at once. He felt the full force of Avilov's duplicity like a slap in the face. Avilov had launched on them, bracketing the *Jacksonville* above and below. He had been suckered before, but never with such bald nerve. Where the hell was that reactor? He needed power.

"Man battle stations. Helm, on my order we will execute a one-hundred-eighty-degree high-speed turn to starboard. Mr. Randall, maximum cavitation. I want a big knuckle for the torpedo's sonar. Steer to course zero nine zero. Maneuvering, all ahead flank."

"Maneuvering, aye."

"Conn, sonar. Contact's still closing. Lot of sound out there."

"Fire control, keep tracking the *Star*, and let me know the minute you have a solution."

"Fire control . . . aye." Danvers sounded harried. MacKenzie wished he had Flynn, Bell, and Carter, but he couldn't rescind his order.

Where the hell was that reactor?

* * *

When the silent battle alarm flashed, Carter's first impulse was to rush to the conn. The ship was in danger. Battle reports were coming over the PA speaker. Danvers sounded shaky. MacKenzie needed them. A hundred and fifty lives were at risk because he hadn't told Ransom to go to hell.

"Withdraw group two," he ordered. He was standing apart from himself and watching himself do things he never dreamed he could do. He justified it to himself that he was helping Bell. Ransom's way would have left him nothing. This way he could move on. Start a new life free of pursuing devils. When group three was withdrawn the reactor would begin to go critical. Fatal. But if Carter held it a few seconds before it did, he would accomplish his purpose. Bell was surely listening to the startup over the PA and dying a little more at every command. Was he clawing at the walls till his hands bled, like some Poe character entombed by a madman?

"Sir, group three ready."

Danvers said over the speaker anxiously, "Upper stratum torpedoes have acquired us."

Carter heard fear in the fire control boss's voice. It reached down to the core of his being and the basic values the navy had instilled since his Academy days. His ship. A fellow officer. A friend. In the end it was a line he could not cross. It was one thing to plan it, even to execute part of it. He realized each step had taken him farther down the road of corruption till he thought he was lost, but even now he still had a chance to make amends. He couldn't do this no matter how far Ransom pushed him, no matter what he would do to him. He'd hate himself forever, hate the man underneath—and deserve it. He pulled back at the very last second.

"Wait! We left a wrench inside. I'm sure of it. I have to retrieve it."

"Sir?"

"Secure the reactor." Carter was already on the lower level cycling the hatch open. A frightened and exhausted Bell spilled out. Quickly Carter shut the hatch and completed the reactor startup. Power flowed into the ship.

"Reg, what the hell happened?" demanded Bell breathlessly. "Didn't you know I was in there? The reactor almost—"

Carter told him. All of it.

". . . God, I'm sorry, Mark. I tried to tell MacKenzie the other day, but I couldn't. Ransom kept coming at me till I couldn't think. The threats. The pictures. I just couldn't."

"I know Ransom," Bell said bitterly. "He came to see us after the accident. Told me my father was to blame. I threw him out of the house."

"He never forgot," Carter said. "He's insane."

"Christ, Reg, how could you? I'm your *friend.*"

The ultimate condemnation. Carter's pain radiated like heat. "I'm going to be asking myself that for a long time. But not now. C'mon, we gotta get Jamie."

"Conn, engineering. We have full power, skipper."

"Acknowledged. Helm, execute a one-hundred-eighty-degree high-speed turn to starboard. Mr. Randall, maximum cavitation."

"One-hundred-eighty-degree high-speed turn to starboard, maximum cavitation, aye."

"Sonar, conn. Where is the *Star?*" MacKenzie demanded.

"They've gone deep, sir, and quiet. But there's something . . . I can't be sure yet. We're picking up some weird noises. Could be her own fish turning deep. Something's going on down there. I need some more time with this. We're still tracking the two upper-stratum torpedoes closing on us."

So this was how Avilov had figured to make the final leg of his run, MacKenzie saw—by tricking his enemy into letting him. What a mind. Suddenly showing himself had been just the right trick to call off the hounds baying at his door. They had given him safe passage through the straits, and now only the *Jacksonville* stood between him and Cuban waters. Two torpedoes were closing on the *Jacksonville*. MacKenzie put down his fury at the betrayal. Coldly, that was how he had to respond.

"Fire control, make a quick reaction shot back on the torpedo bearings. Shoot units from tubes one and two."

"Tubes one and two. Fire control, aye."

"Conn, maneuvering, answering all-ahead flank."

"Acknowledged. Helm, hard right rudder steady new course zero nine zero. Swing her as fast as she'll turn."

The helmsman pushed the steering yoke all the way to its stop. "Hard right rudder, aye."

"All stop."

"All stop, aye."

"Fire control, firing point procedures. Match sonar bearings and shoot."

"Fire control, aye. Tube one . . . Set. Standby. Fire. Tube two . . . Set. Standby. Fire."

"All ahead flank," MacKenzie ordered.

The *Jacksonville* ran to top speed, turning as fast as her mighty reactor could push her. Pivoting around through a full one hundred and eighty degrees, she blasted the ocean with her props, churning enough bubbles to create a cloud. All over the ship men grabbed handholds to fight the pull.

"Passing zero eight zero," announced Randall. "Shifting rudder to steady on new course."

"Conn, sonar. Contact four hundred yards aft and closing."

MacKenzie felt the hot torpedo breathing down his neck. "Sonar, go active. Max power in omni mode. I need three hundred and sixty degrees coverage. Torpedo room, reload tubes one and two."

"Sonar, aye."

"Torpedo room, aye."

In the sonar room the sonar chief flicked the sonar onto active and turned the gain up to maximum. Sound beams at the height of their decibel range shot out. The undersea mountains magnified the screeching pulses, making them fragment and reverberate. The locator in the torpedo's warhead suddenly had a hundred different sites to choose from. It chose the wrong one. Heading straight for the cavitating cloud MacKenzie's maneuver had created, it burst through the bubbles, ran straight into the undersea mountain, and exploded.

"Conn, sonar, first tracking unit explosion. It missed us, Skipper."

"Conn, sonar. Sir, it doesn't make sense, but the contact we're tracking doesn't seem to have any cooling pumps, and there are some weird frequencies on our screens . . . much quieter. We don't know what to make of it, there's so much sound in the water. Sir, what's going on? How could the *Star* change like that?"

"Tracking second upper-stratum torpedo," said Danvers. "Closing on us at three thousand yards."

There was no time to think about the *Star*'s changing act. "Emergency deep," MacKenzie ordered. "Make our depth one five zero zero feet, Mr. Randall. Thirty degree down bubble."

The *Jacksonville*'s bow dropped like an express elevator, and the ship plummeted at full speed. The hull popped, and there were creaks and groans as the floor buckled slightly from the increased pressure.

"Second upper-stratum torpedo still closing," said Danvers.

"Countermeasures, release decoys."

The noisemakers sped from the ship and burst into staccato firecracker sounds to fool the tracing torpedo's sonar. MacKenzie waited.

"Conn, sonar. It's not buying it, skipper. Still on our tail."

"Still closing," said Danvers, his voice cracking.

MacKenzie had no choice. He took the *Jacksonville* deeper.

"Make our depth two thousand feet, Mr. Randall."

"Sir, I must advise that is below crush depth," said Randall nervously.

MacKenzie figured somewhere Avilov was grinning. *Well, he thought, the bastard didn't count on me—and I'm just the nasty-ass son of a bitch to ram that torpedo right back up his props.*

But first he had to shake the torpedo. He said, "Take her down."

Bell and Carter found Flynn doubled over on the floor, pale and ashen-faced.

"Get the doc, Reg." Bell kneeled beside Flynn. He winced in pain. His eyes were glazed.

"Wha? Oh, you. Mark, just lemme . . ."

"Lie still. Doc's on his way. What happened?"

Flynn coughed, and there was blood in his spittle. "Fell last night. Off a girl's balcony. Drunk. Felt bad over . . . over . . . I can't have Jessica, Mark. Just *can't.*"

"Don't talk, Jamie."

Bell lifted Flynn's shirt and winced. He was a mass of black and yellow bruises. Ribs felt broken. He must have been in incredible pain. Why the hell hadn't he said anything? Why hadn't he let his friends help? Because he was Flynn, that was why, the proudest of them all, and in spite of his brogue and blarney, the most vulnerable. He couldn't handle falling in love for the first time with Jessica and losing her. The dark side he never showed anyone had taken him up to that balcony, and the pain had tumbled him off.

Bell wondered if you could ever knew what anyone was really feeling inside. Jamie tore himself up over Jessica. Carter had been suborned by Ransom, and really, how did anyone know what they'd do in a similar situation? Bell's inner demons had destroyed his ability to command. *"Everyone is a moon and has a dark side which he never shows to anybody."* What was important now wasn't what had been done, but how to make amends for it.

Carter ran up with Doc Price, the pudgy Afro-American pharmacist's mate who probably knew as much about trauma as any mainland surgeon. He kneeled over Flynn and probed. "Broken ribs. Shock. Internal bleeding. He's banged up bad, sir. Maybe punctured a lung. He's got to be MedEvac'ed to a hospital."

"We're under attack," said Carter firmly. "We need him up and around."

Doc hesitated. "I can wrap him up and pump him full of antibiotics and painkillers. If that doesn't do it . . ."

"If that doesn't do it," said Flynn weakly from the floor. "A little whiskey might."

Bell and Carter lifted Flynn. "Let's get him to your office, Doc," said Carter. "On the way, Jamie, I got a story for you."

MacKenzie was worried. The torpedo continued to track them, a hound that even depth could not shake off. He couldn't take the *Jacksonville* any deeper without stressing her hull beyond its limits. And he hadn't had a second to spare for a larger problem: where was the *Star* now, and how vulnerable was the *Jacksonville* to a second attack?

"Keep tracking that fish, Mr. Danvers. I—"

"Sir," cut in Bell. "Permission to return to duty."

"I thought I told you to—"

"Sir," said Carter from behind him, "if my old job's still open . . .?"

"'Tis a fine mornin' for a little spat, is it not, Captain, sir?" Flynn said with a soft brogue. He was bandaged from neck to waist under his torn shirt. He was still pale, but stronger than before.

For a moment MacKenzie almost refused. But he had

learned, too. Nurture and you get it back. Life returns life. That's what being PCOI has taught me, he thought. "Take your stations, gentlemen. We've got a hot fish on our tail that doesn't want to be shaken loose. You're relieved, Mr. Danvers."

Danvers *was* relieved. "Aye, sir. Welcome back, Mr. Flynn."

"Good to be back, laddie. Now what have we got here?"

"Conn, sonar. Torpedo two thousand yards and closing."

There had to be a way to shake this fish, MacKenzie thought furiously. "Engineering, increase reactor power to one hundred and ten percent power. Shift to battle short."

"Reactor in battle short, Captain," said the chief engineer, worry in his voice.

"Conn, sonar, distance to torpedo?"

"Increase in speed's doing it, Skipper. Two thousand yards, no longer closing. Holding steady. No differential."

Stalemate. As long as he could hold this speed the torpedo couldn't catch him. But it was a race against time. Could *Jacksonville*'s shaft handle the excess torque until the torpedo ran out of fuel? If they slowed at all, the torpedo would catch them.

He needed a way out, and he needed it fast.

Adri

Avilov had been so compliant up till now, Zilah just didn't see it coming. He thought the *Northern Star* was having engine trouble when it stopped so short. It was a costly error. When Zilah ordered hard right rudder the *Star* had turned on him and launched her torpedoes. His delay cost him more than positioning. His boat was far slower than the *Star*, his top speed only twenty knots underwater. He had no choice. He had been outmaneuvered, so he ran. One of Avilov's torpedoes misfired and sank to the bottom. The other ran out of power and fell away. Zilah heard the

American fire on the *Star*'s last position, but the *Star* was long gone, vanished off his screens. Another of the Hawk's tricks. They named him wrong, Zilah thought. He should have been called the Ghost.

Zilah's superiors would never accept his failure. Demotion, maybe even prison would follow his loss of the *Star*. Unless he brought back another prize. He liked that. His hunter's instincts were happier fighting than running.

"Sonar, where is the American submarine?"

"Very deep, Captain. Running from the *Northern Star*'s last torpedo."

Avilov had played them both like fine fish, thought Zilah. Sent them both running while he escaped. Well, *Adri* would run. But not before finishing the American.

"Make ready forward tubes two and three. Prepare to fire."

Chapter Twenty-six

Northern Star

THE MOMENT AVILOV FIRED THE TORPEDOES HE DIVED THE SHIP hard for Morey Pass. If he'd worked it right, the *Jacksonville* would think the *Adri* was the *Star*, and both subs would be too busy avoiding torpedoes and engaging each other to notice him slip away or come after him.

"Formation two hundred meters."

Avilov slipped the sonar headset over his ears. No sighted pilot had ever run the pass. Eyes weren't sufficient. You couldn't react quickly enough to avoid those jagged, hull-tearing edges. But ears were another matter. Bats were blind, and they navigated openings no sighted creature would dare try. From his throne the blind Poseidon reached out to his realm.

"Sonar, go active minimum," he ordered. "Narrow beam only, Mishkin."

A narrow active sonar beam shot out from the *Star*'s bow, covering a very small field in front of her, a cone of sound with as much tactile feel as any hand. The sound bounced back to Avilov and he built up a "picture" of what lay ahead. Pachenko had gone over the charts with him, too, giving him his own impressions of how the charts read. He heard the change in pitch. There was the opening, a cave mouth that opened into an underwater valley beyond.

"Fifty meters," said Stepov.

Avilov was one with his ship. "Right five degrees rudder. All ahead slow."

The *Northern Star* plunged into the jagged opening like a sausage into a toothy mouth. Avilov felt them slide in. Sonar was a steady pulse beat sent out and reflected back. Out and back. Out and back. Each pulse had its own rhythm. Timing was everything. The hull crunched against a rocky wall. Concentrate, he told himself.

"Left five degrees rudder . . . no, don't repeat it, Mishkin, there's no time. Just do it."

"We're entering the first valley," Pachenko said softly, and Avilov heard the awe in his voice. He led them deeper. He "heard" the tube coral swaying on the valley floor, "felt" the tiny bounce off the school of fish who, frightened, darted off.

"Come up five meters. Back off a bit . . . there. Steady as she goes."

The sound ranged ahead and gave him sight. The opening to the next passage was a tube only fifty feet taller than the ship itself. He thought about slowing and abandoned the idea. Losing momentum in here was as dangerous as having too much. He waited, feeling for it, and when it came he knew it.

"Right three degrees rudder. Up another five meters. Another three. Zero bubble . . . faster! All right, steady."

"There's a five-knot current," Pachenko warned.

The *Star* slipped into the tube like a man into a woman. The sound of things dragging along the hull was steady all the way. God knew what had grown here since the Russian aquanauts had first been through. Jagged stalactites pointed down at the *Star* like daggers. Their stony points could easily penetrate the hull. All at once a grinding sound could be felt as well as heard. Something was being chewed up by their prop. If it broke the blades, they were doomed. No EPM could propel them out of this place against a five-knot current. Just as abruptly it silenced. The *Star* continued its eerie journey.

"Stop whispering!" Avilov said sharply to Stepov. "It distracts me."

Stepov stopped in midsentence.

"Left five degrees rudder. Come down three meters. Now five more degrees left. There is a turn here. Back off a bit . . . there. Steady as she goes."

He felt the daggers growing smaller. Heard the echoes more clearly.

"We are coming out of the tube, Pari," said Pachenko. "Next is the Sea of Storms."

The next cavern was trickier. Time and water pressure had eroded hundreds of channels into the vast canyon inside the mountain. As the currents changed out in the open sea they flowed inside in a hundred different directions. It was like a mixing bowl fed by a hundred different spigots, and the effect was a melee of currents, often conflicting, totally unpredictable.

"Left five degrees rudder. Come down ten meters. Now steady as she goes."

A vast trench cut perpendicularly across the floor. Avilov sensed almost endless depth under him. It went down for miles. It felt like they were flying across. Then danger. All at once they were struck by a vicious current of at least ten knots that flung the *Star* around as if slapped by a giant hand.

"Pari, we're off course. The current!"

They were descending. The combination of currents was forcing them down. If they struck the trench wall, they might be sucked down into its depths and not recover. He fought to right the ship.

"All ahead two thirds."

"Pari, at that speed . . ." Pachenko warned.

Avilov knew. At that speed if he didn't hit the exit opening across the canyon just right, he would strike the wall and break the *Star* in half.

"Maintain constant speed. Steady on that power output. Right five degrees rudder. Come up ten meters. . . . Now five more. Three degrees left. Mishkin, get our stern up. Maintain zero trim. I want zero bubble. The opening is very small. Fight the current. Use your hands, man!"

The ship was buffeted from side to side. Seven thousand tons does not sway easily. The currents were as powerful as any they had ever felt. Stepov leaned over the diving officer's chair to help. Together they fought the ship back on course.

"Back off a bit . . . three degrees left. Up another five meters. We're going to hit. Up, damn it. Up!"

With a sickening crunch the keel rammed the lower lip of the opening. A sharp dragging sound came from below. Then they were in, and the sound stopped.

"We are inside the last tunnel, Pari," said Pachenko. "It's long, but comparatively straight. Three miles."

"Ahead one third," Avilov ordered. He was shaken after the trip through the Sea of Storms.

Three more miles through this tunnel, then the most difficult passage of all. The charts called it the Canyon of Skulls. There was no notation as to why, only the word *Opasno*.

More than dangerous. Deadly.

Chapter Twenty-seven

Jacksonville

THE TORPEDO CHASING THEM WAS STILL HOLDING STEADY AT two thousand yards. Only running the reactor in the red zone was keeping it at bay.

Bell said hesitantly, "Captain, was there a thermal layer close by?"

"Three hundred feet. Looks like a twenty-degree drop. Why?"

"Nothing. I was just thinking, sir."

He couldn't risk the ship on what he had in mind. Not with a torpedo homing in for a kill. Last time they were in combat he'd snagged the helo and almost killed the pilot. Just yesterday Jamie had tricked him with a maneuver an ensign would have spotted. He was a Jonah, doomed to fail. MacKenzie was in charge now. He would save them.

"Mr. Bell, look at me. We don't have much time. I need help." It was something MacKenzie had never said before, but he knew it was true. Avilov had gotten the better of him. Any minute their shaft might fail, and the pursuing torpedo would catch and kill the ship. He saw Bell's indecision, his doubt.

"Mark, listen to me. The way you go now, it's what makes

213

the difference. There aren't any guarantees. Believe me. You've still got to *try*. You make your bet, and you live with it. It's all any of us can do. If it matters, my faith in you still holds."

"It matters a lot, sir," Bell said. But could he do it?

"Torpedo two thousand yards."

"Mark?"

Bell took a deep breath. "Sir, I was remembering an old football play."

"Excuse me?"

Bell went through it in his mind again. He had to be sure. Conditions looked right. An upper layer of the ocean warmed by the sun. A colder, denser layer lay below. The juncture of the two was a line that reflected sound. Sitting just under it, a submarine could not be heard by surface sonars. Sitting just *over* it . . .

"With your permission, Captain," Bell said slowly, "I'd like to try a handoff."

"You've lost me, but it's your show. You have the conn."

Bell gripped the railing tightly to steady himself. "Jamie, do we still have an exercise torpedo on board?"

"Yes, sir."

"Load tube one with an Mk-48 Extorp."

"Load Extorp, aye."

"Mr. Randall, get ready to play angles and dangles for real."

"Yes, sir."

"Torpedo room ready, sir," reported Flynn. "Extorp loaded."

The Russian torpedo couldn't have much fuel left. Bell first wanted to try and shake it with a roller-coaster ride through the ocean.

"Mr. Randall, twenty degree up bubble! Take us up to three hundred feet. I want a tight curve. Reg, prepare for ultra-quiet. We're going to secure the main engines."

"Mark, with a torpedo chasing us?" questioned Mac-Kenzie.

"Yes, sir. Maneuvering, prepare to shift propulsion."

"Maneuvering, aye."

"Mr. Randall, call out that depth."

"Eight hundred feet . . . seven-fifty . . ."

"Unit set to fire, Mark," said Flynn.

"Six hundred . . . five-fifty . . ."

"Approaching thermal layer," said Carter.

"Conn, sonar, torpedo closing fifteen hundred yards."

They couldn't shake it. "Maintain zero bubble."

"Zero bubble, aye."

"Five hundred . . . four-fifty . . ."

MacKenzie was beginning to see what Bell planned. It was brilliant. Timing was everything. A seven-thousand-ton ship had tremendous momentum. He'd have to cut his power perfectly.

"Depth four hundred feet."

Now, MacKenzie thought . . . and at just that moment Bell gave the orders.

"Five degree down bow angle. Maintain full rise on stern planes." Bell's commands put the sub in the rare configuration of rising with the bow lower than the stern. "Shift propulsion to the EPM. Secure main engines and prepare to hover. Jamie, fire unit one."

"Set . . . Standby . . . Fire. Unit one away."

Still rising, the *Jacksonville* shot the Extorp down through the thermal layer in the exact instant that she rose above it. Bell had shut down the main engines and secured the reactor coolant pumps. They were carried over the thermal layer by momentum alone. This was his handoff, passing their sound from the *Jacksonville* to the Extorp, now the sole "noise" below the thermal grade.

"Two nine zero feet. Stable hover," Carter reported. "Main engines secured."

The enemy torpedo sped up from the depths. Bell held his breath along with everyone else in the conn.

"Looking good," MacKenzie said softly.

"Conn, sonar. The Extorp is sounding loud and clear. Enemy torpedo is slowing . . . Its sonar is in search mode . . . It has acquired the Extorp, sir! It's moving away from us. Tracking . . . contacts merge. Explosions, Skipper!"

The conn erupted like a Texas whorehouse on a Saturday night. Cheers echoed and reechoed throughout the boat. Carter pounded Bell on the back.

"Well done, Mark," said MacKenzie.

"Thank you, sir." The smallest hope was rekindled inside him. Not a Jonah this time.

"A quote for us," yelled Flynn.

" 'By the Shadow of Death, he's a lightning pilot!' " Bell offered, barely able to stand.

"Captain has the conn," said MacKenzie. "Maneuvering, answer bells on the main engine."

"When you have a moment, sir," said Carter.

"Of course. Mr. Flynn, who or what hit you and ran?"

"Oh, you mean the gift wrapping? Small spat with a stronger man, sir."

"Who might that be?"

"Myself, sir. It's over now."

"Conn, sonar, still no sign of the *Northern Star.*"

Carter said, "Skipper, would you look at these?"

MacKenzie looked at the tracings Carter had drawn from the sonar data. "Sir, when I plot those points where sonar says he picked up that contact, well, the point is moving in a straight line at three knots. Sir, if it isn't the *Northern Star,* could there be another sub out there?"

MacKenzie considered. "We'd have picked up the frequencies."

"Not if it's a diesel," said Carter.

The light went on in MacKenzie's mind. A diesel. Of course. And it meant they were in danger.

"Maneuvering, status of main engines?"

"We're working on it, sir. They are warming up now."

"I need power."

"We have a small vibration. Still, ninety seconds, sir."

MacKenzie waited impatiently, every intuition telling him that Carter was right, and that death was stalking them again.

Adri

Zilah listened to the American's maneuvers with growing respect. He's a clever one. And bold, he thought, sitting with his pants down while the torpedo came at him. Only in the last seconds did Zilah hear the Extorp and understand what the American was doing. He suspected the American would be an outstanding poker player. Bluffing a torpedo was quite a feat.

Adri's computers identified the American ship as the *Jacksonville*. She was fast and powerful, but *Adri* was far quieter. Even now they were closing on the American ship without being detected. The *Adri's* engines ran on silent batteries. There was no mechanical noise, and they could stay submerged for days without resorting to a snorkel. Without cooling pumps or couplings she was as quiet as light. These advantages cost her, however. To achieve these conditions she could only make a speed of three knots.

"Captain, we have a firing solution on the *Jacksonville*. They are completely unaware of us. They remain in a hover."

"The advantage is with the mouse this time," said Zilah. "Fire tubes one and two."

Jacksonville

"Skipper, torpedoes in the water! Two high-cycle motors bearing one eight zero coming at us from the south."

217

The conn burst into action again. Men who just seconds before had been lounging at their stations in the aftermath of defeating Avilov's torpedo rushed back to their consoles to defend the ship again.

"Maneuvering, I need power now," MacKenzie demanded.

"Thirty seconds, sir."

"Conn, sonar. Torpedoes two thousand yards and closing."

"Acknowledged. Helm, on my order give me hard right rudder. We'll pivot at flank speed, turn her as fast as you can."

"Aye, Captain."

"Conn, sonar. Torpedoes eighteen hundred yards and closing."

"Fire control, status of tubes three and four."

"Tubes three and four loaded with Mk-48 torpedoes."

"Mr. Flynn, snapshot tubes three and four. Match sonar bearings for that contact and make a shot back on that torpedo bearing. Open outer doors tubes three and four and shoot."

Flynn found his bearing. "Ship ready. Solution ready. Torpedoes ready . . . Tube three away . . . Tube four away."

"Enemy torpedoes fifteen hundred yards and closing," called sonar.

"Maneuvering, conn. Get ready to kick her in the tail. Max power."

"Ten seconds, Captain," responded the chief engineer.

"Conn, sonar. We have identified the hostile contact. It's a Libyan Kilo–class diesel sub, the *Adri.*"

"Acknowledged. You were right, Reg. Now listen, all of you. We're in a sticky situation. We've got torpedoes closing on us, but if we move, the *Adri* will fire again. I don't give us much chance of beating four torpedoes all closing at once. So we stay put for now."

"Conn, sonar. Torpedoes one thousand yards and closing. Our own torpedoes are ranging away. No contact, sir."

"Acknowledged."

"Captain, maneuvering. Ready to answer all bells, sir."

"Prepare to answer all-ahead flank in ten seconds." He turned back to Carter. "Mr. Carter, I want a constant course solution plotted on the *Adri*. Head on to her bow. Collision course."

"Head on, Captain?"

"That's right. And when I want it, I'll want it fast."

"Aye, sir."

"Mr. Bell," he continued. "We'll be turning fast and diving right at him."

"Sir?"

"You heard me. We move, we draw more torpedoes. We have to take him by surprise. He has to move damn slowly to stay so quiet. That's our advantage."

"Conn, sonar. Enemy torpedoes eight hundred yards and closing."

MacKenzie made a silent prayer. "All right now. For the money. Maneuvering, all ahead flank. Helm, hard right rudder. Pivot at flank speed, turn her as fast as you can. Sharply now."

"Helm, aye." The *Jacksonville* shot forward, pivoting at top speed.

"Conn, sonar, contact depth."

"Adri is at two hundred feet."

"Conn, sonar. Torpedoes are closing at six hundred yards. They've turned with us, following close in aft."

"Good. Now, Mr. Carter. Give us a course."

Adri

Zilah was crouched worriedly over his sonar operator's console. One second before he had been watching his torpedoes home in on the hovering *Jacksonville*. The next second the American captain had turned his ship like a race car and headed straight for him with the torpedoes following like angry dogs.

"Sonar, what is he doing?" he shouted.

"Captain, the *Jacksonville* is on a collision heading."

Well, Zilah would put a stop to this. If he could slow the *Jacksonville* one bit, those angry dogs would catch him and bite his props off and send him to the bottom. *Adri* couldn't shoot. A bow shot stood almost no chance of hitting, and the Americans were too close anyway for the torpedo to arm itself. But if he charged, the American would have to slow in order to turn, and then the torpedoes would have him.

"All ahead, two thirds," he ordered.

Jacksonville

"He's not turning," said Bell anxiously.

"Maintain course and speed," MacKenzie ordered. "Sonar, range to contact."

"Five hundred yards, Captain."

MacKenzie faced his PCOs firmly. "The captain of the *Adri* expects us to turn aside. That way he can fire, or slow us enough to let the torpedoes astern catch us. Either way would be disaster. So I have already decided I will not turn aside. It's the only chance I can give us. I've made my bet, and I'll stand by it. There's not a lot more I can teach you except that. It's something you can't fully understand till you're here. Good luck to us all."

"Conn, sonar. Thirty seconds to collision."

Death was riding hard to put his bony hands on them. Orders you learned. Systems you traced on paper. This was deeply personal. This was what he had lived for, what they had made him put aside . . . till now. He could see it in their faces, the final understanding of command. *I've made my bet*. Were they going home, or would they implode two hundred fathoms below the ocean? Were you callous to risk them, or were you sublimely gifted? There was nothing in the Book to tell you how to do it. You either could, or you couldn't.

For a moment he was back on the *Riga* in the middle of the Black Sea running head on at a Soviet admiral. He felt power rise inside him now as he had then, coming from the abandonment of everything to one final turn of Fate's wheel.

MacKenzie said, "Maneuvering, maintain turns."

Adri

"Captain?" The sonar officer was worried. "They are *increasing* speed, coming straight at us."

"What?"

"Collision in fifteen seconds . . . fourteen . . . thirteen . . . twelve . . ."

"Maintain our course," Zilah ordered. He was sweating. Had he guessed wrong? The American was playing a very Russian game with him. It just wasn't their tactic to run at someone like this. He should have turned by now. Avilov himself had taught him that in his Academy days. The first tendrils of fear reached for his heart.

". . . ten . . . nine . . . eight . . . collision imminent."

Zilah broke first. "Emergency! Hard left rudder! All stop on port engine, helm."

Adri pulled to the left.

Jacksonville

"They're turning hard left, Captain," yelled Bell.

"Torpedo two hundred yards aft and closing."

"Now, Mark, hard port. Maintain flank speed. Straight at him. Hold steady . . ."

221

"One hundred yards to collision . . . fifty . . ."

The torpedo was still closing on the *Jacksonville*'s stern as they headed straight for the turning *Adri*. MacKenzie waited till he could thought he could *hear* the damn thing, and at the last second he ordered, "Emergency surface! Full rise on all planes!"

Bell grabbed the chicken switches and blasted air under full pressure into the main ballast tanks. The *Jacksonville* shot up like a balloon. The torpedoes tracking her stern took a few seconds to react before they began to rise in response, but by then it was too late. The *Jacksonville* was no longer in their plane. Dead ahead, the *Adri* attracted them like a magnet. Passing fifty feet under the *Jacksonville*, the first torpedo blasted into the ship that had birthed it.

The *Adri* exploded. Flame burst down her main corridor, incinerating everything in its way. The force of the explosion snapped her keel in two, sending her to the bottom. But relief inside the *Jacksonville* was short-lived. The explosion that claimed the *Adri* was too near. The second torpedo was forced upward by the pressure wave and exploded only yards from the *Jacksonville*'s hull. The ship was shaken as if by a giant hand, and shock waves rolled down the corridors. There was the shriek of tortured metal. The hull buckled. Valves exploded. Icy water poured into the ship. Men were crushed against the bulkheads by the force of the water. Electronics shorted out and fires began. Smoke filled the air.

The torpedo room took the main force of the explosion. Nineteen-foot Mk-48s weighing over thirty-five hundred pounds broke from their moorings and burst free like a cupful of pencils. Men were crushed beneath them. They rammed the torpedo tube inner doors, wrenching them out of line. Seals ruptured, sending water streaming into the boat.

In the control room the pressure wave threw MacKenzie aside and smashed his head into the fire control console.

Blood flowed into the water flooding the deck. Bell reached him first. The ship was listing to port and had a fifteen-degree down angle on the bow. MacKenzie was lying on his side, eyes closed. "Captain . . ."

"Commence damage control," MacKenzie managed. "Mark . . . find it in yourself . . . Have faith. . . . Promise me!"

"I promise, sir."

"The ship . . . I couldn't . . ." A black fog swirled into MacKenzie's mind. He lost consciousness knowing that he had sailed one mission too many, and then he knew no more.

Fires had broken out. Bell peered through the smoke, saw Danvers dragging himself off the deck. "Danvers, get the captain to his cabin."

Chief Crowley had been killed when a high-voltage electrical cable from the ceiling tore loose and landed around his neck like a snake. Smoke poured from his eyes, and the smell of him burning was a thing no one who survived would ever forget. The blast had also overturned the plotting table on Carter, trapping his legs. Rising water swirled around him. Flynn was hanging on to the railing, pain contorting his features. God, Bell thought, what he must have felt being thrown around like this with broken ribs.

Water cascaded down from the sail. Randall was wiping blood from his face.

"Mr. Randall, are you all right?" Bell asked.

"I can manage, sir."

"Help me."

Randall slid awkwardly down the incline and they sloshed over to Carter. Together they moved the big plotting table back toward the nav center. A jagged edge of bone protruded from Carter's torn pants. They propped him against the table. His face was drawn and tight from shock, but he managed, "Mark, the ship . . . depth."

The depth gauge read one hundred feet. With her deep wounds the *Jacksonville* mustn't go any deeper. They had to get her back on the surface and reestablish control.

"Captain's in his cabin," said Danvers, back in the conn.

"Take the helm. Jamie, can you take the chief's board?"

"Okay, Mark." Flynn began removing the burned body.

Bell stepped over the debris and grabbed the MC channel. "This is the captain. Compartments report status."

They called in slowly. The torpedo room was completely out of commission. The engine room reported steam leaks and broken valves, but they thought they could answer limited bells within the hour. Communications was gone. The explosion had cut all hydraulic power to the masts. There was flooding all over the ship, and pumps were working at maximum. The crew had suffered extensive injuries. Doc Price was treating them as best he could. Bell ordered him to get up to the conn for MacKenzie and Carter as fast as he could.

"We got trouble." Flynn was pumping water out of the tanks, but the down angle of the sub had not decreased.

Danvers was fighting with the control yoke. "Captain," he said, alarmed, "I can't get any response on the planes. One hundred thirty feet . . . one hundred forty . . ."

The planes were jammed in a down angle. They couldn't stop the dive, and they were already too deep. "Engine room, I need all back emergency now. Jamie, take the conn. I'm going aft."

"Right. Blowing forward emergency ballast again," Flynn said, grabbing the chicken switches, but they had blown their pressure evading the *Adri*'s torpedoes. There wasn't enough charge in the air banks to blow the ballast. They needed those planes.

Gratefully, Bell felt the vibration of the engines as he ran back. It was a nightmare. Men were lying in the corridors being treated for cuts and burns and bruises, many in terrible pain. He saw several sheet-covered corpses. Groans of pain seared through air that was already burned and foul. The decks were flooded. The ship was still at an obscene angle. Bell spoke to them as he passed, doing his best to restore confidence, but they all felt the angle, heard the depth. They knew.

Bell had to save his ship. It was his responsibility. Carter and Jamie were hurt. MacKenzie was unconscious. No matter what he felt, it was up to him now. He ordered three unhurt crewmen to follow him to the engine room, where he ripped at the manual control valves for the stern planes. The blast had jammed the planes in a down angle. They had to pump them back up manually.

"Parker, with me," he said to one young mate with a blond crew cut. "You two get the other one."

"One hundred sixty feet," came Carter's voice over the PA, tight with pain. Bell was amazed he was still functioning. The noise of the engines became a loud whine as they strained in full reverse.

"One hundred seventy feet."

They pulled at the control valves heroically. Bell's muscles felt like they were ripping. The planes moved an inch. They were making progress, but it was slow.

"Two hundred feet." Even the intercom couldn't mask how pained Carter sounded. They were well below the depth at which the pumps could keep up with the flooding.

Bell pumped. Nothing was going to take this ship from him. If he had to swim it home, he would. This was what he had seen in MacKenzie and never fully understood till now, that beyond effort there is only a tenacity of will. Never giving up. Never stopping. The sea could hurt him, but it couldn't make him surrender. It would have to kill him for that. The hull popping grew louder. The planes moved another inch.

"Two hundred feet." Carter's voice held a tentative note of hope.

"Planes at zero," Parker said.

The muscles in Bell's arms and legs were on fire. They fought the planes up another inch.

"We're slowing! One hundred ninety feet!" Carter's voice was jubilant. "One hundred eighty! All stop. All ahead two thirds."

They fell to the deck, exhausted, gulping air. They had done it. Bell felt blessed relief. Not Ahab. Not any longer. No more curse. The ship was dying, and he had saved it.

"We gonna make it, sir?" Parker asked.

Bell clapped him on the back. "You bet we are."

Bell made his way forward. Men cheered. Everything seemed fresh and new, as if he had died and been reborn. This time, worthy.

They gathered in the wardroom. Bell was cut and bruised. Doc had treated his head wound and set the break in Carter's leg with an air cast and given him enough painkillers to anesthetize the fleet when he refused to come off duty. Flynn's movements were constricted, and every cough racked his body with pain, but he also refused to go to his bunk. MacKenzie was still unconscious in his cabin. Doc had bandaged him and treated his head injury as best he could, but concussions were tricky. The degree of damage was only a guess without an MRI scan. They couldn't MedEvac him to a hospital till radio communications were restored.

"We're a pretty sorry lot," said Flynn wryly.

Bell drank some coffee. The warmth soothed his parched throat. "Here's the picture. We've got two thirds power. No offensive weapons. Sonar's got about half the hydrophones left, but communications is out, and Avilov's got a three-hour head start to Sabaña Key."

Carter laughed without humor. "What's the good news?"

"We're alive," said Flynn.

"I'd say that about covers it," agreed Bell.

"What I want to know is where Avilov went," mused Flynn. "And why the second sub?"

Bell was thoughtful. "Let's conjecture a little. I've been thinking. The captain assumed the *Adri* was a watchdog to help the *Star.* But what if the Libyan sub wasn't a watchdog at all, but a *guard* dog to make sure Avilov finished his run to Sabaña Key? He had the drop on the *Star,* so Avilov drew us here by popping up in the AUTEC range, and when we came to investigate he fired on both of us. It takes us a while even to figure out he's gone and we're fighting the *Adri.* While we play tag with each other he makes his final run."

"Through the Morey Pass," said Carter, eyes bright with understanding.

"What?"

"Back in the conn I kept saying to myself there was no way he could have gotten around Cay Sal so quickly," Carter said. "Not without some noise. Well, I don't think he went around. He went *through.* We've got Morey Pass listed on our charts, and he probably does on his."

"Through Cay Sal? I've heard guys say they thought it could be done," said Flynn.

"Which makes it pretty damn likely Avilov would," said Bell.

"Can we catch him?" wondered Flynn.

"No way to tell," said Carter. "He might pick up more time, he might lose some. It can't be smooth sailing in there."

"Under normal circumstances going after Avilov would be Captain MacKenzie's call, but he's out of commission, and we can't radio COMSUBLANT for orders," said Bell. "We have wounded on board, including the captain, and the ship is badly hurt. We're the senior officers. I think we should take a vote. Jamie?"

"I want Avilov for what he did to us," Flynn said defiantly. "I say go."

Carter nodded tightly. "I've got a lot to atone for. Maybe this way . . ." He shrugged. "You understand, Mark. Go."

Bell grinned. "All right, I say we go, too." He hesitated. "Just one more thing. We need a CO. With the captain down we don't have one."

Flynn gave Carter a meaningful look. Carter nodded.

"Yes, we do, Mark," he said quietly.

They surfaced the ship in the darkness and held burial services on deck. One by one the dead were laid to rest in the glistening sea. Up on the sail Bell watched them go with deep sadness. He had learned many things since coming to Andros Island. Foremost among them was the deep humility men who command must have, for their mistakes, for their losses, for their isolation. He wished MacKenzie would awaken. He needed his advice and his solace.

The moon was a pale, bright disk lighting a channel through the sea. The silver waters were calm and smooth all the way to the horizon. Bell addressed the ship's company over the MC channel.

"This is the captain speaking. We have come a long way together in a short time. Our ship is battle-scarred, and we are weary, but we have a mission, and I plan to complete it. I know that's asking a lot of you who have already given so much, but you are navy. That is reason enough. Captain out."

Chapter Twenty-eight

Camelot

THE DARK WATERS OF THE NICHOLAS CHANNEL AT NIGHT swirled around *Camelot*, still mated to *Augusta*'s escape trunk. Scotti had brought them as deep as he could into the winding inlets and tiny islands comprising Sabaña Archipelago. With dangerous shallows ahead it was time to let the SDV do what it was designed for.

"Ready to disengage," radioed Jessica. Justine, Lee Jackson, and Pepper Torres squirmed in their cocoonlike seat pods. They had all donned wet suits in the sub.

"Ten seconds to release," radioed back the conn. "Safe trip, *Camelot*."

"Roger, *Augusta*." Jessica applied power, and they broke away from the sub. She had to go slow in the darkness. *Camelot*'s lights only gave them about twenty feet of forward visibility, barely illuminating the bottom rises. She was sweating after ten minutes, but they completed the first mile of their journey without incident. One mile to go. Moonlight began to filter down as the water got shallower. Jessica checked their heading. She was piloting by dead reckoning. When she was closer to the island she was going to surface and get a visual fix.

She was concentrating so deeply she jumped when Justine put a hand on her arm. She pointed to the surface. "There."

The bottom of a surface craft was clearly visible in the glare of its own searchlights. It was trailing a small wake, going no more than two or three knots. Jessica cut the forward floods instantly.

"Too big for a fishing boat," said Jackson, craning upward. "Patrol boat. That bulge in the hull looks like a hydrophone pod."

Justine frowned. "Can it hear us?"

"I don't know," said Jessica. "They're damn close."

"It's stopping," said Torres, worried. Beams of light slashed through the water like swords.

"How deep is this water?" Justine asked.

"Sixty feet."

"Bottom us out," said Justine. "Fast."

Jessica took them down. The crunch sent up a cloud of silt. They would be impossible to distinguish from the reef itself. The patrol boat remained overhead.

Justine looked up to the surface. The lights were still visible. "Let's talk options," she said.

Northern Star

"We're coming out of the tunnel, Pari," said Pachenko.

"Slow to one third," Avilov ordered. The three-mile tube had been almost as nerve-racking as the Valley of Currents. Several times it made tortuous turns, and he thought the *Star* might be stopped. Sometimes they had only inches of clearance. The *Star* slid into the Canyon of Skulls, a vast water-filled cavern lined with jagged spires leading up to a roof of stalactites. He could feel how huge it was.

"Up ten meters. Right ten degrees rudder."

He wished he had eyes to see this unique world within a world. They would have to see without light, though, for none penetrated here. The fish, if there were any, would be stark white, as alien to the surface as the surface was to the moon.

"Up five more meters. Right ten degrees rudder. We're coming to a turn."

Avilov quested out. The sonar pings were like his heartbeat. One beat at a time. Pulse, echo . . . pulse, echo . . . pulse, echo. And suddenly they told him of the danger ahead.

"All stop," he ordered.

"What's wrong, Pari?" asked Pachenko.

"The cavern, it just . . . ends."

"It can't."

Avilov shook his head. "I can't see a way out. There is a huge wall . . . and then it ends."

"Pari," said Pachenko desperately, "there's not enough room to turn in here. And we don't have the time to back out even if we could. Can you tell me what you see?" asked Pachenko.

"Ahead the canyon walls slope down to a great wall. It is . . . not smooth. It is . . . pitted. I can hear one, two—no . . . four great depressions. Yuri, is there a current in here?"

Pachenko checked. "Yes, two knots. So there must be an opening if the water is passing through."

"Yes, and the more I hear . . ." Avilov let his mental picture build. "The four holes are arrayed two above and one in the middle and one below. Do you see it?"

"Like the eyes, nose, and mouth of a face or a skull!" said Pachenko triumphantly.

"But which one leads out?" wondered Avilov. "Each of them feels like it ends in a stone wall just inside. Which one goes through, and how?"

It was maddening to be so close to the end and yet unable to move. Avilov could not discern which cave to take the *Star* into. And it was too easy to damage the propellers backing out if they chose the wrong one. The empty grinning eyes of the skull mocked him. They could try to clear the way with a torpedo, but the resulting explosion might bring half the mountain down and seal them in this cavern forever.

"Pushkin, give me the narrowest beam possible and scan the far wall. Begin with low setting and bring it up to maximum power slowly."

Pachenko regarded Avilov listening to the sonar pings. He was no longer a sighted man. He felt/heard the sonar pings as if they emanated from *his* brain. A transformation had taken place before his eyes. Avilov was no longer a hawk with keen, penetrating vision soaring in daylight. He was a bat gliding through an endless night, screeching his sounds to return to sensitive ears, blind and alone.

For hours Avilov sat in almost cataleptic silence. Finally he began to mutter. At first it was unintelligible, a kind of singsong hum of rising and falling tones; then Pachenko realized with a start that he was actually singing what he was hearing. The differences in pitch were the differences in the echoes coming back to him.

It came to Pachenko that he envied Avilov's blindness for the sight it had given him.

"Yuri?" Avilov's voice came from far away.

"Here, Captain."

"It is going to be a close thing. Have Stepov prepare a course for the right eye."

"Our right, or the skull's?"

"The skull's. There is a subtle difference there. I cannot describe it."

Stepov bent to work. The man standing on the periscope station was his old captain, yes, but since telling them he was blind, he was also something more. How could a blind man be capable of all this? He seemed more linked to the supernatural than to the human. He was glad Avilov spoke to Pachenko to speak to him. He didn't know how to respond to a god.

"I have our course, Senior Lieutenant."

"Lay it in, Stepov." Pachenko moved to the engineering controls. "On your order, Captain."

"All ahead one third. Steady as she goes."

The *Northern Star* moved forward in the black crystal cavern with its blind captain at its helm.

"Another five-meter rise," ordered Avilov. "Left five degrees rudder."

"Fifty meters to the canyon wall," Pushkin called out.

"Left five degrees rudder. Maintain trim."

"Twenty meters."

"Steady as she goes. Yuri, I want you on the helm. Prepare to pivot hard right as fast as she'll turn. Don't stop for anything, no matter what you hear."

"Yes, Pari."

"Five meters . . . we are entering the cave."

It would have been a sight to see the hundred-and-thirteen-meter length of the *Northern Star* sail into the cave in the face of the undersea cavern. Avilov could feel the bow slide in. He had picked well. There was space. But ahead, abruptly, a wall of solid stone. In less than a hundred meters the cave ended. There had to be a turn. It had to be as he pictured. But which way? Right or left?

"Captain!" Pushkin was yelling. "Obstruction ahead."

"Silence, Ivan." It was Pachenko's voice, cutting like a whip.

"But—"

"Remain at your post."

Avilov felt the opening at the last second. "Hard right rudder, Yuri. Turn her!"

The *Star* made a raucous shriek scraping against the walls. Stony projections dragged along her hull until the men inside grabbed their ears and believed for certain that the rocks must claw the *Star*'s belly open.

"Maintain speed," ordered Avilov.

The scraping went on till there could not have been an inch of hull tile left, till surely even the most fragile further touch would expose her to open ocean . . . and then the *Northern Star* slid out of the cave in the mountain and into the final channel leading to the clear green sea.

"Captain?" Pushkin was awed. "We are through the canyon. Almost to the sea outside. We made it."

"You all did very well," said Avilov tiredly. "Pari, I will be in my cabin. I need to rest. Lay in a course for Sabaña Key."

Pachenko knew Avilov couldn't see the salute, but he made it anyway. "Yes, Captain."

Chapter Twenty-nine

Sabaña Key

MISHA AVILOV FISHED WHERE THE BIRDS GATHERED OVER THE water, the way his father taught him. He had already caught several good-sized ones. A lithe, raven-haired boy of sixteen, Misha was glad this day of two things. His married sister, Vascha, had not come on this trip, and his father would be here soon.

He shot a quick glance back to where his mother and the Arab were sitting on the beach talking. He felt no danger from the man, so he was content to fish quietly, enjoying the solitude, a trait he shared with his father.

Down the beach Epstein knew that Misha was watching him and Katcha. The boy was protective of his mother, just enough to make Epstein like him. He could see Katcha in her son. Her eyes and smile. The father's gift was probably the posture and carriage. It would have been a pleasant day for Epstein with this surrogate family if not for the urgency of the *Star*'s arrival. Less than a day left till Avilov got there. Fancy planning was out. He needed an ally if his plan was to work, so he waited till the boy moved down the beach and then took the unprecedented step of telling Katcha Avilov everything, including who he was.

True to his estimate of her, she had not broken down or run away like some frantic schoolgirl. She had listened attentively, and when he had finished she sat deep in thought for a long time.

"How can I know any of this is true?" she asked him.

"There is one simple way to find out," he said. "Tell Sayid what I just told you, and I will be dead before morning. Will that be proof enough?"

"If it's true, you know I can't go to Sayid. But you, Israeli?"

"Hath not a Jew organs, senses, dimensions, passions?"

"Don't mock me. I know that. It's Shakespeare."

Epstein looked at her closely. "Tell me you haven't wondered why you're here on this island."

She shrugged. "I'm a military wife. I've met Pari at bases before."

He reached into his pocket. "You know Sayid's voice?"

She nodded.

"Listen." He clicked on the tiny Dictaphone.

"What about the Avilov woman and her friend?"

"In due time . . . we'll get to them after the husbands are gone."

He felt her grow cold. There was a silence on the tape for a moment, then he heard himself ask, *"What's the word on the Northern Star?"*

"Get your wire transfers ready, or however it is you pay out the exorbitant sums of money you're trusted with. Avilov will be here any day now according to Fasah."

"We're reaching big now, aren't we? A nuclear submarine. I thought our leader had given up trying to beat the Americans at their own game. Next time he might be in his tent when they send one of their smart bombs in."

"It's a new era. Desert Storm taught us one thing."

"How to get Arab asses kicked?"

"Start and don't stop. If Hussein had taken Riyadh, we'd be telling half the world what to do now."

He stopped the tape. "Enough?"

"But—"

He held up a hand. "Yes, I could have faked it. You can edit things like this. It could be a test. Katcha, I swear I'm trying to save your life. I'll even do my best to help your husband. But that sub has got to be destroyed first. You're the only ones who aren't watched too closely. Now decide."

Her hesitation vanished. "All right, I'll help you."

He was taken aback. "Just like that?"

"My husband always says you must count on your own judgment. As you say, any proof you offer could be faked. So what I have to decide is about *you*. Can *you* be trusted."

"And?"

"I think you can."

"Why?"

Her eyes bored into him. "Because I see how lonely you are, how much you would like to think of Misha as yours. And me." She said softly, "I can feel it. I'm sorry, but a woman knows."

Epstein turned away. "You're embarrassing me."

She touched his hand. "I don't mean to. You are very unselfish. You have given up a family to be what you are. That is why I trust you, because I feel you want the best for us."

"You're a remarkable woman."

"I don't think so. But Pari has taught me a lot over the years."

She turned to watch Misha reel in yet another fish. "Tell me what you want me to do."

Camelot

"Remember to breathe out all the while you're ascending," Jackson advised, "or you'll burst your lungs."

Justine said darkly, "Last time out it was a camel, then an F-15, now this. I get back, I swear I'm walking. Jessica?"

237

"I know. As soon as I surface I'll make straight for the beach and wait like you said. Even though I'd like to go with you."

"The beach," Justine said firmly. She adjusted the knife strapped to her calf. This close in they'd have to take the boat quietly. It eliminated a threat and presented a transportation advantage they couldn't pass up. "Lee, Pepper?"

"Any time, boss."

"Okay, Jess," Justine said. "Crack it."

One of the hardest things Justine had ever done was to wait while the seawater flooded over them. Every instinct rebelled at letting it happen, every nerve screamed for her to get out and scramble to the surface. The water creeping up her body felt like cold and clammy hands. Jessica was handling herself well, holding her head up inside *Camelot*'s top half to get the last air before making the ascent.

"Now," said Torres. "Push."

They shoved *Camelot*'s upper half hard, and the craft split like a clamshell. Justine pushed out and waited till she saw Jessica emerge and kick upward, trails of bubbles streaming from her nose and mouth, before doing the same.

Justine's lungs were exploding by the time she broke the surface, but she forced herself to breathe quietly, treading water in the shadows. Jackson and Torres surfaced without a sound next to her with the waterproof weapons bags. Jackson had a silenced pistol in his wet suit.

The patrol boat sat quietly in the moonlight, an eighty-footer with a bridge amidships, a forward cannon, and twin machine guns mounted on the afterdeck. Justine pointed to her watch and signed five minutes. She waved Jackson to the other side, Torres to the stern, and drew a finger across her throat. They nodded and slid under the water, moving off as sleekly as their acronym.

Justine readied herself for action. Old fears rose as she struggled to become the creature who had been forged in

238

wars since childhood. It wasn't so easy anymore. Civiliza-tion was more than a veneer, it was a series of increasing layers of guilts and inhibitions. Once she would have scampered over the side of the patrol boat and killed without a second thought. Now she thought of the men's families, of her own mortality, of not coming home to Mac.

She pushed those thoughts aside because they weakened her and she couldn't afford that now; she had to do her job. She sought the animal inside, the primeval fearing/hating thing that let her kill without remorse. Treading water in the moonlight, she became what she once was. Good-bye Mac and your talk of children. An inner heat ignited and she shed her civilized manner and became the leader of the Angel's Chorus, the children whose eerie screams frightened the hated National Guardsmen into running so the guerrillas could kill them; then later, the leader of an entire group, a trained killer, a violent revolutionary; and finally, the one the soldiers sang songs about by the firelight, who broke her brother out of the Sandinistas' jail with her machine gun blazing and rode out of Managua itself with half the army chasing her.

A different woman put her hands on the patrol boat. She got a foot up on a port, levered herself out of the water, and slid her fingers over the gunwale. She looked over the deck. Two sailors were smoking by the forward cannon. Four more in the wheelhouse, playing cards. Another one on the afterdeck by the machine guns, lying on some coils of rope strumming a guitar.

Jackson appeared on the other side of the boat. She pointed him to the cabin, herself to the foredeck. He nodded and dropped out of sight. She couldn't see Torres, but he would know without being told to take out the guitarist and anyone else in his area.

She pulled herself along the gunwale. Two men were dressed in Cuban military uniforms—caps, short-sleeved khaki shirts, pants bloused into black boots, side arms. Baseball gloves and a hardball lay on the deck. In the distance she could see Sabaña Key.

One finished a cigarette and flicked it into the water. It landed with a hiss. She rubbed her feet dry. She couldn't afford to slip on deck. The second man flicked his butt into the water. They talked in her native Spanish about their families, baseball, the stinking weather, and women. She drew the knife from her leg sheath and felt the comforting friction of its ribbed handle. One soldier took out his pack of cigarettes, gave one to his friend, and took one himself. He fanned his lighter into flame and held it between their faces. They leaned together to light up.

In that moment they were totally night blind. Justine went over the side and was moving on them before the first sailor had finished lighting his smoke. She grabbed the hair of the man closest to her from behind, yanked his head back, and drew her knife across his throat. Blood spurted from the artery, and he died with a helpless gurgle. She lunged at the other man, but he had recovered too fast. Her knife thrust missed. He reached for his gun.

Part of Justine's mind registered the sound of breaking glass and the soft *pfhut pfhut pfhut* of Jackson's silenced pistol, but she couldn't divide her attention. The soldier's gun was half out of his holster. She leapt forward to deliver a kick but slipped on the blood on the deck and went down hard. The soldier's gun swiveled toward her. She was about to execute a shoulder spring when she heard clearly, "Yo! Catch!"

The baseball came flying out of the darkness and the man instinctively reacted to it, taking his eyes off her for a split second. It was enough. Justine spun around on her hands as if on a pommel horse and slammed her foot into his knee. He shouted in pain and fell. She chopped him hard, and he lay still.

"Yer out," said Jessica Moran.

Justine sprang off the deck, furious. She caught Jackson and Torres's high signs. The boat was secure. "What the hell are you doing here?"

"Helping."

"What about my orders?"

Jessica wasn't cowed. "Look, I told you you've made a big impression on me. That day on the *Ortolan*. Watching you here. I want to be a part your mission. That's why I volunteered to drive the SDV. I saw a whole new set of options. Ones I never dreamed of. I think I can handle it. I'm a fine submarine commander. I'm a great pilot, too, but I'm ambitious. I admit it. Being a CO could be a good future for me. But I've thought about this. It's sexy what you do. Exotic. Mysterious. I think I might like to try it. When are you gonna see it? I want to try being *you*."

"Jesus," Justine said. "You're serious."

"I am."

Torres said out of the darkness, "That was a nice move with the baseball." He added hastily, "Not that you wouldn't have taken him, ma'am."

"You're both crazy. Lee, can you drive this boat?"

"Yes."

"Take us into the beach *now*."

"Yes, ma'am."

She turned back on Jessica furiously. "You shouldn't have disobeyed my orders."

"He was about to shoot you," she respond indignantly. "I don't expect thanks for that, but I don't think I oughta get my ass reamed for it either. You never disobeyed an order?"

Justine looked at her narrowly. "When I find the flaw in that, I'm going to be all over you."

"Fine," Jessica said coldly.

"Look, I'm just trying to get you through this," Justine said by way of reconciliation.

Anger flared in Jessica's eyes. "No, *you* look. I'd like you for my coach and all that, but if you expect me to be a good little girl who's going to cry when you yell, you don't know me very well."

"You have no formal training," Justine said, exasperated.

"Neither did you when you were my age."

Justine choked. *"Your age?"*

Jessica shrugged. "You get older, you forget a lot. That's what I figure."

Justine took several deep, calming breaths and decided to let her live. "Very well, then. Finish this man."

"What?"

Justine's voice was fierce. "You heard me. You wanna be one of us? It's more than throwing baseballs, girl. You think you could have gone into that cabin and pulled the trigger on four men whose only crime was that they're in your way? Or slit a man's throat and not be sickened by the blood all over you? How do you think their wives and children are going to feel when these guys don't come home? You think you can live with that?"

"Maybe. I don't know."

"Well, you're about to find out. You heard me. If you can't get your lily-white Anglo hands dirty, don't come to me and tell me you're like me. I do my own killing, thank you."

Jessica looked down at the man. The breeze ruffled her hair. She wiped the strands away from her face.

Justine said tersely, "You want the responsibility, you got it. Pepper, give her your gun."

"Ma'am, I—"

"Damn it, doesn't anybody follow orders around here? Do it."

Pepper handed his gun over.

Jessica hefted it and felt the power handguns convey. The great equalizer, the ultimate in control. She was familiar with guns. In her neighborhood they were a way of life. But always they were connected to some vague idea of self-defense in a harsh world. This was legal murder, sanctioned by her country, but murder nonetheless. Her emotions rebelled while her mind sought an answer. As a professional military woman she was just doing her job. Was there any moral difference between pulling the trigger of a battleship's sixteen-inch guns and killing this sailor? Here and now she had to make up her mind. What was the cost if this man got up and sounded the alarm, and if in sounding it Avilov's family died, and since they could not be rescued the *Northern Star* fell into Libyan hands, and what if the Libyans used its destructive power on the U.S., say, and her own family died? In the end, it came down to what you believed, and what you were willing to do to protect those beliefs. Justine was right about responsibility. Up until now she had just been a spectator. She felt a roaring inside her head.

Justine sneered and turned away. "I knew it."

The sound of the gunshot spun her around. Jessica's gun was smoking, and the man on deck was dead. Jessica stared wide-eyed as blood bubbled in the hole in the man and the full realization of what she had done hit her. She had ended a human life. The gun hung limply from her hand. Tears coursed down her cheeks.

Justine wanted to reach out to the girl to comfort her, but she was ashamed of herself and that made her vicious. "All right. It had to be done," she said harshly, "Go help Pepper dispose of the bodies."

"Fine . . . *ma'am.*"

Justine heard Jessica's contempt. The girl wiped her tears and bent down to help Torres drag the dead men away.

Justine walked into the wheelhouse, where Jackson had the controls. He flicked a switch and the engines throbbed into life.

"You did the right thing," he said quietly.

She stared out to sea. "Yeah? Then why do I feel so shitty?"

"It's a terrible thing to take away a person's innocence. Makes you feel the loss of your own. But you had to. She had to know. Now she does. It's not a game. Either she can live with that or she can't."

"I have to live with it, too."

"She did it for you," said Jackson, steering for the beach. "She wants your approval."

Justine's anger bubbled over. "Why is this on my head? Who the hell is she to appoint me God?"

"Can't you see it? You're her idol."

Justine cursed.

"She could do worse," Jackson said sincerely. "Look, it was her choice. Let her live with it a while."

Justine's voice betrayed her hurt. "Whoever said I had any choice?"

"Funny thing about that," Jackson said, cutting the wheel hard. He gave a friendly pat to the woman who had once saved his life. "The older I get, the more I realize how none of us do."

Pepper finished tying weights to the bodies. "This way they don't come to the surface and betray you. Got to do it."

"I'm gonna be . . ." Jessica reached the gunwale and threw up.

Pepper waited patiently and helped her clean up. The girl had balls.

"Don't feel bad," he said. "My first time I got the shakes so bad I started to cry."

"Yeah?"

He nodded. "Then somebody said to me, 'Pepper, you gotta remember something. Killing's not new. It's been around since time began. Remorse, that's new."

"You feel bad about it?"

"Sure. I'm human, too." He exaggerated a hurt face. "Didn't you think so?"

She laughed. It was a relief. Part of her had wondered if

244

she would ever laugh again. "I guess I just lost my other virginity, huh?"

"Just remember we're out here for a reason. It's a good one, too."

"I'll try."

"Take this gun. Better for you. Smaller grip. Browning 9mm. Thirteen rounds including one in the chamber. Safety's here. Change clips like this."

"Thanks."

"No sweat."

Jessica slid the gun into her wet suit. They were almost to the beach. "Excuse me," she said. "I gotta do something."

"Sure."

Before they moved onto Sabaña Key she wanted to go find a mirror and look into her eyes to see if anything had changed. She found one in a cabin below deck. They didn't seem to be different, but she was. Irrevocably.

She unzipped her wet suit and bathed her face and shoulders in cold water from the basin. She pulled her nylon tank suit down to wash her sweaty chest. She felt such a strange combination of things. Sadness, excitement, guilt, exhilaration. Her heart was racing. She remembered the sound the silenced gun made, soft in the night.

"Jess, I came down to see if . . ."

She turned. Pepper Torres was standing in the doorway. He met her eyes. She made no move to cover herself.

". . . if you were okay," he finished. His wet suit was open. His muscular chest rose and fell.

"I feel . . ." she started.

He came over to her. "I know. It does something. Lights a fire." He kissed her deep and hard.

"Do it," she whispered. "Now."

They tumbled onto the bunk. His hands roamed freely about her body, and hers did the same. A panther in her belly awakened and slowly uncurled and extended its claws.

Her eyes were bright with it. Her breathing grew quicker. His hand drifted lower, stroking, stoking. Her hands found him, and she gave out a little gasp of pleasure.

They tottered on the edge. She laced her fingers in his dark hair. His head was fuzzy, filled with her. His hard member had a life of its own. She pressed her lips to his and drew him to her, and they tumbled over the edge.

Chapter Thirty

Jacksonville

THE FLOODING WAS SECURED, AND REPAIRS WERE COMPLETE.
Bell made a trip around the ship to check their final status.
They had no weapons or communications, but sonar was
working tolerably well, and he could get full power if he
needed it. They remained on the surface long enough to
recharge the air banks, then ran submerged to the other side
of Cay Sal to try to pick up *Northern Star*'s trail.

"Make our depth three zero zero feet, Mr. Randall. Sonar,
full sweep."

"Sonar, aye."

Bell turned back to the plotting station. "What do you
think, Reg?"

Carter was still studying the charts. "Hard to say. It all
depends on what he found in there. We're fifteen miles from
Sabaña Key now. There's twelve miles of deep water, then
the shallows. If he's had two hours lead he's already there. If
not, he'll be coming soon."

"Plot us a course for the middle of that twelve-mile zone.
We'll remain on station there."

"Aye, sir."

247

Flynn pointed to his downed fire control boards, frowning. "He picks us up and we're sitting ducks, Mark. We couldn't throw a towel at him."

"The battle group shouldn't be more than twenty miles northwest of us," suggested Carter.

"Transit time?" asked Bell.

"Two hours there, two back. Avilov would be long gone."

Bell felt the never-ending weight of command again. "Reg, take the conn. If there's any change, call me at once."

"Okay, Mark."

The door to MacKenzie's cabin was closed. Bell knocked and pushed it open slowly. The lights were dimmed, and Doc was sitting by the captain's bunk. MacKenzie's head was bandaged. He was still unconscious.

"How is he, Doc?"

"Concussions are funny things, sir. I get the feeling he's trying to come awake but just can't seem to make it."

"I'll watch him for a while."

Doc left the cabin. Bell pulled a chair next to MacKenzie. He was quiet in repose, only an occasional tightening of his facial muscles, or his mouth would move as if he were trying to say something. It was like Doc said—like he was trying to wake up.

Bell leaned closer and spoke quietly, giving vent to the feelings he had hidden from the others.

"Sir, I don't know if you can hear me, but I've got some decisions to make, and I'm not sure what to do. Jamie and Reg say I'm the one to be in charge, but frankly, I don't know. I already lost to Avilov once. Maybe somebody else should try this time. Besides," he said grimly, "no matter what I come up with, we've got no weapons, nothing to stop him with. This guy's the best. I'm nobody. Even with the handoff when the torpedo was chasing us I had you there to fall back on. Who am I kidding? I should be running for help."

Bell ran a hand over his face tiredly. "But . . . sir, I got an idea. I don't know if it makes sense. It could cost us everything. I wish I had you to talk to. The only thing we got left is the ship itself. She deserves better than what I have in mind. Better than me, sir.

"If this were the movies, you'd wake up now and tell me what to do. Give me some clue so I'd see how to do it right. But like you said, practice is over. I got to call my own shots. You taught me a lot, sir, but no one can teach you what this is like. I guess you knew that. Whatever happens, I want you to know how much I appreciate the chance to prove myself. I wasn't sure after what happened in Australia anyone would ever believe in me again, or that I'd believe in myself. But you did. So I'm gonna give it one last shot. Whatever happens, I'll try to deal with it like you would, sir. He won't pass us. Not this time."

Bell reached over and adjusted the covers. "That's about it, sir, I guess. Thanks for the talk. Doc?"

The door opened. "Here, sir."

"Stay with him."

Northern Star

Avilov's darkness was complete. Not a pinpoint of light showed in his field of vision, but he was satisfied. A few more miles to Sabaña Key. His Atlantic run was almost over.

His plan was simpler now, of necessity. He would anchor off the key and bargain with Lerner. The *Star* for their families. Once they had been released to Pachenko and flown to safety, Avilov would set the self-destruct detonator on the *Star* and stay on board till Pachenko radioed him they were all safe. Then he would blow the ship. His own death couldn't be helped. They were too few to do anything else.

Pachenko had objected at first, then seen it was the only way.

He had to admit, though, it had been a hell of a run. He was the master of his craft. Past the *Augusta* and the carrier group. The *Adri* gone. The *Jacksonville*. In a way it was fitting to end it now. What could he ever do to top this? Half the American fleet had tried to stop him and couldn't. He had played tag with whales, rammed a carrier, and sailed through an undersea mountain. The Hawk had beaten them all.

"Pushkin, area scan."

"Nothing, sir. Small diesel noise. Surface boat one mile ahead."

Avilov ignored it. "Stepov, make course for Sabaña Key. All ahead two thirds."

Jacksonville

On the surface Bell heard the words that electrified the conn.

"Conn, sonar. Contact bearing one eight zero. It's the *Northern Star,* sir. We have a good solution. Speed twenty knots. Range one mile. Depth two zero zero feet."

"Two zero zero feet, aye," responded Randall.

Bell tried to slow his racing pulse. His trick had worked. He turned to those in the conn. "Here's where we pay him back. Jamie, take the helm."

"Helm, aye."

"Reg, plot us an intercept course."

"Coming up."

"Mr. Danvers, secure the emergency diesel and prepare to submerge the ship."

"Ship rigged for dive, sir. Straight board."

"Maneuvering, stand by to answer all bells in twenty seconds. I'm going to want a flank bell in a hurry. No matter what, keep that reactor on line. This boy is fast."

"Maneuvering, aye. We can deliver, skipper."

"Diesel secured, sir."

"Very well. Mr. Randall, submerge the ship. No noise.

Use only the auxiliary pumps. Make our depth two hundred feet."

"Two hundred feet, aye. Go get him, Captain."

Bell felt an adrenaline rush and his mind was running at fever pitch as the *Jacksonville* dived. Avilov was crafty. He had beaten everyone by doing the unexpected. Bell had figured he'd have to come up with something totally original to beat the Russian, and it looked like he had. Avilov logically expected pursuit underwater. Submarines were faster there, better able to maneuver. So Bell surfaced the *Jacksonville,* secured the main engines and turbine generators, and ran the ship on her emergency diesel alone to shadow his presence. All the *Star*'s sonar could hear was another one of the countless diesel engines that ran fishing boats all over the area.

"Contact one thousand yards," called sonar. "Still on course."

Bell kept the *Jacksonville* dead quiet, all her systems shut down. "Prepare for all ahead slow. No cavitation. We'll come in astern of him. Sonar, prepare to go active. Max power. Continuous ping."

"Sonar, aye."

Bell gripped the steel railing. It was all or nothing. If the *Northern Star* heard him and fired, the *Jacksonville* was dead. He was committed. He had given MacKenzie his word, chosen his course, and made his bet. He would not turn back. Ten seconds more, he prayed silently. Give me ten seconds, God. Then not all the power in the world could protect the *Star*. Ten seconds more and Avilov would be beaten.

"Contact is passing five hundred yards off our bow. Heading one eight zero. Speed twenty knots."

Bell's fist tightened. "Helm, hard right full rudder, come to course one eight zero and stay in his baffle. All ahead full."

"Helm, aye. All ahead full."

Bell made the plan. Carter called out the course. Flynn steered it. The *Jacksonville* turned in behind the *Northern Star* and charged toward its stern.

"Sonar, go to max power. Continuous ping. All ahead flank."

"Sonar, aye."

The *Jacksonville* picked up speed. Sonar beams at full power shot out and raked the *Northern Star*.

"Mr. Flynn."

"Twenty yards to his stern and closing, Captain."

I am a pilot. I scratch my head with lightning and purr myself to sleep with thunder. Sired by a hurricane, dam'd by an earthquake.

Bell said, "Ram him."

Northern Star

The screech of the sonar beams raking the control room set teeth on edge like nails along a blackboard.

Avilov grabbed his ears in pain. "Sonar, what can that be?"

Mishkin's panicked voice called out, "Captain, it is the American submarine *Jacksonville*. Directly astern. We never heard them."

In that moment Avilov knew two things. First, that the Americans had beaten him around Cay Sal, and second, that the final round went not to him but to the captain of the American ship. The *Jacksonville* had taken the *Adri* and then come around Cay Sal fast enough to set this trap for him. The diesel up above. It had to be. It was damn clever. He was a man of honor, too. Signaling his presence gave them a few seconds' warning.

"All ahead flank. Sound the collision alarm. Yuri, shut all watertight doors. We are about to be rammed in the——"

The shock when the *Jacksonville* rammed them threw Avilov to the deck. There were cries of pain as they were tossed around like rag dolls. Systems shorted out, hydraulics shut down completely. The stern hull crumpled like paper, and the engineering compartment flooded. The reactor shut down automatically. Emergency lighting went on as the power failed. All the electrical systems went down, including their ability to shoot torpedoes. In one brief instant the *Star* went from a healthy ship to a floating hulk as she lost her motive power forever. Crippled, her stern dropped, and she filled with water.

Avilov floundered on the deck in his own internal darkness. "Yuri," he yelled. "Yuri, come help me. We have to save her!"

There was no answer.

Jacksonville

"She's heading for the bottom, skipper," shouted sonar. "Propeller's smashed. Pumps on maximum. Heavy flooding. Reactor's down. There, she hit bottom *hard*. She's dead, skipper."

"We got her!" yelled Flynn jubilantly.

Carter gave out with a yell as cheers erupted all over the ship. "Way to go, Captain. Way . . . to . . . go!"

The *Northern Star* was finished. Ramming her at that speed had damaged her beyond repair. Her electronics would be fused solid and her aft ballast tanks crushed. It was impossible for her to shoot. She would never be a fighting ship again.

"Damage control reports," ordered Bell.

Danvers called in, heading the damage control party. "Flooding is secured, sir. But the forward sonar sphere is gone, and the vent valves for main ballast tanks one, two, and three are jammed and can't hold any pressure. I wouldn't count on much depth control, sir."

"Very well."

"Mark, we're too heavy," said Flynn at the main board

worriedly. "Maybe the forward trim tank is flooded. I recommend surfacing."

"We're still in Cuban waters."

"If we bottom out here, we might not get to the surface again. And we've got no radio."

For Bell it was another calculated risk. He understood what MacKenzie must have felt in those last few moments heading for the *Adri*.

"All right, surface the ship. Be ready to cap the main ballast tank vents manually so we can stay up if the low pressure blower can't keep up with the leak rate through the damaged tubes. Reg, plot us a course for the battle group. Let's hope we can sneak out of here as quietly as we snuck in."

Chapter Thirty-one

Sabaña Key

EPSTEIN WRAPPED THE TAPE HE HAD SMUGGLED OUT OF THE main house around two sticks of waterproof explosive and inserted a detonator. "You understand where these go?"

"On the posts. You showed me," Katcha said.

"They're radio controlled, all set to the same frequency. Hide the detonator in your room and don't blow the charges till I give you the command, your name, Katherine."

"That's my name?"

"In English."

She smiled. "I like it."

He measured her waist. "Pull up your shirt."

"Excuse me?"

"I need to see how many you can carry without looking pregnant." When she hesitated, he said, "You have a better way to get them to the pier?"

They were standing in the deserted work shack. Cases of explosive lay against one wall. Dust motes danced in the light filtering between the planks on the windows. It was quiet inside. The surf was a low rumble far away. Katcha had on a white cotton blouse without a bra. She bared her belly, modestly trying to keep her breasts covered, but he saw the swell of flesh under the rumpled cloth. That gentle curve aroused him and sent a sharp tingle across his scrotum. He tried to maintain a businesslike attitude, but this close to her his breath was coming hard. He laid the explosives flat against her skin and tucked them into the waistband of her skirt. The back of his hand brushed up against her breast.

His breath came faster through flared nostrils. Her sexual energy encompassed him. He put his fingers on her stomach, let them ride up to her breasts.

"Please, no," she whimpered. She felt his loneliness as one feels hunger, and it penetrated her defenses as no other emotion could have. She would have been blind to ploys, cold to the thought of any other man raising the love in her that Avilov had. She could not violate her trust. But the terrible emptiness of the man called her the way a mother is called by her hurt child. She felt . . . pity.

Epstein saw it in her eyes, and the pain of it made his hands drop away.

"Banker? Where the hell are you? Banker!"

Sayid's voice penetrated the shack like a knife blade. They broke apart. Her eyes were wide and frightened.

"Here. Quick." Epstein pulled her behind the crates and down on the dirt floor. She clutched her shirt closed. He slid his gun out. If Sayid came in here, he was going to kill him. He fantasized taking Katcha away to Israel. He had enough money. He could make a life for her. . . .

"Banker, damn it. Where the hell did you go?" Sayid muttered something too low for Epstein to hear. For a second the door rattled. Epstein had swept their footprints off the sand, but if Sayid looked too closely at the door, he would see the hasp was broken. He raised his gun. Katcha's eyes were wild and frightened. But the sound of Sayid's footsteps dwindled, and when he called again it was from far away.

Katcha broke into sobs.

"He's gone," Epstein comforted her. "We have to hurry now."

There were still tears in her eyes. "David, I'm so sorry. I can't—"

"Shhh, I know." He put a finger to her lips. "Forgive me. For a moment I thought . . ." He shook his head, still filled with her.

She kissed his cheek gently, and he took a lifetime of tenderness from it.

"Let's go. Sayid may come back."

"All right, David."

She stood and lifted her shirt again, but it was different this time. She couldn't go against her nature and still be the woman he had fallen in love with. She was Avilov's wife. Betraying him would damage a vital part of her. He couldn't do that to her. So he sealed himself up, and when he touched her again he was as cold and controlled as when he had shot the Mossad boy what seemed like eons ago.

And as sad.

Sabaña Key

Justine wasn't sure what was more distant, a cool breeze or Jessica Moran. It wasn't the first time she had fallen from grace, Justine reflected as she wiped her sweaty face. Just the one that seemed to hurt the most.

She and Jackson had run the patrol boat into a small cove and camouflaged it as best they could. They had gone over the terrain, and she had told them about the big snakes and the vicious little alligators Cubans called *caymans*. Jessica pretty much stayed with Pepper Torres. Justine was glad she was talking to someone. The girl was bold, she had to give her that. And fearless. Maybe she did have that rare combination of talent and skills and the mind-set that would let her survive in Justine's world. But it remained to be seen.

All four changed into combat fatigues and moved inland. The swamp was a steamy place of brackish water and trailing vines. They waded from dry hillock to hillock. Bugs ate their exposed skin, and a raucous buzz filled the air. After a mile or so Jackson held up a hand. The smell of cigarette smoke came in on the breeze.

"Cover," he said quickly.

Justine made sure Jessica was properly concealed in the hollow of a rotted tree and pointed a finger at the girl. "Stay put unless you see us come out. Move and you could kill us all. Got it?"

"Yes, ma'am."

Justine took a fix on Jackson's position and plunged into the undergrowth, drawing vines in to cover herself.

Birds screamed overhead. Insects made their buzz-saw sounds. The guard patrol walked into the clearing lazily. This was hot, boring work, and they showed no liking for it. One soldier had a burnoose over his head and shoulders, adapting the hooded cloak to the swamp. They were heavily armed. Justine caught Jackson's hand signal. *Take them?*

No, she signed. There were six, and they looked like pros. She didn't think they could do it quietly enough.

The men smoked and talked. One urinated. Another squatted against a tree to move his bowels. Long inactivity had made them careless, but there were still too many. Justine was concentrating on them so much, she almost missed the flash of movement above Jessica.

The boa constrictor's head was as big as a shoe box, and its body was as thick as her thigh. Jessica felt its touch against her shoulder, and it almost made her cry out, but she stifled it in time. The snake slithered down the tree and dropped over her shoulder. She fought the panicky urge to leap out and run. The snake moved around her body, completing one coil. Jessica grabbed the head and tried to fend it away. It was too strong. The forked tongue slithered against her cheek. She gagged, but the soldiers were only a few yards away, and she had been given an order. She stayed.

Justine didn't know how much Jessica could take. Constrictors were lazy killers, tightening their coils each time their prey inhaled till the animal couldn't expand its lungs any longer and died of suffocation. Then they devoured them whole. Jessica got an arm under the coils and tried to lever them off to give herself breathing room.

The soldiers were still lounging on the hillock. Justine raised her silenced pistol. She signed Jackson, *If I shoot, go.* The boa slid around Jessica's waist and completed a second coil. Unable to make any noise, Jessica was losing ground. Justine raised her weapon in a target shooter's stance. When the head appeared over Jessica's shoulder again she was going to shoot.

On the other side of the clearing the soldiers were packing up and moving off. It was going to be close. The first guard disappeared back into the brush. The insects were screaming. She wished she could get off a target round to see how the gun was sighted. The guard plunged into the dense undercover. Justine held her breath and sighted along the barrel, emptying her mind of everything but the image of the snake's head. Jessica's eyes fluttered closed. The last guard strode out of the clearing. Justine pulled the trigger.

The gun kicked softly, and the boa's head exploded. Justine plunged out of cover, but Torres got to Jessica first. He laid her on the ground and rinsed her face and hair with water from his canteen.

"She's okay," Torres said as he cleaned away the muck.

Justine holstered her gun.

"Tough kid," Jackson said admiringly.

"Leave us alone for a few minutes, okay?"

"Sure. We'll scout ahead." Jackson and Torres moved off.

Justine sat and put her arms around Jessica, who was coming to. She stiffened as the memory came back fully.

Panic surfaced in her eyes. This was what she got for killing that man. This was how God punished her, letting her be eaten by this terrible monster snake. Then realized she was safe, and her face crumpled, "Oh, God!"

Justine held her while she cried. "It's all over now."

"I didn't move," Jessica said. Sobs racked her.

"You were brave. I'm sorry." Justine felt tears leak from her own eyes.

Jessica quieted. Sub command seemed damn good about now.

"You okay now?" Justine asked.

Jessica looked around. The boa's thick carcass ended in ragged tatters. "You?"

"Yes." Justine pushed wet hair off her face. "Look, we have a lot of things to talk about. Hang on till we get back, okay? I wasn't wrong back on the boat. What I said was true. But you shouldn't have had to face it like that the first time. I'm sorry. I forgot. It was easy for me to tell Mac how to teach. First time you tried to show me what you have, I blew up."

Jessica sniffed. "I had it coming."

"You've done fine so far, better than anyone could have expected. You're damn tough. But this might help. Think of things this way: It's all inside. You have to learn to be naked *inside.*"

"I don't understand."

"Out here you give up all protection. No submarine, no DSRV, no grand tradition to give everybody a fine old glow. Just you and your business. Get the mission done and survive. It helps to be afraid of everything, 'cause that keeps you smart, but no matter what, you're naked. You came with nothing, you go with nothing."

"Nothing to lose, sort of?"

"Everything to lose. Nothing to regret. Not invisible. Naked. On the line. Think about it."

"I got a lot to learn."

"Maybe less than you think." Justine tousled her hair. "Now c'mon. These men get too far ahead it just makes 'em feel superior, and then they're harder to manage."

Jessica managed a weak smile.

Sabaña Base

Katcha Avilov got into the rowboat stiffly. The dynamite was a hard corset under her shirt. She was still unsettled by what had happened with Epstein. God, such hurt in him. Maybe she could have given him comfort. Was it a kind of love she felt? Did he represent another choice, one a different, younger girl might have made many years ago in a different place? Should she have slept with him? Maybe Pari would have understood just one trespass in all their years together. But she knew he wouldn't, just as she wouldn't. She went to help him as she had promised, leaving Epstein with pity only, and a deep and bitter pain smoldering in his eyes.

"Where you going, Mom?" Misha asked.

"For a quick ride. Go fish down the beach."

"Okay."

She rowed out along the pier. Halfway down, as Epstein had told her, she rowed underneath it into the shade of the big log pilings and tied up the boat. She brought out the first of the charges from under her shirt and taped it fast.

Misha saw her disappear under the pier and thought it was an odd place to take a ride, but he didn't concern himself further. The security guards were down the beach kicking a soccer ball around, and he decided to join in. He milled around them, waiting for an invitation, and when it came he plunked down his fishing rod and ran into the melee with his usual enthusiasm.

The ball came to him, and a soldier tried to take it. Misha

flicked it sideways with the side of his foot and dodged around the man, who tumbled into the sand. There was great laughter.

"Sayid, even the boy is faster than you!" yelled one.

"Shoot him if he does it again," spat Sayid. When Misha looked genuinely worried, he winked and clapped him on the back. "Good move, boy. Play hard."

Misha grinned. "That's what my dad says."

He got the ball again. It felt good to play in the hot sun, sweat dripping off his back. He moved up the beach. Suddenly he saw the goal open. He set up his shot and kicked it with all his might just as the man they called Sayid flung his body in between. The ball rocketed off his chest into the trees beside the beach. Men cheered.

"I'll get it," Misha shouted as the soldiers sank to the sand to rest.

He poked around trying to find it. It must be further in than he'd thought, he concluded. He crawled deeper through the underbrush and looked up, straight into the barrel of a gun held by a woman who looked almost as surprised as he was. Misha's father had taught him to shoot at the military range years before. He knew the long tube on the end was a silencer. He froze.

"Don't cry out," Jessica whispered. "We're friends." She didn't know what to do. She saw his indecision. Christ, it was bad luck. One second Justine, Jackson, and Torres were up in the trees counting guards and fixing positions for their strike, the next the boy came plunging through the brush. She knew Misha Avilov from his picture in the dossier. Logically, she should shoot him. One call and he would give them away. But how could she kill the boy they'd been sent here to rescue?

All of a sudden the boy was up and running. He would summon the soldiers on the beach. Her finger pulled back slightly on the trigger. She had him in her sights. One shot would bring him down—and she couldn't. She plunged after him. If she could just get to him, she'd have half their mission accomplished. She sprinted through the trees. Her legs were longer. She was just about to close on him when something hit her legs and she went down hard. When she recovered a man was holding an automatic pistol to her head.

"I am Sayid. One word . . ." He cocked the trigger.

Other men moved into the forest. Jessica opened her mouth to shout a warning, but the man hit her and things went far away. She heard a single shot, and then they dragged her forward semiconscious to where Justine, Pepper, and Jackson were surrounded.

Misha ran to Sayid, frightened. He patted Misha proudly. "You did well, Misha. These people are here to hurt your father and his fine boat."

Justine looked to Jackson but got a quick negative. There was no play they could make. *Stall.*

"We're here to rescue you, Misha," Justine said. "They plan to kill your mother and father as soon as they get his submarine."

"Quiet, liar," hissed Sayid. He took two steps forward and slapped her across the mouth. Justine went down and stayed down. No use getting hit again when she couldn't fight back.

"Bring them to the house," Sayid ordered.

Lerner lit a cigarette and regarded them curiously. Justine recognized him and al-Zawi from their CIA-supplied dossiers. She looked over the rest of the men in the room. Somewhere on the island they had an ally. He might even be here. She had to give him time and room enough to make a play.

They yanked her to her feet in front of Lerner. He said calmly, "Tell me why you're here."

She stopped trying to untie the knots binding her hands behind her back. They held fast. Across the big living room Jackson, Torres, and Jessica were covered by soldiers.

"Well, Frankie, we're damn sorry, but you can't have the submarine." She said it contemptuously, as if he were a slow child. "We just dropped in to tell you so."

Lerner's face didn't change, but al-Zawi exploded behind him. "You said this could not happen, Franklin. I will not pay a single dollar till—"

"Quiet, Fasah," said Lerner coldly. "She's bluffing. What's she going to say? That she got caught with her pants down by a sixteen-year-old kid and please don't shoot us?"

"The fleet is sitting off the coast of Cuba," Justine said. "Call Havana, see how they're taking the news. Blockade's nothing new for us, remember? You were probably a citizen back then, right, Frankie?"

His patience snapped, and he hit her again. She spit blood and smiled. "Temper shows inability to cope with the situation."

Lerner looked at her, and a mean little light went on in his eyes. "You're here to hit the sub. That's it, isn't it? Avilov was too good for you. He's still on his way."

"Sub's dead," she lied. "We're here for you."

She saw she had finally gotten to him. It was one thing to abandon your country, another for it to pronounce a death sentence on you and send a team to carry it out.

"That isn't done. It's assassination," Lerner said.

"Snow White, that's my other favorite fairy tale, Frankie. Say bye-bye to all your pretty toys."

He hit her again, hard enough for Justine to decide she was winning on points and losing just the same. He would keep hitting her as long as she made smart-ass remarks. It was beginning to hurt.

Sayid turned to al-Zawi. "I don't think they stopped the submarine *or* came for Lerner. I think they came for the hostages." He grew more certain. "That's why they chased the boy instead of killing him. Maybe they want to use them to deter Avilov. So this changes nothing. Avilov will still come here for his family, and we will still dispose of them all when he delivers the *Star*."

A voice from the doorway cried, "She was right. *You* lied!" It was Misha, his face a mask of rage.

Sayid couldn't be bothered. "Get him out of here."

Misha was no cowed child. He came at Sayid with elbows and teeth and fists. Sayid cried out as Misha sank his teeth into his forearm, and he raised his gun to strike the child. The man who had spoken before grabbed the boy away.

"Get out now. Go," he said. Misha ran out crying.

"He bit me, banker," said Sayid angrily.

"Forget him."

Lerner looked his prisoners over, "I want to know what they know, Sayid, but keep them alive for now."

Justine had expected it. More than for herself or the SEALs, she was frightened for Jessica. They had been interrogated before, but Jessica . . .

"Just tell him everything," Justine said to her. "You hear me?"

The girl was terrified, she could see it.

Sayid was a pro. He knew. He took Jessica first.

Chapter Thirty-two

Northern Star

THE *NORTHERN STAR* WENT TO THE BOTTOM, CRIPPLED BY THE *Jacksonville*. Silence settled over the control room.

"I'm here, Pari," said Pachenko, lifting himself slowly off the deck. "Don't move."

"The ship . . ."

"We were rammed."

"Yes . . . I remember. The men?"

Mishkin was leaning heavily on his console. Vashovsky crawled out from under a fallen console. Pushkin's lifeless eyes stared out into space. A headphone cord from his console encircled his neck and had hung him when he fell. Stepov lay unconscious on the deck. Pachenko searched for equanimity in the face of death, tending to those left alive.

"Vashovsky and Mishkin are all right. Stepov is hurt. Pushkin is dead."

"I'm sorry," Avilov said.

"Can we raise her, Pari? There's still our families."

"What is our depth?"

Pachenko checked the gauge. "Seventy feet."

"Try the emergency pumps."

Pachenko threw the switches. "Nothing."

"Switch to auxiliary batteries."

There was a sudden vibration. "Emergency pumps working."

"Try the manifold air pressurization. Let's see what we can blow out of the tanks."

Pachenko moved with increasing energy. The ship was close to dying, but if anyone could blow a last breath of life into her, it was Avilov. "We're getting a response. It's working, Pari."

"Try to answer bell on the auxiliary motors," Avilov advised him.

Pachenko shifted power. The *Star* would never fight on the high seas again, but she shuddered and groaned and strained to get off the bottom. Seventy feet of water left only twenty feet above the sail. If the crash had not driven them too far into the sand, they might make it.

Pachenko said excitedly, "Pari, I think we can move her."

"Full pressure on all blowers," ordered Avilov. "Surface the ship."

Straining mightily, the crippled *Northern Star* rose from the bottom and broke the surface. The sun shone once more on her deck and the deep scars on her stern where the *Jacksonville* had rammed her.

"What's our speed?" asked Avilov.

"We can make three knots. Enough to get us in."

"Very well. Set the detonator now."

Pachenko left the conn only to storm back in minutes later. "Look at this," he demanded.

"Yuri."

"Sorry. I'm holding the self-destruct detonator. It's been sabotaged. You could pound on the charge till doomsday and it won't blow."

Avilov could barely believe it. "Lerner's last fence. The man is amazing. He's beaten me at every turn. Our families, the *Adri*, now this."

"What do we do?"

"What we must. Put Vashovsky, Stepov, and Mishkin in a life raft, but make them promise not to use the radio to call for help for two hours. You understand?"

"Yes."

"Tell them . . . tell them I never sailed with better men. And that someday we will see one another again. Then take me up to the bridge."

"Why?"

Avilov's face was set. "I swore we'd make it, Yuri, and so we will."

"But—"

"Have we come so far only for you to lose your faith?"

"No, Pari," said Pachenko softly. "Never that."

Pachenko helped the men into the life raft and told them what Avilov said. He extracted their promise in Avilov's name. He knew they would keep it. He saw them off with a final salute, then returned to the conn, where he worked the damaged sail hatch open and helped Avilov up to the bridge. After two weeks undersea the hot sun felt wonderful. Pachenko ran his fingers through his hair and opened his jacket to the breeze.

"Feels good," said Avilov.

Ahead an island grew out of the ocean, green and bountiful. "There's Sabaña Key," said Pachenko. "No one but you could have gotten us here, Pari."

But Avilov was lost in thought. *Sail the* Northern Star *into Sabaña Key by the first of July and you are a rich man. I give you my word your families will be waiting on the pier to see you surface.*

"Yuri, radio Lerner we are coming in."

Jacksonville

Bell took the ship to top surface speed. All he had left was reactor power, but at least he had enough of that. Standing in the sail bridge, he savored the awesome force of the

Jacksonville as it surged through the sea. At a full bell she buried her bow in the water, and the wave came halfway up the sail. The sound of it was like the crashing of a mighty waterfall.

So far the skies were clear. They hadn't picked up anything that indicated they were the target of hostile sonar or radar. If they could maintain this speed, they would rendezvous with the fleet outside Cuban waters in an hour.

"Mark?" It was Jamie on the bridge phone. "The captain's come to. He's asking for you."

Bell slid down the bridge ladder. The captain's door was open. He walked in to find MacKenzie weak but conscious.

"How is he, Doc?"

Doc shook his head. "Don't stress him."

Bell turned to MacKenzie. "Hello, sir."

MacKenzie managed a ghostly grin. "Mr. Bell, didn't we train you better than to run into things?"

"Like you said, sir. I made my bet. You were a good teacher."

MacKenzie fought to stay alert. Bell had done the job. The transformation was complete. A commanding officer stood in front of him. Old instincts died hard, but he had learned. The old order changes, yielding to new—and God fulfills himself in many ways. His eyes closed. "Get us home" was the last thing he said before sliding back into unconsciousness.

All in all Bell had about ten seconds of relief till the intercom sounded harshly.

"Captain to the conn. Enemy contact. Trouble, Skipper."

Bell ran.

Chapter Thirty-three

Sabaña Key

SAYID WAS ROUGH, BUT JUSTINE HAD BEEN THROUGH ROUGHER, and the security chief was under instructions not to kill them. He was just getting down to some serious work when one of his soldiers walked in and whispered to him. He shrugged and closed her shirt.

"It seems Mr. Lerner wants you in plain view in case we missed some of your friends. The *Northern Star* is coming in. If anybody tries to stop it, my men will execute you."

"Sorry our time together was so short."

"It won't be."

The soldier dragged her outside. Her hands were still bound, and her face hurt. Lerner and al-Zawi were already at the end of the long pier with Misha and Katcha Avilov and the senior lieutenant's wife and daughter. To all intents it looked like a parade reviewing stand. Except for the guards with their guns.

"Just a minute, Sayid," said the tall Arab who had gotten Misha out of the room earlier. He came over and spoke in low tones. Sayid grinned. "Thirty seconds, banker."

Together they pulled her around a tree. The Arab stepped up and kissed her hard. She tried to bite him. His hands were all over her. He held her head and licked her ears. He squeezed her breasts and reached down to feel between her legs. She tried to kick him, but he slapped her hard and had Sayid hold her legs while he explored her behind.

"Sayid, where are you?" Lerner was yelling for them.

"Come on," Sayid said. "That's all we have time for. Later. I promise, banker."

"Remember me," said the Arab.

Justine fixed him in her mind. "I will."

The gray dot on the horizon grew slowly at first. Lerner paced anxiously. This close to the fulfillment of his deal even he could not contain his excitement. Beside him al-Zawi saw his dream steaming toward them. This was power once undreamed of. Twenty yards behind them, very aware of the soldiers' guns, Irina Pachenko and her daughter Kara waited stiffly. Katcha Avilov held Misha to her, watching closely, whispering to him. She knew the odds her husband had fought to get here. He had come back to her, as he always had.

Justine was held back on shore with Jackson, Torres, and Jessica. Four men guarded them. Jessica stood on shaky legs. Her clothing was torn. They had been hard on her. Justine tried to get through.

"Hey, Skinny. You look beat."

Jessica squared her shoulders and grinned around a missing tooth. "So says the old broad."

Justine was relieved. She would be okay.

The *Northern Star* showed her dark sail as she made for the channel. She moved slowly. The guards and everyone stared at the sight of her churning toward the pier. Lerner looked like a triumphant merchant watching his cargo ship come home.

Justine used the knife the banker had put in her hands when he molested her to cut the ropes on her wrists. Jackson was watching her carefully. He leaned ever so slowly toward her.

There was cheering from everyone on the pier as the *Northern Star* made her grand entrance. Avilov waved from the sail. Senior Lieutenant Pachenko showed the Russian flag. The *Star* rolled in like the queen she was. Lerner smiled and waved. He pointed to the women and children like a showman. See? I kept my promise. Here they are.

"So, Fasah," Lerner said. "I told you it could be done. The *Northern Star* is yours. Please instruct your banker to release the money as soon as it docks. I will be going at once."

Al-Zawi was delighted. "Of course. I'll see you in Tripoli in a month, and we'll discuss our next order."

Lerner almost bowed. "My pleasure."

The *Star* was only a hundred feet from the pier now. Avilov blew his foghorn loudly. It sounded like a prehistoric monster come home to its final resting place. In that instant Justine knew what he was going to do, and she was already moving as the giant ship surged to its destiny, to dock and die on Sabaña Key.

Her foot lashed out into the soldier's rifle next to her, smashing it up into his face. She caught it as it fell and chopped sharply across his windpipe. Jackson spun and took out his man. Torres had already slammed the palm of his hand into his guard's nose. Blinded, the man spun into Jessica's knife. She gutted him, and Torres pushed him off the pier. Jackson grabbed the final guard, and his shout died in his throat.

But it was enough of a sound that Sayid heard it. They had gained precious seconds while everyone's attention was on the boat, but Sayid was fast. He had his gun out and his soldiers moving back down the pier at once. He turned his back on the submarine. It cost him dearly.

The *Northern Star*'s seven thousand tons shoved aside the pilings and rammed the pier, tearing it from the sea bed with a giant cracking sound. Men went flying. Lerner put up his hands as if he could possibly stop this monster, and it crushed him as he stood there. Al-Zawi was flung into the water along with Sayid. The bow of the *Northern Star* rode high up onto the pilings before crashing down and impaling itself on the pier. Smoke poured from its ruptured hull.

Justine, Jessica, Jackson, and Torres used the soldiers' guns to lay down a pattern of fire. Burning, the *Star* ignited the rest of the pier.

"Look," said Jackson.

Statuesque, Avilov remained in the sail, silent and unmoving, the ghost of a smile on his face.

Justine couldn't help but admire him. He had made it all the way. She wondered hastily what it meant for the *Jacksonville,* but Sayid and his men had regrouped on the splintered pier and were firing. They moved forward, ten in all, Sayid leading and al-Zawi, no coward, firing steadily.

Out on the pier Epstein saw Pachenko come around the submarine in a small boat. For the moment Sayid's attention was on the Americans. Epstein pushed Katcha and Misha and Pachenko's wife and daughter from behind a splintered piling to the edge of the burning pier. Katcha turned to him and looked into his eyes. In that moment she knew.

"No . . . you can't . . . please . . ."

Sudden gunfire plucked wood chips from around them. He pushed her into the water. Misha dived in after her. Irina and Kara followed. Pachenko pulled them into the boat and rowed away. For a moment the water beckoned to Epstein. He could make an escape. But when he looked to Katcha in the rowboat her eyes were on the *Northern Star,* on the sail where her husband still remained.

Epstein pulled back from the edge and climbed over the broken pier onto the *Star*'s deck. Bullets plucked at him. The fire was spreading. The ship would soon explode. He went up the sail ladder and pulled himself into the bridge.

Avilov looked at him with sightless eyes. "Who's there?" he asked. "I'm sorry, but I can't see."

The enormity of it staggered Epstein. Blind? And still capable of all this? "You must come now," he said. "Your ship is burning."

"Will you help me?"

Could God have a drier sense of humor? The man possessed the only thing in this life Epstein had ever truly wanted. One push and . . .

Epstein said, "I'll help you."

He led Avilov over the sail and down onto the deck. Pachenko saw them and swung the boat around.

"Swim," Epstein said, "For her." He pushed Avilov into the water.

Sayid saw the rowboat and fired on it. Epstein rushed back onto the pier, grabbed a fallen gun, and fired back. Sayid's face registered his confusion, but there was no mistaking a bullet. He fired at Epstein as Epstein crawled over the broken planks to get to a better position.

Back at the foot of the pier Justine said, "There are too many. We're losing it."

Jackson's gun clicked empty. "That's all she wrote." He drew the knife and lay waiting.

Torres fired till his hammer fell on an empty chamber.

Jessica sent Justine a death's-head grin and dropped her empty rifle. She yanked a pistol from a dead guard. She understood. Naked *inside*. Clean. Clear. Whatever happened.

"Wouldn't have missed it, ma'am. Let 'em come."

Justine looked at her with fierce pride.

Sayid felt their fire wither and rallied his men to charge, but Epstein fired steadily, keeping them pinned down. Sayid stood and fired. A bullet passed through Epstein's shoulder and spun him into the sharp end of a plank. It speared through his leg. Blood poured from him. He managed to raise himself to his full height, dying as he stood. Sayid fired again.

"Kather*innnnnne!*"

Two hundred yards away Katcha Avilov closed her eyes and pressed the detonator.

The pier erupted in a burst of explosive fury, sending Sayid and al-Zawi and their soldiers to their deaths. An orange-red fireball rolled two hundred feet into the sky. The *Star* lifted into the air, cracking its keel in half, falling back with an enormous crash onto the burning timbers. It was the final funeral pyre for the *Northern Star* and her enemies.

Justine stood in the silence. Pieces of debris floated back to earth. The air smelled scorched. Jessica wiped her sweaty face. Jackson and Torres swung back to make sure there were no other soldiers.

"The pier, the way it blew . . ." Jessica said aloud.

"We have more to thank the banker for than just a knife at the right time," she said. "He was a brave man."

Jessica said with a sense of wonder, "I didn't think we'd make it."

Justine put an arm around her. "That's how it plays sometimes." The pier was a sheet of flame now. "Smell how sweet the air is, even with the burning? How clear you feel?"

Jessica understood. "Everybody came back."

Justine nodded. "This time."

The rowboat slid onto the beach. There was a lot of hugging and kissing and tears. It might not always be so clean.

"Let's go home," Justine said.

Chapter Thirty-four

Jacksonville

BELL RACED INTO THE CONN. "SONAR, WHAT HAVE YOU GOT?"

"Skipper, we have a contact identified as an M-12 *Tchaika* aircraft. Cuban coastal patrol flies them."

Bell heard the news with dismay. The *Tchaika* was a Russian subsonic "flying boat" built for coastal and ASW patrol. It carried torpedoes, depth bombs, and mines.

"Reg, where's the fleet?"

"Ten miles, Mark. We've got them on the screens. But we're still in Cuban waters. They can't cross the line."

"Lay in a course to them. Maneuvering, increase reactor power to a hundred and ten percent. Push it to the red line."

"Maneuvering, aye."

"Jamie, can we get any depth at all?"

Flynn shook his head. "I can't guarantee we'll be able to hold her. Flooding those forward tanks might send us to the bottom. We're barely maintaining positive buoyancy now."

"Conn, sonar. *Tchaika* twenty miles and closing."

Bell thought furiously. So close to home, and now this. One more threat. It was a race to get to the fleet before the *Tchaika* caught up with them. If not, its torpedoes would blow them out of the water. He couldn't hide and he couldn't shoot.

All he could do was run.

Tchaika M-12

The Cuban pilot knew something was up when his radar picked up the hostile contact in his patrol zone. It was on the surface. He had a justified target if he could catch it in Cuban waters. He called in to base. Jets were scrambled. In ten minutes they would be there.

He pushed the two Ivchynko turboprop engines mounted high on his wings to their max and leveled off at two hundred feet and three hundred kilometers per hour. The Soviets had leased this plane to Castro back in the mid-eighties. It had been on duty ever since. Its torpedoes were on a pylon under each wing.

"Radar officer, lock onto target. Weapons officer, match bearings and prepare torpedoes for launch."

Red Lion Squadron

Colby was a half mile away from the carrier, flying patrol, and he could hear the stuff coming from the carrier's combat information center as well as anyone. The *Jacksonville* was in trouble.

"What's their range, X-ray?" he asked the ASW controller.

"Ten miles, Colby. But that *Tchaika* is coming on fast. I don't know if they'll make it."

Colby put his helo into a stable hover. "So we're just gonna sit here and let them take a shot at one of ours?"

"If you mean are we going to invade Cuba, the answer is no." X-ray's voice was dead tired. "Look, we've tried every way we know to raise her, but she's deaf to the world. We don't know what her condition is. We've got orders to stay put."

"That sucks," said Colby flatly.

"Hey, since when are you a fan of the sub force?"

"Fuck it," said Colby, fuming. He broke his dip and turned out to sea. Ten miles. Somewhere in that silvery gleam were the guys who had saved Rico's ass. And he'd made a jerk out of himself blaming them. He seethed. One F-14 off the carrier and that *Tchaika* was history. Of all the pussy shit. Like there was some kind of *line* out there. Rear echelon motherfucker crap. "Breaking dip, X-ray. *Nada.*"

"Red Lion 615, you are clear to freelance."

"Roger, X-ray."

Colby moved out to sea mad as hell.

Jacksonville

"Captain, *Tchaika* five miles and closing."

Bell picked up the mike. "Reg, you ready down there?"

"Ready as we'll ever be. It could blow up in our faces."

"Countermeasures, all set?"

"Countermeasures, aye."

"Captain, *Tchaika* three miles and closing. Sir, we're picking up a flight of jets right behind him."

"More good news. Jamie, where's the carrier?"

"Three miles, Mark. You can see it from the bridge."

"I'm going up. You, too. Wire me."

They passed the cable up to the sail bridge, and Bell and Flynn climbed the ladder.

Jacksonville surged along at more than twenty knots. The sun was dazzling on the sea. The wind whipped at them. The carrier was a tiny oasis in the desert, three miles north. The helos were buzzing around it like flies. So close . . .

"Captain, *Tchaika* closing one mile."

278

Bell heard it now. Flynn pointed. The gull-winged flying boat came tearing down at them and made a pass overhead.

"Bastard's probably grinning like a kid in a candy store," said Bell.

"He's coming in," Flynn warned. "He's made his drop." A single black stick dropped off the *Tchaika's* starboard wing and hit the water with a big spray.

"Conn, sonar, torpedo in the water. High-speed motor."

"Everybody ready," said Bell. "Hard right rudder. Fast as she'll turn."

The *Jacksonville* turned *towards* the torpedo. It was a move of desperation. Torpedoes were set not to "enable"—to be able to explode—until the motor had made enough rotations. That way the weapon couldn't go off too close to its mother craft, or from the impact of hitting the water. If he could get to the torpedo before it enabled . . .

"Torpedo still searching, Captain."

"Reg, let her rip," Bell ordered.

"Trash away," radioed Carter from below.

The sudden booms off the port and starboard bow sounded like depth charges, which, in fact, was what Carter had turned the metal trash cylinders into, packing them with explosives from one of their Mk-48 torpedo's warheads.

"Torpedo turning. Still has not acquired us. Range one hundred yards and closing."

"Countermeasures, release noisemakers."

The decoys shot out the small "torpedo" tube in Doc's office and burst into noise. By the time the torpedo's sonar recovered, *Jacksonville* had made another fifty yards.

"It's still looking . . . looking . . ."

"This is it," said Bell. "Sound the collision alarm. Prepare for explosion."

The *Jacksonville* smashed the torpedo head on, and it did not explode.

"We got it," yelled Flynn. "It didn't complete enough rotations to get hot."

Bell pointed. "He's coming around again. He's firing!"

"Mark, down!"

Flynn threw himself over Bell as the *Tchaika* strafed the *Jacksonville*. Twin streams of fire laced over the sail. Flynn jerked once hard.

"Jamie? Jamie?!" Bell worked his way out from under Flynn and got him face up. There was blood all over. Flynn's eyes were far too bright.

"Don't move, Jamie. Doc! Help me lower him down!"

"Try it . . . a second time, Baby Bell," said Flynn. "And say good-bye to . . ." Then he was gone.

Bell wiped his eyes and looked into the sky. "Sure, Jamie. Sure."

But not this time. The pilot had figured it out and launched from too far away.

Red Lion 615

Colby saw the second torpedo drop and gunned his helo over the line.

"615, X-ray. Negative, negative, negative. You are not cleared to cross into Cuban waters, Colby."

"Sorry, X-ray. Rotor malfunction, I'm out of control."

He shut off his radio.

It was going to be close. The *Tchaika*'s torpedo was heading right for the sub. *Jacksonville*'s captain had done the only thing he could after that crazy stunt ramming the first torpedo, which was to turn tail and run like hell for the carrier. He looked back. Men were lining the decks cheering for it to come over the line. Nice thought, but the sub wasn't going to make it. Any fool could see that.

By his screens, the torpedo had already enabled and acquired the sub. It was at five hundred yards and closing. He was going to get just one shot. Either he got it or the sub was a goner. It hadn't dived or fired one of its own torps. The blackened scar along her side by the torpedo room and the crumpled bow told most of the story.

"Sonar, pilot. Prepare to jettison our MAD."

"Skipper, what the hell are we doing?"

"We're going fishing," Colby said happily.

He squinted through his windscreen. He was the best. He could put them down on a dime and keep them there. This was no different from leading a big six-point buck with his bow and arrow, like his father taught him when he was a kid. He flew straight in over the *Jacksonville*'s sail and saw the surprise in the bridge as he blew by.

The Cuban fighters were coming in fast. Colby darted over *Jacksonville*'s stern and shot into the open ocean. The *Tchaika*'s torpedo was running hot, straight and true. He dropped close enough to the water that he could see their reflection.

"Jettison the MAD."

The ASQ-81–towed Magnetic Anomaly Detection Radar stored in the helo's right sponson weighed over two hundred pounds. It hit the water with a big splash.

"Jettison the smoke launcher, too, and anything else that isn't nailed down," Colby ordered. "Drop all the sonobuoys."

The rotors whipped the sea into a hazy spray. The crew tossed out everything they could lay their hands on. It rained parts out of the helo. Everything from chairs to sonobuoys. All of it sank beneath the surface, a screen of metal debris to draw the torpedo.

It was enough. Less than a hundred feet below them the torpedo ran smack into the debris and exploded. It lifted a pressure wave of water ten feet high. Colby didn't have time to get them out of the way of the shock wave. It rocked the helo hard, and he lost control. The blade hit the water, cartwheeling the helo over. It flipped into the sea. Water flooded in. Electrics shorted.

"Everybody out. Let's move," Colby shouted.

He got his copilot and the rest of his men into the water. They linked up and flashed the okay signal. But it wasn't over. Enraged, the pilot of the *Tchaika* was diving on them to pay them back for robbing him of his kill. Bobbing in the water, they were an easy target for his machine guns.

Colby hadn't seen many things he would call beautiful, but that was what he yelled when the rest of his squadron flew over and encircled them in a protective screen and a pair of A-6 Intruders rolled by, heading straight at the Cuban jets. The *Tchaika* and the Cuban fighters knew a bad deal when they saw it. They pulled up just half a mile away and ran for home.

"Whooowheee! Beautiful, guys," he yelled. "Hey, everybody okay?"

"Skipper, you are one crazy maniac," said the sonar chief admiringly. "And that was one helluva stunt."

Colby grinned. They all linked arms in the water, heads held high by the flotation vests. He expected the roar of the SAR helos and was mildly surprised when a voice rang out.

"Hey, helo puke. Taxi? CO's treat."

The small boat from the *Jacksonville* was making its way across the low chop.

"Send a limo," he shouted back.

The sub was waiting for them a hundred yards away, bright blue water washing forward from its props.

Colby floated back and stuffed a sopping wet stogie into his mouth. Not a bad day, he thought. Not at all.

Epilogue

ADMIRAL WALTON RANSOM WAS HAVING BREAKFAST WHEN THE phone rang. It was his most private line, one used only by those at the very center of Ransom's web. He put down his fresh-squeezed orange juice and motioned to his orderly to leave the silver tray and his newspaper and go before he picked up the receiver.

"Walton?"

Ransom recognized the voice. "Morning, Senator. What could be so important this early? I'm just having breakfast."

The voice was tense. "Have you seen the *Washington Post* yet?

"Got it right here. But I never read dirty books till after lunch," Ransom joked dryly.

"Walton," the worried voice went on, "they got it all. The Pershing deal, the carrier stuff. All the way back. Even the oil stock. How could they, Walton? How could they? There's going to be a congressional investigation."

Ransom felt the first feathery shift in his chest. "I don't know, Fred. You're sure?"

"It's *my* goddamn committee!"

283

A bass beat somewhere inside him was getting louder. It rang in his ears. Pounding. Faster now. He touched his forehead. His skin felt like parchment, crisp and dry. His hands trembled as he unfolded the paper. The word SCANDAL jumped out at him. It took him only a few paragraphs to know someone had done a complete job on him. But who?

"Walton, are you there? Walton, talk to me!"

Ransom stumbled into the library. His long, bony fingers could barely press the electronic keypad to unlock the cabinets. He saw at once files were gone. Damning ones. No one but a top professional could have gotten past his security.

His vision blurred. There, in an empty file. Something shiny. Who had put it there? He reached for the tiny object and held it in his aged, almost translucent palm. Geedunk, sailors called it. Junk. The kind of stuff you gave out to wives and kids visiting a ship. Caps, whistles, T-shirts . . . or a tiny stainless steel folding knife with the *Jacksonville's* insignia on it, and her designation, SSN-699 . . .

It was a message, and he knew it. His mind flashed into defense mode at lightning speed. The *Jacksonville* was Carter's ship. And MacKenzie's . . . wasn't his wife? . . . Yes. Justine MacKenzie. CIA. She had the skills. If Carter had broken and told his captain . . .

It's time to rest. Father.

No, not yet. But the pounding was louder now. He had to sit. Revenge. He knew who his enemy was now, knew they had doomed him completely, but there was still time for a counterstrike, still time to take them with him. Maybe there was even a way out. . . .

Father, come to me.

The pounding inside his chest reached a crescendo.

I've missed you so.

He clutched at his heart, only to realize with acute surprise that the beat had ended. The silver knife dropped from his hand. He slid to the floor like paper crumpling, dry and empty.

Inside, the Senator's voice called plaintively. "Walton, are you still there? Walton?"

The line went dead.

Andros Island

They took MacKenzie to the base hospital and treated the concussion. By the time Justine got back from Washington she was able to move him back to the Q. Within a week he was walking on the beach, and by the time they held the next fish fry the doctors pronounced him fully healed.

Mark Bell, Reggie Carter, and Jessica Moran came. The graduating members of this PCO class were altogether different people than the ones who had first set foot on Andros Island. They had been tested under fire and not found wanting.

Jessica had resigned her commission and would join Justine MacKenzie at the Central Intelligence Agency. Bell was going to Norfolk to be CO of the *Key West*. He had buried Flynn at sea that day. Crews had lined the carrier's deck and all the other ships as the *Jacksonville* sailed by slowly. Bell hadn't known so many men could be so silent. Flynn, the dark pirate. The man in secret pain who had given his life to protect him.

Warm summer sun, shine kindly. . . .

This last night made for fond farewells. Justine felt a secret smile grow. More than just Jessica's new career and Bell's command status had been born here. She and Mac had gotten through another difficult time. They had both grown. She felt freer and happier. They wanted to make him an admiral in the Pentagon, but he was fighting it because he wanted to stay in command of PCO final training. She watched his charges across the clearing. Confident, battle-toughened veterans.

285

"I don't know who learned more from whom," she said.

"They threw out the rule book," Mac said philosophically. "It's why they won. I don't know that I could have," he said honestly.

She took his arm and laid her head on his shoulder. "I love you, Mac," she said.

He felt the richness of what they had together. "I love you, too."

They were still standing close when Bell came over. "Hi, sir. Ma'am. How are you feeling?"

"Fine, Mark. Back to D.C. tomorrow. They want to make me an admiral."

"Nobody deserves it more, sir."

"I heard about the *Key West*. Congratulations."

"I couldn't have done it without you, sir. You showed me how to live. You had faith."

"Did you meet Avilov?" MacKenzie asked.

"Yes, sir. He came to see me before he and his family got on the plane to the States. Told me he had spoken to you also."

MacKenzie smiled at the memory. "Two old pros. We spent the afternoon comparing notes. The doctors think they can fix his sight. I hope so. Remarkable, what he did."

"He told me why he suckered us with the *Adri*." Bell said. "It made it easier for me to understand. If my wife and kids were at stake, I might do the same." He motioned to Carter. "What will happen to Reg?"

"We can't ignore what he did or didn't do. Ransom was a powerful force, but Reg should have come forward. I think he knows that now. But he'll get a chance to make amends. He's earned that much. Maybe he'll be in my next class. Good luck, Mark."

"Thank you, sir. Ma'am. Just one more thing to take care of before we go. A kind of side bet we made before all this started. We kind of dedicated it to Jamie. We can't actually figure out who won it, though, so—well . . . if you'll excuse me?"

They shook hands warmly.

Justine watched him go. "Reminds me a little of you," she said.

"How so?"

"Needs a good woman to loosen him up. By the way, here," she said, "hold this."

MacKenzie took the little tube. "What is it?"

"I got it today. You like the color?"

"Sure. Blue. Very nice. So?"

"Before I explain it," Justine said, "can you tell me what exactly's going on over there?"

Colby was an ugly man, and he was even uglier in drag. Jeers and cheers followed him as he walked into the clearing in a dress. His hairy legs looked like a spider's, and his bonnet would last in memory for a long time. And if that wasn't enough, he was followed Easter Parade–fashion by Rico, the rest of Red Lion Squadron's pilots, and Bell and Carter, all of whom had changed from their uniforms and were similarly clad. Jessica wore a man's suit.

Colby plunked money down on the bar. "We're buying."

Bell said, "Nope. We're buying."

Many beers later a compromise was reached. They raised their glasses, and Bell's voice floated across the clearing.

"'Haint we got all the fools in town on our side?'" he said loud and clear. "'And aint that a big enough majority in any town?'"

MacKenzie turned to Justine, "So what is this?"

"What do you think of Peter Sebastión Miguel Segurra MacKenzie, Junior?"

He looked at her wide-eyed. "You're kidding."

"Nope. The package says it turns blue when you are."

"You're *kidding.*"

"Stop grinning. You already said that."

A few minutes later somebody noticed that the captain and his wife were still kissing.

It was late. Justine turned out the lights. Mac slid into bed beside her. His skin was back to coppery and his eyes were soft and crinkled like they got when he looked at her and thought she wasn't looking.

He said simply, "Other challenges."

"Yes." She ran a hand over his chest, felt the hard muscles. "I can still count the ribs, Captain."

She felt him smile as he reached for her.

Good indicators.

BART DAVIS

"Bart Davis is a rare talent....His novels are extraordinary."
—Gerry Carroll, author of *North SAR*

RAISE
THE
RED DAWN

★★★

DESTROY
THE
KENTUCKY

★★★

ATLANTIC
RUN